VIRTUALLY IMPOSSIBLE

ONCE AND FOREVER BOOK 2

LAUREN STEWART

The Hyde series

Hyde, an urban fantasy

Jekyll

Strange Case

The Heights

Unseen

Unearthed

Once and Forever

Darker Water

Virtually Impossible

Deeper Water

No Experience Required

Second Bite

Stick around to find out how to sign up for Lauren's mailing list and get exclusive extras from the *Once and Forever* series.

For the people whose support and encouragement reminded me that life isn't about being perfect—it's about being who we really are. Thank you from the bottom of my flawed and crazy heart.

Once Upon a Time...

...THERE WAS a woman who made the mistake of trusting the wrong man. And that mistake led to another. And another and another, each more damaging than the last. But the woman was as ignorant of her mistakes as she was of the damage they caused. Until she was punished for them. But because all knew she'd acted out of youth and naiveté, imagined love and true stupidity, her punishment was not grave.

However, the woman believed she had not paid enough for what she'd done and how stupid she had been. So the punishment she gave herself was far, far more severe.

She locked herself behind glass, only coming out from behind it when she was forced to, which wasn't often. And the longer she stayed behind the glass, the safer she felt until she didn't see it as a prison at all. Until she loved it for its beauty and depended on it for its clarity.

For, you see, her cage was made from one-way glass, and the mirror faced out, so the woman never had to look at her own reflection. And when she saw the world beyond the glass, things were clear and simple and fair, for she was not part of the world, but separate from it. And from behind the wall, there was nothing hidden from her and everything to hide behind.

Day after day she toiled, working hard to repay the wrong she'd unwittingly done and the people she'd unwittingly hurt. And thus, she became so focused she didn't feel how the glass pressed in on her, how hard it became for her to breathe. And when she finally did realize, it didn't matter anymore, for she believed the tiny box was what she justly deserved for believing the lies told to her.

So of her own volition, she remained behind the glass, knowing that one day she would have no more mistakes to make, no one left to hurt, no more sins to pay for, and no more air to breathe.

1

ANDI

"He fired me, Andi. That fucking foot-freak fired me."

"Who? Wait, what?" I picked up my cell phone, took it off speaker, and held it to my ear. "When did we start speaking in alliteration?"

"Never. That'd be weird." Sara sighed. "Can you believe that bastard?"

"Well..." Honestly, it wasn't a huge surprise she'd gotten fired by— "A fucking foot-*what*?"

"The foot-fetishist," she grumbled. "Jon-Jon. Who names their kid Jon-Jon when their last name is Johnson, anyway?"

"Maybe his parents wanted him to go into politics." Or die in a tragic airplane crash. Man, they must have been so disappointed when their little Jon-Jon turned his kinky fetish into a very successful, high-end women's footwear company.

"I thought he was your favorite client." The virtual assistant agency we worked for was doing really well, but little Jon-Jon had been her biggest account. The problem: Sara was all kinds of wonderful things, but neither 'hard worker' nor 'normal' had made it into the mix. She claimed it was due to size constraints —she was tiny and weighed practically nothing. I'd always believed it was because she came from an obscenely wealthy family and never had to pray our boss would forget it was July and give out Christmas bonuses early. Since I weighed a lot more than nothing, came from nothing, and prayed for Christmas every day, I'd had to make up for it in hard work. I'd given up on being normal years ago.

"He was. Right up until the moment he fired me." She paused. "I hope he doesn't expect me to give back all those shoes."

"He gave you shoes?" Eww. "Tell me you didn't send him pictures of your feet or anything."

"Gross. No."

Thank goodness—I wasn't sure Sara actually knew what 'boundaries' were. "So what happened?"

"His wife happened."

"Oh shit, Sara." I guess in Sara's world, kinky pictures of feet crossed a line that intercourse didn't. "What did you do?"

"He told me he was divorced! I should've looked him up. I should've." No, she shouldn't have slept with a client at all, or even met him face-to-face...or whatever-part-of-hers met whatever-part-of-his.

Damn it, that was not the kind of visual I wanted before my fourth cup of coffee or, you know, *ever*.

"What does it say about me that every guy I've ever slept with more than once has been a total dick?" she whined.

"That you should seriously consider abstinence?" The chance of her considering it was only slightly higher than the chance she'd actually *try* it. But I had to mention it, seeing how well it was working for me and how amazing my life was. Oh wait, my life sucked. Right.

"Take heart, Sara, I'm sure the men you only sleep with once are assholes, too."

"Gee, thanks, Andi. I'm such a fan of your pep talks."

"Don't worry about losing one asshole. Emilia will assign you another one right away." A good friend tells you what you need to hear. A *great* friend tells you the truth, whether you need to hear it or not. "Just, you know, try not to sleep with him."

I shoved my chair back from my desk and spun around, blinking to get rid of the afterglow of the computer screen. I realize it's not actually called 'afterglow,' but it's the closest thing to it that I've experienced in a really long time.

And I'll say it again: My life sucks. But only for the last...say... twenty-three years of it or so.

If I'd known how it was all going to turn out, I would've never left the womb.

"Honestly, we should be celebrating that you're rid of him."

"I hate men," she said. "I'm going back to one-night-only status. Updating my Facebook profile as we speak." Thankfully, that wasn't an option...I don't think.

"Why don't you wait to make an official announcement? Tonight I'm taking you out to find a couple hot guys who will fawn all over us and ply us with liquor like we deserve. Then we can tell them we're purity club recruiters, and ask them if they'd like to join. Do you still have your ring?"

"Unfortunately, no. I gave it to Jon-Jon to use as a cock ring— it fit perfectly." She laughed. "Do you really want to go out drinking? You said you weren't doing that anymore."

"When did I say that?"

"Last Friday night."

"Was I drunk?" I asked, knowing full well I'd said it. I was tired of tagging along, pretending to have a good time. "Because there's no way I would say that on a Friday. Monday maybe, sure. Wednesday, probably. Saturday's fifty-fifty. But no way would I *ever* say that on a Friday." The truth was, I hadn't been drunk in public in eight months and four days, but not even Sara knew that. It's easy to convince a drunk you're drunk—just laugh at their terrible jokes and say, 'I'm never drinking again' every once in a while. "Plus, when a friend needs to celebrate getting rid of a loser, who am I to not support her?"

"Best. Friend. Ever."

That wasn't even a little bit true, but it did no good to correct her. If I were the best friend ever, I wouldn't be using her name to avoid getting arrested. Again.

I brushed another lock of disobedient hair out of my eyes, wishing I'd grabbed a stronger clip before I left the house, or maybe a hacksaw. Naturally curly hair is a misnomer—no naturally occurring substance on earth can restrain it. Mine could only be controlled with industrial-strength anti-frizz, leave-in-forever conditioner made from totally unnatural chemicals. The kind that didn't come cheap, which was why I almost always wrapped a hardware store rubber band around a messy ponytail and pretended it didn't exist. Damn, how I envied Sara's long, straight, well-behaved locks. While she, naively, wished she had mine.

About a year ago, she'd tried dying her hair the same auburn color mine is. Since I wasn't willing to saw off a lock she could bring to her hairstylist, and a picture wouldn't have shown what Sara referred to as my 'subtle lowlights' or something equally bizarre, she'd dragged me to the salon with her, promising to pick up the tab for both of us to get prettied up. It was an experience best forgotten, since the stylist, who had obviously never dealt with hair like mine before, was faster with her scissors than I was at screaming, 'No, please, no!' Thankfully, the bangs she'd chopped had now grown out just long enough to be annoying.

"You should wear that dress more often," Sara said to me

while holding onto the arm of the guy who'd handed her a new drink. "You look hot."

"I *am* hot." And grumpy. And tired of pretending to be enjoying this. I can't believe I ever actually liked these kinds of places. Although, 'like' might be too strong a word. 'Used these places to forget how much I hate my life?' Yep, much better. Far more accurate.

Nowadays, I preferred to stay safe and sober in public and drink myself to sleep at home. Even if I did have to pay for my own booze, I was never nervous I'd slip a roofie into my glass or have meaningless sex with myself, and—

Well, the meaningless sex with myself happened, booze or no booze, but I'd never do drugs. I already had too many problems.

"Come to the bathroom with me," she slurred.

"No way. I'm not going through that crowd again. Go. I'll be here, finishing my drink."

I wondered if Sara would ever notice that, in the two years we'd known each other, I'd gone to the bathroom with her twice. Minus the times I knew she'd need someone to hold her hair back for her—the true sign of a great friend.

I'm not a go-to-the-bathroom-in-a-herd kind of girl, I guess. I'm more of a totally-not-a-surprise-I-only-have-two-friends kind of girl.

Which meant those two friends were extremely important to me. Now that one of my two friends was at home, happily married and boring, it meant my protectiveness was focused solely on Sara. Especially near the end of the night, after she'd picked out the guy she was going home with.

So when my friend decided to drown her intelligence in liquid courage, it became my responsibility to make sure her lapse in judgment didn't end with her in the wrong guy's lap.

Sara leaned in. Probably to whisper, but I cringed at the

volume of her voice and her boozy breath. "Watch him for me, Andi. Don't let him get away."

I sloppily saluted her and nodded. "I'm on it."

"But not him."

Big sigh. "No, Sara, not him."

As soon as the crowd had sucked her in and I couldn't see her anymore, I turned toward her new playdate and dropped my mask of drunkenness. "I'm going to need to see a picture ID and a major credit card."

He squinted and leaned closer. "What?"

"She's not a whore, so you can stop looking at me like that." No, she was much cheaper than that—she was going to do him for free. "But I still need to see your ID and credit card."

"Why?"

"Because I'm not going to let my friend go somewhere I don't know with a guy *she* doesn't know." He stared at me, not comprehending that I was totally serious. "I'm not here to judge anyone, but I need to know she's safe. So if you're planning to screw with her, I want to know who you are and where you live." I was always surprised by how many men would hand over their credit cards. Sadly, it might be a direct reflection of Sara's taste in men, but I didn't judge that either. All I wanted was to know my friend wasn't walking off with a guy who was a serial killer, or a rapist, or had thirty cats—Sara was allergic to all of the above.

Once I'd made it clear to a guy that I could—and would—find him if he decided to cause any trouble, and if he was still standing there when Sara got back from the bathroom, I knew my friend would be okay. The major credit card was just a joke. A bad one, considering *I* was the one making it, but if you can't laugh at your own felony, whose can you laugh at?

I typed his name into my phone, did a quick search through a few databases, and then held it up to show him.

"You're supposed to update your address with voter registration every time you move, Matthew Hadley. Did you know that?" I clicked a few more times. "Who's Rebecca Holt? She doesn't like you very much, does she, Matthew? Seriously, she wrote an entire blog post about you last November." I tsked. "Bad breakup, huh?"

His jaw dropped as I quickly scrolled through all the information a suspicious computer geek could find in 3.6 seconds. Nothing too terrible—besides breaking up with Rebecca by text, of course. But since Sara probably wouldn't even give him her phone number, that jerk-move could be overlooked for the evening.

When Sara came back, I pulled her to the edge of the dance floor and pretended to dance, which was basically step-touch, step-touch. Seriously, my version of 'dance like no one is watching' isn't for the squeamish.

"You sure about him?" I yelled at her.

"Yes, *Mom*. I'll be fine."

I loved the girl, but I worried. She hadn't always been like this. It was a fairly new thing, actually—sometime in the last year anyway. We'd never talked about it, but I didn't need an advanced degree to know she was using booze and sex to cope with something...badly. Whatever it was had changed my behavior, too—I'd added her to my list of things to be paranoid about.

"I'm meeting Emilia for breakfast at Morning Grill," I said. "You'll need food, so meet us there."

"Okay. Are you staying here for a while?"

"No. I think I've had enough." We walked back to her suitor of the night. I gave him a warning glare but spoke to Sara. "I'll be calling you first thing in the morning to see how you are. You better answer your phone. Have fun!"

I took a cab home. Alone. Then I made myself a drink and had wild, meaningless sex with myself all night long.

Morning Grill was packed by the time I got there the next morning. All I could make out was a dramatic wave and Emilia yelling my name from a table in the back.

I slid into the seat across from her and patted Sara on the shoulder. "Have you guys been here long?"

"Not too long. I had to wait for a table to open up." Emilia adjusted her ponytail and nodded toward Sara. "And Grumpy got here just before you did."

"Water," Sara groaned without lifting her head. "Orange juice. And more aspirin."

"When are you going to realize you're not eighteen anymore, Sara?" Emilia set her enormous purse on her lap and fished through it until she found a small pill case that she handed across the table. Leave it to our boss-slash-bestie to come prepared.

Sara grunted.

"Did that mean 'thank you' or 'screw you?'" I asked.

"Yes."

"Ok-ay." When the server came over, I scoured the menu for side dishes. I'd budgeted exactly three dollars for breakfast out with the girls, which meant bread and water on this side of town. "An English muffin. Lots of butter. And I'm fine with just water."

"Please ignore my friend—she hasn't had her coffee yet," Emilia said. "She wants a latte and an omelet. The um...Spanish or Florentine, Andi?"

"Em," I hissed in warning.

Emilia excelled at many things, one of which was ignoring me. "Spanish or Florentine?"

"Neither. I'm not that hungry."

"She'll take the Spanish then. Orange juice." Emilia looked up briefly. "Or apple?" When I didn't say anything, she continued as if no one was trying her best not to jump across the table to shove an expensive saltshaker into her mouth. "Orange it is. And she'll also have"—her finger traced down the menu —"a side of fruit."

"No, I won't."

"Fruit is important, Andi. You won't grow up big and strong without it." She didn't even look at me, but smiled sweetly at the confused server. "I'll have the same, but with egg whites, no oil, no toast, no juice, and I'll take a black coffee instead of the latte."

"That's not at all the same," I mumbled.

She shrugged. "And an orange juice for my pitiful friend over there, in case she wakes up. That's it. Thank you."

"Emilia."

"I'm buying," she said, her eyebrow raised. "Once you've built up your high-paying client list, you can treat me. Or bring me breakfast in bed."

"Every day for the rest of my life?"

She smiled. "That'd do."

It's not like I was impoverished. I'd been working at Emilia's virtual assistant agency for almost a year. It had started out as assisting an assistant, but as the company grew, so did my workload. Unfortunately, even that wasn't enough to cover all of my financial problems.

"Seriously," she said. "I asked you to come to my favorite restaurant without thinking about whether or not you could afford to spend thirty-five dollars for brunch. So, how about you shut up and let me do something that will make me feel a little less like a jerk?"

"You're not a jerk."

"Well, duh. I know that. Because when I screw up, I fix it. Just like someone else we both know and love."

"And who would that be?"

"I love you, girl," she said quietly.

"Me, too." We'd been friends since high school, thick and thin—metaphorically and literally. When we'd met, Emilia had just finished packing on forty pounds of stress eating weight from when her mom had died. Funny how death could bond people. Well, not *funny*, but...

Being equally pitiful and our mutual love of unhealthy coping mechanisms had created an impossibly strong connection. We'd lost our moms within a week of each other. At least, she'd still had her dad—mine had left before I could say 'dada.' So when my mom got sick, we moved into my grandma's house. The same place I lived in now, except now I was completely alone.

But somehow Emilia had found willpower and had lost all the weight, which meant I was the only one left coping unhealthily—regardless of how hard she tried to curb my attempts to, as she put it, 'close myself off from the world.' Honestly, I took unwarranted pride in how far she'd come and how well-adjusted she was. Almost as much pride as I had in my ability to close myself off from the world.

'Never be afraid to celebrate your success,' as Grandma used to say.

"Besides," Emilia said, "you need the calories for a new boot-camp-in-the-park class I found. It's this afternoon."

Someone groaned—either me at the thought of exercise, or Sara because of her hangover.

"Please, tell me boot camp is a rich-girl expression for shoe shopping."

"Not even close. We can meet there. Bring lots of water. Oh, and you're going to love me even more when I tell you my other good news."

"Uh-oh." Her good news always seemed to be to my emotional detriment because she was constantly trying to better my life. Not that I could complain. How can you complain when someone is trying to help you? Except when it makes you wonder if she doesn't think you'll ever be able to handle it without her.

Because that makes you wonder if she's right.

"I found you a new client. He might very well be a pain in the ass, but I think you, out of all my staff, will be able to handle him."

"Hey," Sara said with her head still in her hands. "I heard that."

"Drink your breakfast like a good girl while the grown-ups talk," Emilia said. "This guy has never had a virtual assistant before, so you'll have to train him. But he should have tons of work for you to do because he lost his regular assistant about two weeks ago."

"'Lost' as in, he just can't find her? He should check under the sofa cushions. Seriously, I keep my TV remote there permanently now since it always ends up there anyway."

"He's been 'borrowing' the secretaries of a few of his co-workers, but I guess he's really picky. And really impatient." She tried to hide her grimace with her coffee cup—unsuccessfully. "I got the impression he's starting to get on people's nerves."

"Wow. How did this dream client find us?" The agency belonged to Emilia, but she had a way of making it feel like a family. The only kind I had left.

"We work with a few of his employees—overflow and that sort of thing—so one of them suggested he try us. Eventually, he'll find someone permanent to put on the payroll, but until then, he's yours." She smiled. "You're welcome."

"Thank you." I couldn't refuse. First, because I owed a lot of people a lot of money, and second, because I owed Emilia everything else. At a time when no one would hire me, Emilia had taken me under her wing, despite the risks that came with it. She knew I would be lost without technology. It was in my blood. My veins were welded copper, my brain a circuit board. Everything but viruses, because it's important to be safe and protect yourself. Ironically, with Trojans or another brand. Not that I'd needed to use *that* kind of protection in...a while.

As strange as it sounds, computers were the only connection I still had to my mother. All my memories of her were tied to them—me sitting in her lap while she worked, watching her fingers move so quickly they blurred. My tenth birthday, when she presented me with my first little Macintosh and taught me how to use it. Working side-by-side—she programmed while I learned how to type, hoping that someday I'd be as fast as she was. As smart as she was. As good as she was.

Then she got too sick to work anymore, and then she was gone. But whenever my fingers were moving across a keyboard, I knew she was still a part of me. It was the only time I didn't feel lonely.

Jump ahead ten years and, because I'd made a huge mistake, I was forced to sign something that took away everything I loved. Part 653-dash-something of the agreement I'd signed to stay out of jail was that I had to stay away from computers. I hadn't realized I was crying until the prosecutor slipped a box of tissues to me.

I'd signed my name because I didn't have a choice, but even while the pen was in my hand, I knew I wouldn't stop. I promised myself I would never hack anything ever again, never hurt anyone again. But to never touch another computer? Impossible. I wasn't alive if my fingers weren't on a keyboard and my eyes weren't glued to a monitor's screen.

Unfortunately, if anyone ever found out I was actually working with them, I could be thrown in jail, and Emilia's business would probably be shut down. Even Sara might get in trouble for letting me use her name. I guess that was the virus I should really be worried about—making my friends into accomplices. Truthfully, I did worry about it. Twenty-four-seven. I just didn't know what to *do* about it.

It had started out far more innocently—just chipping in to help Sara when she was feeling overworked, or overwhelmed, or overly hungover. As Emilia's company grew and I took on more work, Sara started paying me, calling it 'subcontracting.' One thing led to another, and the next thing I knew I was working the equivalent of two full-time jobs, still using Sara's name because I couldn't use my own. Creating a fake identity would've broken that whole 'no hacking' rule I'd set. It was like any other addiction—one small indiscretion would lead to me waking up in a strange place with no idea how I'd gotten there.

So the money I earned went into Sara's paycheck, and Sara wrote me a check every month. In exchange, I paid taxes for both of us and felt equally horrible guilt and gratitude.

I wanted to back out, to stop being a danger to my two best friends, the only family I had left. But they were the kind of people who would do something wrong just so someone else could do something right. And to do the right thing, I needed money. A lot of it. The kind of money I could make a lot faster doing this than if I worked for minimum wage and tips. Not to mention I was hardly what one could consider a 'people person.' In fact, the last few times I'd worked in-person jobs had all ended with the businesses suddenly finding the need to downsize. Me.

Sara shoved her chair back from the table, a look of sheer terror on her very pale face. She covered her mouth with her hands and ran toward the bathroom.

When I pushed my own chair backwards, Emilia grabbed my arm. "She needs to learn her lesson. She did the crime, so she should do the time." Then her eyes grew wide. "I didn't mean—"

"Oh, please. Do you seriously think a cliché can hurt my feelings? Besides, I wasn't prosecuted, so it doesn't even count."

One total and complete moment of horrific judgment had led to a lot of people losing their life savings, among other things. Three idiots who thought they were so special that the world owed them whatever they could take, and the idiot girl who'd completely bought into all her boyfriend's lies. As soon as I'd realized what I'd done and how stupidly trusting I'd been, I went to the police. My ex-boyfriend and his friends were paying for what they'd done, but prison time didn't put money back into the pockets of the people they'd stolen it from or take the feeling of violation away. Not even a *lot* of prison time.

Looking back, all of my ex-boyfriend's bullshit was so obvious, I still couldn't understand why I'd done what he asked me to without asking a single question.

'Just to know which bastard's pocket my tuition check went into, babe.' Sure it was. When I'd balked, he quickly turned it into a guilt trip, a *'I just want my friends to know how fucking smart you are, how fucking amazing'* trip. So, obviously, I had to prove my amazingness to them. I mean, how could I allow them, for one

more second, to think I was anything less than 'fucking amazing?' Besides, it's not like he'd ever do anything illegal.

Somehow, the fact that it had been so easy had made it seem like it wasn't a big deal. What I hadn't anticipated was the damage my ex would do once he had a way into the system. I doubt he even looked at his own file to see where his tuition check had ended up. I doubt he'd even sent a check. He and his friends were too busy going through employee accounts, gathering as much sensitive financial info as possible and skimming off small, easy-to-miss amounts that eventually added up to hundreds of thousands of dollars. And I was too busy being in love and being 'fucking amazing' to realize it.

I'd thought he loved me for my intelligence. Nope. He'd loved my stupidity. And the six thousand, three hundred and twenty-seven university employee retirement accounts I'd handed him and his friends access to.

The experience had taught me a great lesson. Unfortunately, you can't pay your bills with silver linings.

Speaking of...the server put down plate after plate of incredible-looking food, the kind you're never sure is edible or just supposed to be admired.

"I'll pay you back," I told my friend.

"And ruin my attempt to feel less like an elitist snob? I don't think so."

After another minute of staring at each other, I gave up, thanked the server and Emilia, and dug in. "Oh crap, this is actual fruit." I was used to the stuff that came in a can and was more heavy 'syrup' than fruit. And the omelet? "Oh man. These eggs must have come from a golden goose." I'd forgotten that food could taste like something other than the flavor pack it came with.

"Andi," Emilia started. "It's okay to spend a little on yourself, you know. I mean, you work *so* much, and—"

"Tell me more about this guy you're siccing on me."

She sighed. "Have you heard of The Conure Group?"

"Sounds familiar. Was that the bad guy's company in the Fantastic Four? That guy with the metal mask?" I put down my fork to stop shoveling food into my cheeks like a hamster. "Okay, so my duties will mostly be ordering more evil-guy masks, organizing cleaners for when his nefarious plans go wrong, and keeping track of cover-ups or payoffs?" I'd done worse things, but I wasn't that person anymore. Nowadays, even if something seemed shady, I knew it was all in the normal realm of semi-sleazy-but-legal business activities.

"Not even close, although I can't say for certain there aren't any payoffs to track with this one." Emilia shook her head. "The Conure Group is the biggest cargo shipping company in California, and its headquarters is here in San Francisco. It was started by two families everyone knows—the Bennetts and the Chalmers."

"Never heard of either of them."

"Right. I misspoke. I should've said: everyone who comes out of their cave for more than a few hours a week."

"And if you didn't keep dragging me out of my cave to go jogging or boot camping, I could cut those few hours down to none." I'd have to do something about Sara's relationship status too, of course. Find her someone stable so I didn't have to babysit her at clubs.

"And let you achieve your lifelong dream of being a hermit? I don't think so."

"You're a bad influence on me," I said, smiling. "Let's stop talking about my shitty life and go back to this guy I'm supposed to have heard of."

"Right. He co-owned the company before it went public, but now he's VP of New..." She squinted and looked toward the ceiling as if she'd see his job title written on the ceiling. "Projects or something. I'll email you the file later. His name is Hayden Bennett." She looked at me for confirmation. I shook my head. "You have to know them—they're the Bennett Foundation people."

"Oh, yeah. I've heard of the Foundation." Started by an old, rich, white guy. I think. "I looked into a purchase they made from a local artist named Laney." All I'd done is look up a little information for her and be on the other end of a very weird telephone conversation with her and my friend Hillary. "I think she might have been dating a Bennett at the time."

"Carson. Yeah, he and Laney are still dating. In all your time on the internet, you never look at the local news?"

"It's crazy, but I don't actually consider who's dating who to be news."

"She's having a big art show in a couple of months, and..." She stopped, probably mistaking my cringe at the thought that she was going to drag me to an art show for caring about the dating lives of rich people. Not that the latter didn't make me want to cringe, too.

"Never mind. Going back to Hayden. He's a Bennett, like Carson, but is the complete opposite—really old-school, Ivy League type guy. Hayden seems to be tough on his staff, but he agreed to try using a virtual assistant. Of course, as always, it could turn into more responsibility as time goes on." She bowed her head and stuck out her hand. "You may kiss my ring now."

I looked at the ring in question. That I wasn't going to kiss. The diamond was I'm-incredibly-wealthy-and-want-to-spend-it-all-on-you karats and not I'm-a-douchebag-who-thinks-he-can-buy-your-love-and-wants-to-show-off-how-much-money-I-have karats of glittering glory, given to Emilia by the most amazing man I'd ever met. Huge bank account aside, Rob was incredible to her, so sweet and considerate I could barely stay in a room with the two of them without feeling sticky. But the biggest reason I respected him so much was the way he supported his wife while she followed her dreams. Unfortunately, there weren't many men out there like him.

And even if I were lucky enough to meet one, the chance of him being interested in a woman with a very sketchy past whose life might come crumbling down any second was pretty damn slim.

3

ANDI

AFTER BRUNCH, Emilia took Sara home, and I went home to start working. Shocking, I know. Saturdays at Andi Clark's house were wild and crazy. I might even put my Pizza Pocket on a *real* plate tonight. Probably not, though.

I cleared my throat. "We can influence change." Ugh, that was lame. Select entire sentence and delete the bastard. "By holding ourselves accountable for our actions and beliefs, we can affect other's lives in a positive way. Integrity matters. *You* matter." Better, but still iffy.

"Thank you all for working to make this organization the best it can be. I look forward to seeing that 'best' pushed even higher." Not too bad for a keynote speech I'd found out about last night at 6:30. But not quite right either.

A half hour later, I looked up from the screen and blinked. Since my client needed the speech for a banquet tonight, he probably wouldn't even read it until he was standing in front of a hundred people. I considered slipping a dirty joke into it somewhere.

"Oh, so tempting. You can't, Andi. I know you want to, but

you can't." Maybe Emilia was right—maybe I did spend too much time alone.

When the phone rang, I pushed my chair back from my computer and wheeled across the room to get it.

"Hello?"

"I'd like to speak with Sara Antonopoulos." His voice was deep, direct, and none-too-happy sounding.

"This is Sara," I lied. Closing my eyes made it a lot easier to pretend I wasn't lying. Juvenile? Totally. But it worked, and I had no other option. If my clients knew I had a criminal past, there'd be hell to pay. My two best friends and I were deep enough in it that if anyone found out, losing a client would be the least of our worries.

"I'm Hayden Bennett," he said. "I was given your name as some kind of virtual assistant."

"Not 'some kind.' Just a plain old virtual assistant."

"Very well, plain old virtual assistant. I looked up what exactly you do, but frankly, I've come to the conclusion that internet search engines were created solely to cause me pain and frustration. So, on occasion, I prefer real people. You are a real person, aren't you?"

For some reason, I looked down at myself as if I needed verification. "More or less." Although some might disagree. "The main office didn't warn you what you were getting into?"

"They did, but I wasn't listening."

"Okay." Honest. Blunt. Obviously confident, and definitely used to getting what he wants. I'd have to thank Emilia later.

"In my experience, the first person you speak with isn't the one with the answers. They are mediators. When I work with someone, I prefer to hear details and definitions directly from them. In addition to providing the information, I also get a feel for what they consider their strengths and weaknesses, which a mediator probably isn't aware of. Does that answer the question you were thinking but didn't verbalize?"

"Absolutely: You don't trust the first person you speak to, and you're a bad listener. Got it."

He chuckled. Hallelujah! The first sign of humanity. "Exactly."

I gave him the condensed version—he could assign whatever work he needed to be done, anything he would ask a regular, in-office assistant or secretary to do. "Obviously, I can't do any tasks that involve non-virtual behavior, like picking up coffee or dry cleaning. I can order gifts online and have them delivered to whomever you want, but I'd prefer it if you didn't ask me to order anything too...intimate, if you know what I mean."

"Intimate?" he asked.

"Intimate. Like...um..." The first thing that came to my mind —and rarely left it unfortunately—was an old client who'd asked me to pick out something from a particular website for his girlfriend. Until that moment, I'd thought the only thing made from PVC was pipe. Silly me.

I'm no prude. In fact, one of my current clients owns the second largest online adult toy store in the country. But buying fetish gear for someone's girlfriend was a line I didn't want to cross...or get within thirty feet of.

"Anything...um...too..." How to define something sexual without mentioning sex? "Too...um..." I should Google it. "I could send you a link to a definition." Might take me a while to find one without dirty pictures, though.

"Thank you, but contrary to what some might think, I *am* familiar with the word and its various meanings." I could almost hear the laughter in his tone. "Nothing too intimate. Understood. Please continue."

I told him the things I excelled at, namely anything to do

with computers and social media, but I left out the hacking for obvious reasons.

"So basically, you can use me for whatever." Oh man, did that sound wrong. "I mean, whatever you might use a normal, non-intimate assistant—" Crap! That didn't sound much better —as if he had countless other *intimate* assistants, too. Did I forget to turn my brain on today? Seriously, it was like I had no control over what came out of my mouth. "I mean—"

"I understood what you meant."

After I was done stuttering, I said, "So...did that make your head hurt?" *As much as it did mine?*

"Mildly."

"Bummer. Unfortunately, I can't get you any aspirin because that goes against the whole 'virtual' thing."

"So, in effect, you are a genie in a bottle that I can tell to do whatever I need done, whenever I need it done?"

"Right. But I dress more conservatively than your typical genie." And there was no rubbing involved. "You get more than three wishes, though. As long as your checks clear."

"Then more like Siri, the virtual helper on my phone."

"Good comparison, yeah. Although, I don't freeze or tell you to try again later as often. Also, if you ask me a stupid question, I don't have a preset polite response."

"It's always been my belief that there are no stupid questions, just stupid people who ask them."

Oh shit, I was giggling. I should hang up now. Go back to bed. Forever.

"I don't think Siri has that nice of a laugh either," he said quietly. "It's all a little bizarre, isn't it?"

"What is?" Me? This conversation? My sudden and inexplicable girliness?

"Working closely with someone without ever looking into their eyes. Doing everything over the phone."

"Actually, we'll do very little over the phone." Thankfully, because I speak much better in writing. "It usually works better to use email or other chat features like— Does Gmail chat give you a headache?"

"Perhaps it would if I knew what Gmail chat was."

"Oh boy. We're starting at the beginning, aren't we?" I wouldn't have guessed it from his voice, but anyone this tech-deficient had to be in his late-fifties or early-sixties. Slightly balding and hoping his expensive suit covered his paunch. Not that I'd ever be able to verify it, but I gave myself a 90% chance of being right.

"I've just become far less intimidating, haven't I?"

"Of course not, Mr. Bennett. You're highly intimidating. Or you *would* be if you hadn't asked that question—truly intimidating people don't care if they're intimidating."

"Actually, truly intimidating people *enjoy* being intimidating, so they care quite a bit. Believe me, I know."

I blew out a breath. Hayden Bennett wasn't going to be an easy one.

As soon as we hung up, I started investigating the Conure Group. I should've done it before we spoke, to be prepared for his call, but very few of my clients actually call me, and none of them had ever called on a weekend. I would've mentioned my office hours to him if I actually *had* office hours...or a life outside my virtual one.

I Googled the company name, deliberately avoiding images and anything personal about Hayden himself. That was a no-no for me—looking up the actual person I was working for. I didn't need to know what he posted on social media, did in his free time, or what he looked like. In fact, that just complicated things. This was business.

"Okay." Typical stuff—if you consider a gigantic shipping company typical—no mentions of evil plans to take over the world, no big scandals, at least not on the first page. The website said it was founded in a tiny North Beach office in 1984 by two friends who'd met at Stanford. Good for them. But I didn't care. Now publicly owned, although Bart Chalmers and "HP Bennett" as the site referred to him, still ran the day-to-day. I scrolled down past the side-by-side pictures of the two men in their forties, looking very stoic and boring. For a brief moment, I wondered which was Hayden. But I kept scrolling, kept skimming the words, looking for anything that might help me do my job better.

Each division had a different tab—admin, the board of directors, contact form you fill out and hope you get an answer within six to eight weeks. Still bored. Also, moderately impressed that such a large company had hired such a lame web developer. Probably someone's nephew. These kinds of companies were built on nepotism. A link to the Bennett Foundation and the Conure Group's charitable contributions. Nice. Much better website, too.

I went back to the Conure Group site, to the 'about' link. Evidently, the company logo—an ugly bird with wings that morphed into the San Francisco skyline—had been designed by HP himself, in homage to his love of San Francisco's mysterious wild flock of parrots.

"Wow, Hayden, didn't peg you as a bird lover." Good thing he'd decided to go into big business because he had absolutely zero talent with design. Over the last thirty years, the friends had built that small office into an enormously successful international shipping company. Great. Lots of acquisitions and an impressive line-up of clients. According to their announcement page, they'd just signed a contract with the largest steel manufacturer in the country.

And this is why he earned the big bucks. Nothing was stated outright because smart businesses kept this stuff quiet, but a lot of their newer clientele worked in conjunction with the state government. That hinted they had other bigger, meaner clients that they *didn't* mention.

I stopped clicking before my curiosity got the better of me. I'd focus on the work that Hayden gave me and ignore any and all conclusions I made beyond that. The last thing I needed to know was that Hayden Bennett was anything more than what he let me know.

He could keep his secrets, and I'd keep mine. After all, our relationship would be a temporary, purely professional one.

4

HAYDEN

I CHECKED the pads of my fingers for calluses before typing. *'I'll be out of town until Monday night.'* Hiring a new assistant was supposed to mean less typing, not more. But I wasn't complaining.

'Going someplace warm and sunny?' Without fail, my new assistant answered almost immediately, as if she never stepped away from her computer. I wasn't sure why that bothered me so much, but it did. Even while hoping it wouldn't stop.

'It's for work, but I need you to redo a section of the contract proposal. It doesn't sound right.'

'In what way?'

'In the sound,' I typed.

'Hang on a sec. I need to stop laughing.' Less than two seconds later, another message popped up. *'Okay, I'm done laughing.'*

My cheeks hurt from using muscles so rarely engaged.

'But you're going to have to give me more to go on than 'the sound." She was very impressive, by far the best assistant I'd ever had.

Even though the virtual aspect was still uncomfortable and my typing speed annoyingly slow, it gave me an opportunity I'd never had before. Something about communicating through messages in real time, but not being face-to-face, gave me a sense of privacy. Obviously false, because what happened on the internet stayed on the internet. But my reactions and expressions were my own—if I laughed, smiled, or grimaced, no one knew. The perpetual poker face, the one I'd perfected after years of hiding other people's secrets and a few of my own, wasn't necessary.

In business, I'd learned to be quick, decisive, and to speak in a way that got the most out of my employees or clients. I didn't do that with her. With her, I spoke without an underlying agenda. It was freeing. Stupid to finally be myself with someone I would never meet, but it was a nice change.

I typed, *'You're usually so good at knowing exactly what I want.'*

'Stop being nice. I hate that. Maybe I'm having an off day. So how about you share what's going on inside your head for someone who isn't in it?'

I tried to explain, hunting and pecking for the correct letters. If this were to go on for much longer, I'd need to learn how to type properly.

The Inspex project was all mine, start to finish. It had started out simply enough, merely a desire for The Conure Group to be more than just a moneymaking venture for its stockholders. I'd been on the board of my brother's charitable foundation since the beginning and had watched Carson take the money our father had left him and turn it into something good, a way to help families and children. It took me a while, but I finally realized that I was following too closely in our dead father's footsteps. When my father's business partner, Bart, finally retired, I would be given his title and position in a company that hadn't changed in thirty years. A company whose only motivator was financial gain. Regardless of how it was acquired.

Now, after an agonizing amount of networking, subtlety, and

negotiating, I'd finally figured out a way to do both. In a few months, I'd be sitting in a senator's office to present the project, and I'd walk out with a contract that would set Conure on a new path. Create new jobs, ignite an explosion in the company's stock, and help people who would never know about the Conure Group or Hayden Bennett. I had no interest in fame, and if this project went the way it should, my family name would have nothing to do with it.

But in order for that to happen, my name was the only one that *could* be connected to it. Everyone else only knew the pieces they had to know, and nothing more. If I let anyone else in before everything was in place, I wouldn't be able to control the outcome. After this much time and effort, that was a risk I couldn't take.

When I presented the project, first to Conure's board of directors and then to the senators, it had to be perfect. No loopholes, no gaps, no what-ifs.

After a few minutes of trying to convey what needed to be changed in the manufacturing contract, her reply popped up.

'Okay, I think I got it. So basically, you just want me to fix the sound, right? :)'

I laughed. Five minutes of struggle and, *'Yeah, basically.'*

Totally confident she'd figure out what I needed from her, I signed off and pushed my chair back from the desk. After a few minutes of staring at a blank screen, I glanced at the night sky out my window.

When every day was the same, why did it always surprise me when they ended?

Only then did I notice the silence of the building and realize that I was alone in the normally chaotic Conure offices. Everyone else had already gone home.

Home. Yet another place to be lonely.

"Good evening, Mr. Bennett, sir," the security guard said as he took a few steps back from me.

I nodded and headed for the elevator. The luxury apartment building was home to very few families, so it shocked me when I felt something collide with my leg, then looked down at the child clutching my pants.

"I'm so sorry!" a woman, who was probably the child's nanny, said. "Jonathan! Let go of Mr. Bennett right this instant." She didn't look familiar, but I wasn't surprised she knew my name. Clare did an excellent job of keeping our reputation pristine and our secrets well hidden.

The boy, who couldn't have been older than four, looked up at me and smiled. The security guard left his desk and hurried toward us, passing the equally concerned nanny.

"I don't think he plans to hurt me too badly." I stopped them both with a raised hand and spoke to the boy. "Do you?"

Jonathan shook his head.

"Well, what can I do for you then, little man?"

"I need to poop."

Huh. I glanced at the woman. She cringed apologetically and said, "I'm so sorry. He never goes until his dad gets home. And Mr. Coyle is running late."

"Hmm. That makes it tougher, doesn't it?" I asked the boy. "So how do you propose we handle this?"

"I need to poop."

"I get that. Well, the way I see it, you have a couple options, but only one of them would keep those pants looking nice." I blew out a breath, not wanting to laugh. "If you want, I could take you to the bathroom in the security office, and you could see what happens." I looked at his nanny. "If that's alright with you."

Her mouth hung open until she said, "I..." Then I think it got stuck again.

Jonathan let go of my pants and took hold of my hand as soon as I offered it to him. I didn't remember ever having touched a child before. My experience with them was limited to smiles from a few feet away. His skin was so soft, so delicate, so warm, I didn't dare move for fear I'd break him. I swallowed, enjoying the slight pressure as he squeezed my fingers, all he could wrap his tiny fingers around.

"Mary-Anne?" a deep voice called from the front entrance. "What's—?"

"Mr. Coyle!" the nanny said with relief. "Thank goodness. Jonathan needs to go to the bathroom."

The boy's hand disappeared from mine and reconnected with my pant leg, digging in even deeper than before.

"Jonathan? Daddy can take you now," Mary-Anne said. "Let go of the nice man."

My breath caught in my throat, trapped by a memory I'd pushed away long ago. Even as I saw the boy's expression change into a grin as he let go of my leg and ran to his father, I couldn't let go of the panic. The need to stop him, protect him from a father who was nothing like mine.

I stood absolutely frozen, trying to regain control of my breath, my heartbeat, my sanity. The others must have perceived my stillness as annoyance or anger because all three of them started apologizing at the same time.

"It's fine," I said finally, raising the hand Jonathan had held. "No problem at all. Really." I turned around and hurried to the elevator, letting out a deep breath when the door closed and their stupid, unnecessary apologies were silenced.

"I'm...fine."

I went through the foyer of our apartment and down the hall

toward my office to put down my briefcase. I'd do some more work as soon as I'd gotten something to eat.

Clare looked up from her e-reader when I came into the living room, blinking as if she were surprised to see me. As if I hadn't come into this room in exactly the same way, into exactly the same silence, every day for the last three years.

Some nights she was home, and others she was out with her friends, but the silence never changed.

For a second, I was tempted to tell her about the little boy, about my bizarre reaction to his touch and the way he looked at me. But we never talked about kids or our childhoods...or anything much at all.

"How was your day?" I asked, setting my jacket across the back of a chair and loosening my tie.

She stretched like a cat in the sun. "Fine. Yours?"

"The same." Our mandatory eight words spoken, I went to make myself dinner.

I opened up the fridge and pulled out eggs and some vegetables. Great, nothing but the Camembert Clare loved. I looked toward the living room but decided against it. Our housekeeper ordered the groceries to be delivered every Wednesday, I think. I could live without cheese for a few days.

I wrote a quick note to Helen to make sure she included it on the shopping list and then thought of the little boy again. My virtual assistant would get a good laugh from that story. Staring at my phone, I tapped my fingers on the granite. It could wait until tomorrow.

"Can you stop that? I have a headache."

I looked up and saw Clare leaning on the center island. That was unexpected. "Did you take something for it?"

"Yeah, but it hasn't kicked in yet." She nodded toward the ingredients I'd gathered. "If that's for omelets, would you make me one, too?"

"Of course. You're not going out tonight?"

Clare had lots of friends—some with as much money as she had and others she'd bought on the cheap. All of whom enjoyed filling up their very nice, very empty lives with shopping and dinners out.

"Not with this headache," she said. "Plus, I thought it might be nice to stay here with you." She sat down and watched me chop, whisk, and sauté. I tried not to wonder why she was hovering.

"That'd be nice."

"We haven't talked in a while." She came around the island, standing right next to me, her shoulder brushing mine. "Can I help?"

"Sure," I said, turning around to grab a knife and cutting board for the scallions. "Here."

She chopped slowly, in between each cut looking up at me with an expression I didn't understand. We lived under the same roof, attended the same events, she even held my arm occasionally, but there was nothing between us. A life of deceit does that to people.

A single lie kept us together...and kept us apart.

I'd accepted it a long time ago. Was it normal? No. But it was *our* normal, and I didn't have the time or energy for anything different.

There was nothing wrong with Clare. No reason to hate her, resent her, or even be annoyed by her. She was kind, intelligent, and she was certainly generous with her trust fund. When she was surrounded by people, she laughed and cracked jokes, making sure those around her were happy.

I just wasn't one of those people.

She was practically perfect in every way. A Mary Poppins who couldn't sing or do magic. Or cook. Or clean. And thousands of men would kill to have the chance to treat her like a queen. I'd tried. I'd tried right up until the moment I knew she didn't *want* me to try, because all it did was cause her disappointment to grow. Because my mere presence was a reminder of a life she didn't want. Because she could never have the life she *did* want...with the person she wanted.

She set the knife down and switched off the burner under the pan.

"The eggs are still runny, Clare."

When she turned to me, I finally recognized the expression. It had taken a while because it had been so long since I'd seen it, at least directed at me. Lust. Pure and simple, let's-get-it-on lust. I stepped back, confused. She stepped forward.

"I want you," she said quietly. Such a direct statement seemed even more foreign than the expression.

"Do you?" I couldn't even bring myself to hope anymore.

She laughed. "Of course."

"Really?"

Her smile faded as she walked back around the counter and sat down. "You've been different lately." How could she tell? We barely spoke. Barely saw each other.

"In what way?" I looked at the pan that was already cooling. If I turned the burner back on, it would only char the bottom of the omelet. It was past salvaging.

"Is there someone else, Hayden?"

"No," I said, annoyed. Then I sighed. "No, there's no one else. Nothing has changed."

"Well, *something* has changed. You're different."

Was I? I hadn't noticed, other than a few times when I'd caught myself smiling. Yeah, I guess I *was* different. "I feel...I feel awake, that's all." Because I'd had more interesting conversations in the last few days with my new assistant than I'd had in the last few years with Clare. It had nothing to do with romance —if she'd been a man, I would feel the same. Mostly.

"Are you going to leave me?" my wife asked.

"What?" Where was this coming from? "No, of course not. I'm staying right here for as long as you want me." I laughed at the irony. "But you don't want me, do you?"

"Of cour—"

I raised my hand to stop her. "I didn't cheat. But I'm waking up now. And I'm thinking about some things I never did before. You. Me. This." I gestured to all of the trappings that trapped us. "I never questioned it. Or thought to want anything else."

Twenty-nine years, and I could probably count the number of times I'd been happy. All that practice had left me numb to everything—good or bad. That's how you deal with chronic pain —refuse to feel anything else until the grief becomes all you have, all you know.

Until the highs and lows of everyday life constrict into a flat line.

"Am I not enough for you?" she asked.

I sighed again. "How many lovers do you have now, Clare? Just the one, or are there more than that these days?"

She jolted back in her seat.

"You didn't think I knew?" That was a shock. I'd assumed it was just one more of the things we knew but didn't talk about. Just one more lie we didn't verbalize. Why would we? It would ruin our mutual boredom. "If nothing else, we haven't had sex in...long enough for me to know your smiles aren't my doing."

"You've had some, too."

"No, I haven't." No lovers. No smiles.

Her brow furrowed. "You're telling me that you haven't had sex with anyone but me since we got married?"

"Unless my hand counts, no."

"We haven't been intimate for years, Hayden. Are you telling me you haven't had sex in two years?"

I shook my head—both answering her question and

acknowledging to myself what an idiot I'd been. Damn, had it been that long? I'd stopped counting the days when it got pathetic, but two years? Yeah, that was far beyond pathetic.

"Why not?" The question was honest—she really didn't understand why I would've been faithful when she, and almost everyone else we knew, wasn't.

"I distinctly remember the words 'honor and obey' in our vows. Fidelity wasn't mentioned, but I kind of thought that was an unspoken promise."

"I made the same promise, but I didn't keep mine." She pulled her hair back as if to put it in a ponytail. It fell into place as soon as she let it go. "If you knew I was sleeping with someone else, why aren't you angry? Why don't you leave?"

The vulnerability of her expression only added to my shock that we were having this conversation. How could she not realize she was breaking the only rule we lived by? That to not talk about this, give the other an opportunity to hurt us, was an even larger promise than our marriage vows.

"Why are you still with me, Hayden?"

"Because..." Because I'd known what I was getting into with Clare, and I married her anyway. No one forced me. Even before we were married, there was no real passion in our relationship. And certainly no love. We got married because it was expected of us, because it was the logical thing to do. Because I'd wanted to protect her the only way I knew how.

Because I'd failed to protect my mother and my little brother from my father. I'd failed them by leaving them behind. I couldn't make that mistake with another person, couldn't leave her to a different but equally horrible man. Her father was still alive, still part of her life and mine. All I could do was be a buffer, a shield. To make sure I was present. Love wasn't a necessary component of that.

Initially, I'd been naive enough to think that things between

Clare and I would change. No, that's not right. I knew she'd never love me. I guess I didn't see love as being all that important because I'd never felt it before, didn't think it was something I could ever have. Until I had a conversation with Carson. Until my little brother—the one without a single desire for stability or fidelity—had found something beautiful and was happier than I'd ever seen him. That was the moment I realized what I'd been missing, that being numb might not be the only way to be.

"I'm not sure I can express it," I said. "There are a lot of reasons, I guess. Respect, comfort, stability, companionship."

She rolled her eyes. "Oh, Hayden, you do know how to sweet talk a lady."

"Do I need to sweet talk you? Would that change anything?"

"I wish it was different," she said after a moment.

Me, too.

She went to her chair and sat down, curling up her legs and picking up her e-reader. I dumped what was now congealing in the pan into the sink and started a new omelet large enough for both of us.

No other words were exchanged for the rest of the evening. Like normal. A normal I wasn't sure I could manage anymore.

5

ANDI

A CHAT WINDOW popped up on the bottom of my screen. Hayden had gotten the hang of the feature amazingly fast for an old guy, even when we'd had to switch from Gmail to an in-house chat system his company used because of privacy issues.

Not that surprising, considering he was probably one of those people who was good at everything. I hate those people. Although, in Hayden's case, I felt sorry for him—he seemed lonely. An unhappy, old, rich guy, who had no one to talk to other than his virtual assistant. His not-rich virtual assistant who had no one to talk to other than her boss. Yeah, that wasn't sad at all.

'Are you done yet?' He'd sent me about ten documents to proofread—barely anything for him, and about ten times what most of my other clients gave me. No wonder he'd lost his old assistant. But he paid well, and it wasn't like I had anything resembling a social life to distract me.

I laughed and typed, *'I promise to let you know as soon as I am. But please note that every time you ask me if I'm done, I have to stop what I'm doing to answer.'*

'Then stop answering.'

'Then stop asking.' I paused. 'I'm sending you something to keep you occupied until I'm done. Check your email.' Over the past week or so, I'd started researching birds. Not something I'd ever thought I'd do, but according to his bio, Hayden loved birds. That's weird, right? Scratch that—it shouldn't have been a question. Because, yeah, it's totally weird. I sent him a link to the file anyway.

About an hour later, I sent the finished documents to him via email. Then I used the chat box to tell him to check his email again or he'd never do it. How people could live without modern tech, I had no idea. Although, he'd obviously gotten pretty far without knowing how to use it. If nothing else, I could pat myself on the back for teaching an old dog new tricks.

'Did you look at the file?'

His response popped up fast. 'Yes, more birds. I would never have pegged you for a bird lover.'

What? 'I don't like birds. You do.'

'Sure...when they're on my plate.'

Well, I guess everyone lies on their resumes. But, oh crap. I'd been sending him pictures of birds for weeks. Did he think I was a total weirdo? Scratch that. Shouldn't have been a question, and it didn't take a MBA to figure out the answer. Although, having a bird fetish seemed a little too weird, even for me.

'Thanks for the doc. I'll take a look later.'

'I thought you needed it right away!' I'd pressed send before I should have because that one comment could cost me the job. Sarcasm didn't always translate via the written word, and no amount of smiley-faces could convince someone otherwise once they thought they'd been told off. I typed, 'Didn't mean that to sound so rude.'

After a nerve-wracking moment, his response popped up. 'Too bad. I thought it was the perfect amount of rude.'

My mouth dropped open. Oh shit. What did that mean? Was

he joking back, or was he serious about the comment being rude, or was he offended but trying to be nice? I'd gotten too comfortable with him, too chatty. I'd never done that kind of thing before.

I leaned back from the computer, not trusting my hands anymore. "Wait. Just wait and see if he gives you more work, Andi. Don't say anything that might make it worse. In fact, don't say anything at all." I think I'd already given him enough proof I'm nuts. Anything more would just be redundant.

I relaxed as soon as I saw he'd made another comment.

'Having something sent to you. Do the same thing you did with the last one, but more politely.'

Was that sarcasm?

'Okay.' My day was normally a breeze because I was more comfortable on a computer than on carpet. But not today. And not with Hayden Bennett.

So what did I do? The one thing I'd never done before for a very good reason. You don't look up info on your clients because you might find something you shouldn't know. And then you might not want to work for them, or you might start reading between the lines of their documents, looking for bodies or any information the FBI needed to know. All bad things for an assistant to do. Be professional, be polite, never pry. And above all, do not make it personal.

But I did.

I Googled Hayden Bennett, the man.

The first thing that popped up was the company website I'd already seen, followed by Hayden's LinkedIn profile—and no, I did not want to connect via LinkedIn—followed by images. Oh, the images.

"Damn it, damn it, damn it." I couldn't have been more wrong about his age and his hair and every single other thing if I'd tried. He looked to be somewhere in his late twenties, maybe

thirty, dark brown hair without even a hint of a receding hair-
line. No too-many-lunches-out potbelly. Not even a little one.
From what I could tell, his belly was tight...hard...probably had
those underwear-model hipbone lines that point right down
to his—

Oh, this was bad.

Obviously having lost all control, I clicked on one of the
close-ups. At least I wouldn't be fantasizing about his
body, right?

Wrong!

As it enlarged on the screen, I felt myself inhale far too
abruptly. If I kept this up, I might hyperventilate.

"Now that is a man." He was incredible. Model-worthy.
Fantasy-worthy. Bad, dirty-dirty-thoughts worthy. When I
pictured 'old-school, Ivy League, VP, computer un-savvy' this
was *not* what came to mind.

In one image, he was standing next to a guy who looked like
him but a lot more trouble—tattoos, longer hair, a big smirk.
Had to be Carson Bennett.

Oh, shit. If I ever talked to Laney again, I was going to
congratulate her 'cause that boy was a sight to behold. Just like
his old-school, Ivy League, quick-where's-the-fire-extinguisher-
hot brother, Hayden. Damn it. When Emilia had told me they
were related, I'd assumed she meant Hayden was his uncle or a
second-cousin or something. The idea that they were brothers
hadn't occurred to me.

I mean, seriously, how hard would it have been for Emilia to
say 'brother?' It's only two syllables. A small part of me felt like
she'd left those two syllables out on purpose. No idea why she
would've, but those damn syllables changed a lot.

If I'd known Hayden was...what he was... Well, I don't know
what I would've done if I'd known, but at least I would've
known, you know?

The next picture could've easily been confused with an ad out of a wedding magazine. Hayden was wearing a tuxedo and standing in front of the Opera House with a gorgeous blonde on his arm. Of course, he had a gorgeous blonde on his arm. He was *exactly* the type that gorgeous blondes held on to. As would anyone else who had the chance. Except me. Because...because I wouldn't. Hold on to him *or* have the chance.

I closed the page before I could do more damage to an already damaged situation. Why couldn't he have been old and ugly and mean? Now my teasing seemed even more inappropriate. Like I was flirting with a hot, rich guy instead of humoring an old, rich one.

'Are you done yet?'

Oh, shit. I opened up another tab on my internet browser, feeling incredibly guilty even though he couldn't see my screen. Everything had changed. I didn't know why or in what way, but it had. This was exactly why I worked virtually—it was safe. *I* was safe. Just did my job, and that's it. But we'd chatted, something I'd never done with another client. And now, looking back and knowing that those chats were a little too flirty, it felt wrong.

I typed slowly and then reread the word several times, trying to see if there was any way it could be misconstrued. *'Almost.'* Almost. That was good. It would be pretty tough to read into 'almost.' So I pressed send and sat back in dread.

'Almost as in 15 minutes or almost as in sometime tomorrow?'

Before I'd figured out a safe response, another comment appeared.

'Don't have to mention I prefer the former, do I? :)'

Oh, shit. He'd used a smiley face. When did he learn about those, and why was he using it with me?

I typed carefully: *'Somewhere in the middle of those two options.'*

'What time do you get off?'

I groaned. "It wasn't an innuendo, idiot. He meant what time do you get off *work*. He does *not* want to know your masturbation schedule, for shit's sake!" Oh, dear God, I think I actually might *have* a masturbation schedule.

Not wanting to spend any more time contemplating exactly how pathetic that was, I typed, *'I'll try to get it to you by the time you leave the office. What time is that?'*

'8 or 8:30 at the latest, I hope. Thank you, Ms. Aconofoinwwetejubte.'

I laughed. *'That wasn't even pathetically close to my name.'* Or Sara's.

'It's not my fault your surname is practically impossible for a novice like me to type.'

'And yet you typed that last message just fine.' That wasn't flirting, right? I imagined him sitting in his office, looking gorgeous, typing with two of his gorgeous fingers.

'Your name is more complicated. May I call you something easier?'

Something easier and more familiar. I bit my lip until I decided I was reading too much into this—obviously he didn't have a problem with our familiarity, so I shouldn't either.

I wrote, *'That depends on what name you intend to call me.'*

':) Nothing too colorful. I promise.'

I typed slowly. *'You can call me Sara. Unless it's too hard to type as well.'* Then I stared at it, my finger hovering over the send button. Should I send it? It wasn't my real name, so telling him wasn't too intimate or personal. He probably called all of his co-workers by their first names, anyway. I wasn't his kindergarten teacher, for shit's sake.

I was, however, positive that I'd had too much coffee today because I was freaking out over this. I deleted the last comment and then wrote, *'What did you call your former assistant?'*

'Now I call her my former assistant. Or Natasha. I hope the first option won't be under consideration for a while. So should I call you Natasha?'

'You can call me whatever you want.'

'Okay. Don't you have some work you should be doing, Sira? :)' I got it immediately—Sira, a combination of my fake name and the name of the fake person programmed into a smartphone. It fit perfectly, and oddly, I loved it.

'Just as soon as you leave me alone.'

'Testy today, aren't you?'

'Considering I'm not paid by the hour, it's understandable, isn't it?' Then I quickly added a smiley face. Not winking, smiling—big difference.

'I'd like you to send me a list of the various faces one can make as well as the meanings of the common acronyms used in this bizarre form of communication.'

'Now?'

'No. The doc first, the list ASAP.'

'That was impressive.'

'Get to work, Sira. :)'

I was so tempted to look at his picture again. All it would take was one little click to switch pages.

This is why I didn't date, and why I would never date anyone that attractive, even if they *were* interested. This is also why I needed to stop drinking so much coffee.

And start drinking a lot more booze.

AFTER I'D EXPLAINED four or five times using simple, non-technical words, Hayden started recording memos on his smartphone and sending them directly to me to type up. Dictation was something I could do with my eyes closed—literally—but I stopped doing it for his stuff. Because every time I closed my eyes, I started paying attention to the smoothness of his voice, its depth, the way his tone changed when he was speaking directly to me, and forgot to type. Not at all good. I was fantasizing about someone I'd never meet and had less than zero chance with. And even if I did ever meet him in person, my luck was so amazing, he had to be either married or gay. Possibly both.

A message popped up. *'What did you do today, Sira?'*

'I spent all day working on something for a very impatient jerk.'
And I enjoyed his constant interruptions. Despite the fact that it was totally inappropriate, he seemed so relaxed with me, I felt like it was okay to be relaxed back. All I had to do was make sure we never strayed to any risky topics, shared any personal information, or discussed politics, religion, or sex. That last one being the biggest no-no, of course.

'And did you finish what the impatient jerk asked you to do?'

'*I did. He should probably check his inbox.*'

'*He will, once he's done being a jerk.*'

'*I'm not sure that will ever happen.*'

'*You're probably right.*'

I wondered if he was like this with everyone. *I* wasn't—only my closest friends saw my sarcastic side. Or any other side, actually. '*What did you do today?*'

'*Sat around trying to figure out how to be a better jerk. But I got too impatient and moved on to other things.*'

I laughed as I typed. '*I have bills to pay, so send me something else to do.*'

'*You're very demanding.*'

'*And impatient.*' I should be working, not chatting.

'*How long have you been doing this?*'

Um... '*I've been impatient all my life. I've been doing the virtual thing for about a year.*'

'*Do you plan on continuing for long?*' Simple question, really. But for some reason, it bothered me, made me wonder if our chats might be headed toward more dangerous territory.

I typed, '*You're full of personal questions today, aren't you?*'

'*I needed a break. And what better way to amuse myself than to bother you? If it's working too well, feel free to tell me to go away. Anytime.*'

'*It doesn't bother me.*' In fact, I'd probably call it whatever the polar opposite of 'bother' was. Is it 'like?' Yeah, I think it's 'like.' Damn it. '*I plan on doing it as long as I can. Jobs are scarce.*'

'*But there's not much room for advancement in this realm, is there?*'

'*I don't need advancement, just a paycheck.*'

'*I've been told there's more to life than just that.*'

'*Not MY life.*' Work, rinse, repeat. With the occasional meal thrown in or meet-up with a friend I couldn't get out of. '*Yours?*'

There was a pause before he answered. '*It's just something I've been told.'* That's when it occurred to me—what had been missing from all the images of his face I couldn't seem to get out of my mind and, in the interest of full-disclosure, had been scouring the net for. There wasn't a single bad one of him—no eyes closed, no mid-word convoluted expression, no crotch-shots. Unfortunately.

He also wasn't smiling in any of them, and there were no laugh lines near his eyes, not even a hint of them. Hayden Bennett didn't smile, not even with a gorgeous blonde on his arm. But I knew he smiled when he messaged me. I knew it. You couldn't joke and tease like that—even innocently—without smiling.

'What do you do for fun?' Holy hell was that inappropriate, but I had to know.

'Tough question. I'm pretty boring.'

'No way. You're a shipping magnate. I bet you go yachting and drink champagne with your family every weekend.'

'Never use the word 'magnate' around me again, please. Also, fun is actually discouraged in my family. We usually stay on dry land and argue. Occasionally, we argue over wine though. Does that count?'

I would bet my paycheck he was smiling as he wrote that. *'Depends on the wine, I guess.'*

'Ha.' And there was proof.

Proof that made me feel special, proud, like I'd done something miraculous by making him momentarily happy.

I guess that's what made me type what I did next: *'Do you ever wish you could start over? Go back to some point in your life and make a different choice?'* As soon as I'd pressed send, I wanted to take it back. He was my client, not my confidante. I had no right to ask him that.

Then his reply popped up.

'Every single day. You?'

I chewed on my nail for a second, then answered honestly.

Because *he* had. *'Every single day.'* After a deep breath, I added, *'But if I did, I might have missed out on an opportunity to work for a boring, impatient jerk. So things could be a lot worse.'*

'A jerk who wouldn't be able to get anything done without you. Maybe we should both consider ourselves lucky.'

I did. But right now what I *couldn't* consider myself was professional or sane. As much as I liked him, it wasn't worth screwing up the job. I needed his money, not him. I should be thinking about all the people I'd hurt, not myself.

I typed, *'Speaking of getting things done... Remember when you mentioned I could tell you to go away anytime I wanted? Well, now is anytime.'*

'What? I couldn't hear you.'

'You mean, you chose not to listen,' I wrote.

'Still can't hear you. It's very loud in here.'

Damn it. I wish I didn't enjoy this so much. He was my client, and clients were always off the menu. Unfortunately, he was also funny and smart and basically every woman's wet dream. Definitely *this* woman's wet dream, like, every night this week. Good thing he was totally out of my league, and we'd never meet face-to-face. Because if we did, we'd probably have nothing to say to each other. So we'd have to fill up the awkward silence with something that didn't take any words.

"You wish," I mumbled. Yes, unfortunately, I really, really did.

'Have a good day, Mr. Bennett.' Then I closed down my computer and went for a long walk...to the donut shop.

Whether the inventor of donuts knew it or not, she—had to be a woman who invented donuts—had created the world's most perfect coping food. Sugar, fat, bread, and sprinkles. With a hole in the middle so you could pretend you weren't finishing off a big ball of calories all by yourself.

It got a little trickier to play that game after two of them, though. After three, I felt so ill, when the image of him and the blonde popped into my mind, the woman's face had been replaced by a cinnamon roll.

7

HAYDEN

I DICTATED a short memo on my phone, sent it to Sira, then texted, *'Please type this up and have it ready when I get to my office. Need to send it out ASAP.'*

'You're still home? Don't you have a meeting this morning?'

"Oh, damn it." I looked at the time—8:38. I had twenty-two minutes to get downtown for Bart's pointless monthly meeting with the heads of each department. Each of us would share what we were working on, and then Bart would spend the next ten minutes berating us for not doing it right. Regardless of the facts.

Everyone else was probably already there, waiting for the fun to begin. I shoved files into my briefcase, grabbed my jacket and phone, and ran. I took a cab instead of my car—not having to park would get me there faster.

Thankfully, when I arrived, Bart and a few heads of departments were still talking to each other in the hallway outside the boardroom. My father-in-law raised an eyebrow when he saw me rush past. I said a brief hello before setting down my things at one end of the table. Bart still proudly held the official head of the table, even though his role within the company had dimin-ished to that of king—he waved at people from afar and gave an occasional angry speech when someone screwed up, but when it came to actual decisions, everyone knew he yielded no power.

When I set down my phone, I saw another text from Sira.

'Are we there yet?' And another. *'You're wearing pants, right?'*

I chuckled, then texted back, *'Wish you'd reminded me of that earlier.'*

'Oops. You're supposed to imagine other people naked, not be naked. I pray you're kidding but, just in case, I'll write up a sincere-sounding apology letter. Or maybe a forged note from your mom would be better?'

'You've obviously never met my mother.' I imagined Renee's excuse as to why I'd been late—making up excuses and lies were all she knew how to do. But she'd never lifted a pen or a finger to defend me.

'No, but I know she never bothered to teach you how to type.'

'True, but I know which fork to use, which is obviously so much more important.' Actually, most of my education had come from my father's fists, followed by my mother teaching Carson and me the importance of keeping secrets.

"Hayden?"

I didn't need to see Bart's face to know how annoyed he was. When I looked up from my phone, everyone was seated and staring, waiting for me to finish.

Something useful my father had taught me—not on purpose, mind you—was that apologies were bullshit, so I rarely bothered with them. In fact, I decided to do the opposite this time. I pointed at my phone and said, "This is regarding Inspex."

Bart grunted but didn't dare say anything. He understood our positions within the company—he was free to continue acting as if he were in charge, but we all knew my Inspex deal would catapult Conure into a powerhouse position and keep everyone fat and happy past retirement.

'My mother did teach me how to dress though, so I am fully clothed. Don't worry.'

'Thank goodness. I'll just rip up this application to the mental institution then?'

I couldn't smile, but I wanted to. *'Might as well keep it handy.'*

The murmurs grew as the group got restless, so it was time to say goodbye. Although...

"I'm going to record the meeting and have my assistant type up the minutes." I looked at the secretary who'd been assigned the task. "You do a wonderful job, but she's still fairly new. This will give her a chance to see us all in action." I winked. The real reason was that I had no interest in listening to Bart rattle on about things he knew nothing about. I'd let Sira decide if anyone had actually said anything interesting or not.

"Anyone have a problem with that?"

When no one spoke up, I opened the recording app and set my phone face up in front of me.

"Let's begin, then, shall we? Who has the agenda?"

When a new text popped up, I slammed my hand down to cover my phone, so no one could read it. As I typed, *'In meeting. Can't talk,'* my eyes wandered up to what she'd written.

'What are you a 42-Long? I'm shopping for straitjackets.'

I smiled before I could stop myself. Then said to Bart, "Good news about Inspex," in explanation.

His lips tightened, but he didn't say anything, knowing I wouldn't share more.

An hour later, after a meeting that provided no information other than why I should start buying aspirin in bulk, I went back to my office.

About thirty minutes later, Sira emailed me a very short list of relevant points, along with a note that said, '*Your boss sure likes to yell a lot, doesn't he? He's very good at sounding important.*' Yes, he was.

A few hours later, I took a break to stare at the chat icon on my computer screen. How could a tiny picture symbolize so much confusion? I didn't have anything new to give her to work on, so I had no reason to click on that icon. Except to chat. Did grown men 'chat?' Not with their assistants. Not just because he found her interesting and amusing and wanted to get to know her better. Grown men didn't do that.

Before I could make a fool of myself, I shut the damn thing down and shoved tonight's work into my briefcase, knowing I could just as easily make a fool of myself from my phone. Mobile stupidity. Great.

"In fact..."

The head of marketing stopped me in the hall on my way out. "You should try having lunch before three o'clock sometime, Hayden. It's all the rage these days."

"Is taking a three-hour lunch the rage too, Tim? Because you do it really well. Maybe you can give me some tips." I was only partially joking, and he knew it. No judgment—how people did their jobs wasn't my concern, and each of us had different goals. From the outside, it probably seemed like I cared about this. And peripherally, that was true. But, unlike Tim and everyone like him, money wasn't my goal.

I had more than enough in cash, stock options, and outside investments and, when Bart retired, I'd take control of the company he and my father had built. So money had never been my goal—proving my worth to my father had. Before he'd died, and every moment since.

I'd married my boss's daughter, the man who'd been my

father's best friend until he died. This wasn't a job for me. It was a life. And damn, wasn't that pathetic. My career was something that filled the time, my wife and I felt nothing for each other, and I detested her father with every cell in my body. Almost as much as I'd hated my own.

"Are you going for lunch?" Tim asked as he followed me into reception. "Because I could join you. I thought you might want to throw some ideas around for that project you've been working on."

That was never going to happen. I'd never 'thrown ideas around' with anyone, and if I ever decided to, it wouldn't be with Tim. "No lunch, I'm afraid. I'm taking off early to go computer shopping."

"Seriously?"

"Is it that strange for someone to buy a new computer?"

"No, it's that strange that Hayden Bennett is taking off early. What are you looking for?"

A way out, but unfortunately, I didn't think that could be bought. "Something small enough to use for travel. Just enough for email and a few other things." I didn't mention the chat feature because that would expose too much of something I wanted to keep private, particularly from Tim.

"I have some time. Want me to tag along?"

I was instantly on edge. Tim and I shared the occasional conversation but were not what anyone would call 'friends.' He was too cocky and too self-serving to waste time on.

I shook off my paranoia before it started to show. "I'm fine. Thanks, though." Then I headed for the elevator.

"Hey!" Tim called. "How's that virtual assistant thing working out?" Tim's secretary was one I'd given work to before I started working with Sira, and he'd been the one to recommend I try using a virtual assistant to begin with. So his question wasn't unreasonable. In fact, a few people had already spoken with me about it.

"It's fine. Some quirks and things to get used to, but otherwise, it's fine."

"Rosie is starting to bitch. Any chance your assistant could help mine out? What's her name again? Emily or something?"

"Sira. I mean Sara."

His brow tightened. "I thought you'd gotten the owner of the agency, seeing how important you are and all."

I could recognize a backhanded compliment when I heard one, especially since Tim didn't know how to make any other kind.

"Nope. But Sara's more than competent. Unfortunately, she's still pretty busy catching up with everything Natasha left, so I don't think she'd have time to help you out, as well. You might try being a bit nicer to Rosie. Then she won't have anything to bitch about."

"She'll always have something to bitch about," he grumbled.

I'd never been an easy man to work for, but that was due to the amount of work, not the way I treated people. Tim hadn't learned the bees and honey lesson yet, and probably never would.

As soon as the elevator door closed, I leaned against the far wall and closed my eyes. What was I doing? And why did I suddenly feel the need to keep secrets about a stupid computer?

Because it wasn't about the computer. It was about Sira. Our conversations weren't overly personal, but for some reason, I didn't want to share her. My laugh was bitter. I wanted a monogamous working relationship with an assistant I'd never seen and had barely spoken to. That made so much sense. Maybe I should just accept my inner-Neanderthal, toss the computer onto my shoulder, and bring it back to my cave.

I was no less confused by my behavior when I got to the electronics store and explained to the salesperson exactly what I intended to use the computer for. Since I knew nothing about RAM or memory, I took what the man suggested.

A few steps out the door, I stopped. Then I went back in to add a couple more things to my credit card bill.

8

HAYDEN

WHEN I GOT HOME, Clare was out, so I went into my office, took my new laptop out of the box, and plugged it in. I got something to eat and flipped through the instruction booklet. Two hours later, I booted the thing up. That was when my brilliant plan went awry and my self-esteem completely disappeared. I didn't know how to set up a wireless internet connection, let alone the office chat feature. Clare had a computer set up in her office, so I should be able to connect to the internet. I should, but I didn't. Because I had no idea how.

Rarely did I encounter something that made me feel inept, let alone stupid. Why had I never bothered to learn something school children could do? Hundreds of thousands of dollars in education, and I was stumped by three pounds of circuit boards and plastic.

An hour later, I was no closer to figuring it out. Although, if staring blankly at the screen did anything, it should start working any minute. I'd definitely put in the time. When my phone rang, I picked up right away, grateful for something I actually knew how to do.

"Bennett," I said, my eyes never leaving the last error notice that had popped up. "Bastard!"

"Excuse me?"

"Um...nothing. This is Hayden Bennett."

"Yeah, I know. I just got a weird email, Hayden Bennett."

I recognized her voice immediately—Sira. The one time I wasn't happy to speak to her. Because she didn't sound at all happy. "From someone claiming you won a million dollars? Trust me, you didn't."

"No, and it wasn't the male enhancement offer either. By the way, a friend told me that doesn't work. Sorry."

"Are you sure?" I joked. "I just placed my order with them, too."

"The email was from an electronics store, Hayden."

"Oh?" Damn it. I remembered this feeling. I was nineteen, and my girlfriend's mother had walked in on us. I'd had a blanket over my head at the time, but I could still hear the girl's screaming orgasm blend into her mother's much louder shriek of horror.

"Yeah." Sira's tone was mocking. "It seems that I have a few packages waiting for me to pick up there."

"That's nice. Are you telling me this because you'll need more time to finish putting together the Inspex presentation?"

"I'm telling you this because you're going to explain *why* I have packages to pick up."

"Maybe I was wrong. Maybe you won a million dollars, after all."

"Your name is on the order slip, Hayden!"

I leaned back in my chair and sighed. "Well, then, all I know is that their salesman doesn't follow directions very well because I specifically requested he not do that."

"I wish you'd talked to me before buying me anything."

"So you could say no? I don't see how that would've been useful."

"I can't accept it."

"Is it not good enough?" Why else would she sound upset? "If not, it's not my fault. Although, I admit to deferring to the salesman, who I now know shouldn't be trusted."

"You bought me a top of the line gaming computer!"

"So it *is* good enough?"

"It's *too* good. I can't take it."

"Why not?"

"Because it's too much. You can't just go around giving people $5,000 worth of electronics."

"Not 'people.' You." Yes, I'd bought it on impulse, but since then, I'd been able to come up with a few really good rationalizations for doing it. That she was questioning those perfectly good excuses bothered me. A lot. They hadn't been easy to come up with. "I know I'm not your only client, but I deem my work important. The things you do to assist me are integral to my success. It's not a car or a trip to Europe, Sira. It's a computer and some accessories. So, you'll accept the damn thing, say a quick thank you, and go back to doing my work."

"What about the laser printer? I don't even use paper for your stuff."

"True"—and that might actually have been too much—"but I thought it might be useful at some point in the future. Plus, the salesman could obviously see that I was out of my element, and he used that to his full advantage." And earned himself a nice commission off my disinterest and distraction. I hadn't listened to his sales pitch. I'd been too preoccupied by my reasons for buying her something at all.

"I know you can't be out-negotiated by a guy who works in an electronics store."

I wasn't used to people not accepting my gifts. I didn't give many of them, and when I did, the recipients were always happy. "Fine. If you'd prefer something else, then return what I bought and go fight with the guy for something else."

"It's not—" Her tone had softened, obviously in reaction to my increased and irrational intensity. "You're right. You work hard for your money, and deserve to buy whatever you want."

"For *whomever* I want." I waited for her to understand my point and stop arguing. "You work hard too, Sira. I think you deserve to be rewarded for that occasionally. Don't you?"

She laughed quietly. "How often do you really think people get what they deserve?" Something in the way she said it made me think we weren't talking about computers or printers or paychecks anymore.

"I'm not sure, but I don't think life is about that. Or how it's determined. I know a lot of unpleasant people who have more than they could ever need, and good people who don't have enough."

"And other people who try to be good, but who wonder if they ever will be."

Interesting. "Is that who you are?"

"I'm not sure I know who I am, Hayden."

I rubbed my lips together, wondering what to say that would keep this conversation going in the direction it was. Before I'd figured it out, she spoke again.

"Look at me getting all deep and morbid," she said dramatically. "I think the high of receiving such a fantastic gift is wearing off." She laughed. "Thank you for the computer and the printer and all the other things that incredibly talented salesman talked you into. I love it all. It's so much more than I would even ever dream of, but I know I'll love it. Seriously, the only thing that would make me happier is if that erectile enhancement thing turns out to actually work for you."

"I was kidding about that," I said quickly.

My comment only made her laugh harder. "I know, Hayden. So was I. Seriously, I couldn't be any happier right now. So thank you. I don't know what else to say."

"Say you'll help me figure out what the hell to do with the one I bought for myself."

"Oh, boy. I will gladly help you with whatever you need." If only that were true. "What did you get?"

"I wanted a laptop to take on my trip." I read the model number off the box.

"Hmm... For what you want to do with it, you probably shouldn't have gone with that brand. They're temperamental and over-priced. Next time you go computer shopping, call me first."

"Would you have come with me?"

Silence. "No, I can't...but I would've given you advice." Advice like how to get a woman I'd never met out of my head? How to stop from falling back into a walking coma if I ever did the smart thing and said goodbye to her?

"Actually, I don't see very much computer shopping in my future. I hate getting screwed."

She laughed. "You got screwed, but I'm the one with the huge smile on my face." She gasped. "I shouldn't have said that."

"Why not? I'm glad you're smiling." That I *made* her smile.

"There are lines."

Lines, right. As far as the eye could see, going in every direction, except where I wanted them. "Do you ever wonder what would happen if we drew new ones? Ones that led where we needed them to?"

After a moment, she said, "I'm happy to help you with the laptop, but it would probably be easier if you brought it to your IT department."

"It may very well come to that, but I'd like to try with you first."

She led me step-by-step through the set-up, obviously trying not to make me feel like an idiot. She failed on that last part but, thankfully, she realized where I'd gone wrong and got me through it.

"I've now completely obliterated any lingering intimidation you still felt toward me, haven't I?"

"Of course not," she said sweetly. "You did that a while ago."

"Are you sure you can't bring me any aspirin?"

"Positive. But hopefully this will all be over soon. Then you can lie down and recover."

I took a break to get myself a drink, putting the phone on speaker while I poured. "I'd offer you something, but I don't know what you like."

"I'm not a big drinker, but I've been known to enjoy a beer from time to time."

"Beer drinker, huh? Are you sure you're real?" There was something innately sexy about a woman drinking a beer. Maybe the sight of her lips parting and going around the long neck of the bottle, her hand wrapped tightly around the base. Swallowing with a look of satisfaction on her face. Yeah, that's something I'd go through a lot more humiliation to see Sira do.

"I'm so real, it hurts. Unfortunately, so does my head when I drink anything stronger than beer. I'm an ugly drunk."

"I doubt that."

"Someday, after I get that check from the Nigerian prince who keeps spamming me and I'm living on an island in the Caribbean, I may fly you out just so you can see how ugly a drunk I am. And if you're *really* lucky, I might even buy a round."

"Deal, as long as it doesn't come with an umbrella in it. I have limits."

"Oh, come on, Hayden! It's an island in the Caribbean. You have to get girlie drinks in the Caribbean! One?"

"Not even one."

"Are you afraid of umbrellas?" she asked with mock concern.

"Damn, you spotted my weakness. Umbrellas, yeah. I had no idea what a tough negotiator you were."

"Says the man who got played by an electronics salesman."

I groaned. "Ouch, another blow to my ego. I can't take much more."

"I bet you can take a lot more, Hayden Bennett."

When it hit me, it hit hard. Triggered by something in her laugh or her teasing. The feeling itself wasn't new, just the realization. I was incredibly attracted to someone I'd never laid eyes on. All I knew about her was that she had an amazing sense of humor, was smart and hard-working. She was so full of life and, somehow, she'd woken me up, made me laugh, and I wanted more. She *made* me want more—of life and of her.

And I'd never felt a more useless emotion. Or a more troubling one. This was why I'd always chosen to ignore my feelings. My brother had his way, I had mine, and neither of us were any good with them. Not until he'd met Laney, a woman who accepted him for who he was and, just by being there, made him better, happier than I'd ever seen him. Their love had done that, the kind of love I'd never known or could have. Because I'd been asleep too long. Because I'd spent too much of my life doing the 'right' thing and had made promises I couldn't free myself from.

Having what I wanted was impossible. Even if I knew what that was.

"Now that you're hydrated," she said, "restart the computer and see what happens."

Right. Back to business. I slowly walked back to my office. "How do you know so much about this stuff?"

It wasn't a pause—it was a hesitation. Normally, I would've changed the subject. I'd had a lot of experience with small talk, and the point of it wasn't to get the other person to admit or confess something they weren't comfortable sharing. But this didn't feel like small talk, maybe because it was genuine, a sincere attempt to understand her better. So I waited for her answer.

"I grew up on technology," she said eventually. "Like milk and eggs and things that make you strong. I didn't have a lot of friends when I was young, so I played with computers."

"Why didn't you have many friends? You seem like a very likable person."

"Thank you. But...um...my mom was sick for a long time, and I had to help her a lot. Not much time to socialize, I guess. Plus, I was really shy."

"Is your mother...?"

"Shy? No. Dead? Yeah." Her chuckle was half-hearted, too thin to cover her unhealed grief. "She died when I was in high school."

"I'm sorry. I was in high school when my father passed, but it isn't the same."

"Why not? You didn't get along?"

"My father wasn't a nice man." I cleared my throat. "Are you still shy? In real life?" As I said it, I realized how odd it sounded —real life, as if this wasn't.

"Kind of. But we should keep going on the set-up. Is it loading?"

"The...?" Oh, right—the reason we were still on the phone. "Do my questions make you uncomfortable?"

"No, but it kind of goes against the virtual code of conduct."

"There's a virtual code of conduct?"

"No." Her laugh was light, breathy, real but unreal.

"We've been working together a lot lately, and I feel like I know you. But I don't. Not really. I thought it would be nice to try."

"Alright, let's go." The warmth was back in her voice, the confidence. "Why do you know so little about computers?"

I smiled. "Because my mind is so full of useless knowledge, I can't seem to find a spot for technology. But if you ever need to know about ancient Rome or how to convert metric into imperial, I'll impress the hell out of you."

"Thanks, but that's what Google is for." She laughed softly. "Actually, while you may be inferior to Google, you still impress the hell out of me regularly."

"Thank you." The conversation was stunted and awkward as we tested her imagined code of conduct. What would 'too far' be? How much could I learn about her before she shut me down?

"Do you have a lot of friends, Hayden?"

"Just one." Oh shit. Just one. And I was talking to her. Although calling her a friend might not be accurate. "Besides my brother. But calling him a friend isn't at *all* accurate. Pain in the ass might be more appropriate." An occasionally amusing pain in the ass, who was the only reason I'd made it out of my teens.

Who I should've taken better care of.

"Why don't you have a lot of friends?" she asked.

"I don't particularly like people."

She laughed. "Nobody?"

I shook my head even though she couldn't see me. "Not many. They are fine, and I don't wish them ill, but people tend to......this may sound incredibly rude out loud. But, for the most part, people are far too much work."

"Am I?"

I paused. "No. You're no work at all." Because I didn't have to prepare my response, weigh the consequences, lie.

"Hayden?" Clare called from the living room.

And there it was—the 'too far' moment. Too personal. I shifted uncomfortably in my chair. "Speaking of work..."

"Bring it on," Sira said, laughing.

"Hayden! Are you here?" Tapping on the door, Clare opened it and stuck her head in. "Why are you home so early? Are you sick?"

I shook my head and heard Sira say, "Is someone yelling at you?"

"I'm fine, Clare," I said, covering the phone with my hand until she left. "Sira?"

The silence was deafening. Because as soon as Clare had knocked on the door, I'd felt the heat of shame. This was why I didn't lie. Or cheat. Didn't hurt people, purposefully at least. Because of this feeling, of knowing things were wrong but not knowing how to fix them or what I did to make them go bad, of knowing it was my fault at the same time I knew it wasn't. This lack, or lapse, of control ruined me every time it had ever happened. Thankfully, it didn't happen often, because I didn't care very often. I always stayed separate from what or who was in front of me. So why couldn't I do that now? Because this was real. Real life.

I'd never hidden who I was. And it shouldn't matter what a voice on the phone, some words on the screen, thought of me.

But when I spoke, it was softly and with regret. "That was just Clare. My wife."

9

ANDI

HIS WIFE.

His *wife.*

Clare, I think he'd said her name was. Not that I remember a lot of the conversation besides the 'my wife' part. After we'd hung up, I tried to recall what I'd said, if anything. Gone. Nothing in my head but a blank screen with the words 'My wife' written in bold, 24pt font. Italicized with a lot of question marks around it.

It shouldn't have surprised me that he was married—rich, gorgeous, mature men didn't stay single for long. Although from what I've read, when rich, gorgeous, mature men flirt with their assistants, those conversations almost always end with her bent over his desk getting spanked. And then fucked.

Oh man, was I fucked...up in the head. And completely delusional. I shook it off, trying to get rid of the spike of annoyance, or resentment, or whatever it was that I was feeling. He hadn't wronged me or led me on. He wasn't actually flirting, and if he was, it was only because he didn't know me and could make up whatever fantasy he wanted about me. Like a phone sex operator or something.

He was married. Okay. Not a problem. Actually, a good thing because now I knew nothing would ever, ever happen. Fairytale fantasies had all just gotten shot out of the window, because never, in any of them, did the prince dump the woman he'd married for his assistant.

Although, there was probably a bit of *unhappily* in their ever after. I mean, 'ever after' is a really long time.

"Shut it down, Andi."

Hayden and I were never going to meet, but we could still work together and be friends. That'd be perfect. Perfectly perfect friends.

Yep, I was seriously fucked up in the head.

When my phone rang, I checked the Caller ID—it was Sara. Due to the less than stellar work with the foot-fetishist and the complaint the guy's wife had made, Emilia had decided Sara's punishment would be to answer the phone and do other administrative tasks at the office. Any other employer would've canned her ass, but Emilia knew that forcing her to come into work every day was the only way to keep tabs on her. And I knew that the only way I could keep tabs on her was to track her every movement with software I'd installed on her phone and her car. We can only help in the ways we know, right?

Back before I realized how much money and brain cells going out clubbing was costing me, Sara and I used to do a lot of our coping together. It was a beautifully symbiotic and dysfunctional relationship. We'd somehow come to an understanding to never talk about our issues. Plus, self-destructive behavior was always more fun when you did it with a friend. Then I realized that she took it way more seriously than I did and was a lot better at it. The more I slowed down, the more she sped up, until it was impossible to ignore the toll it was taking on her.

I tried talking to her about it—while she was drunk, obviously—but all she said was, 'Family issues,' before going back onto the dance floor and tossing herself at the first guy who approached her. Since then, she'd found new friends to party with, ones who were much shallower and didn't care how low Sara's spiral got, as long as she knew how to have fun.

"Hey!" I said, faking happiness. "What's up?"

After a few minutes of playing life-catch-up, she said, "So, the other day, a man called and asked for your cell number."

Let the panic ensue. "What man? Did you give it to him?"

"Hello? Have we met? I don't even give my *own* number to guys I don't know."

Right. Even after she'd slept with them. "Did he say what he wanted?"

"Well, that's the weird thing. He finally told me who he was —Emilia's husband, Rob. That's weird, right? That he didn't just say that first or ask Emilia for your number."

Yeah, that was weird.

Sara recited the number he'd left, which I already had in my contacts, along with his birthdate, email, and a bunch of other crap Emilia had given me at some point.

"Maybe he wants to surprise her with something but doesn't know what to get. You know how men are with gifts."

"Actually, I only know how to unwrap them." She laughed. "You're the one who gets asked to buy them."

"Don't remind me." Before Emilia had put a stop to the weird requests, I'd had to buy all sorts of birthday and anniversary gifts for wives, mothers, and female 'friends.' Friends. Yeah, right. I can honestly say that I've never bought lingerie, sex toys, or reserved a hotel suite for a friend.

"You want to go out this weekend?" Sara asked. Before I had a chance to say no, she continued. "Let me guess: You're working."

"A girl's gotta eat."

"And drink, which is why you should come out."

"Next time. Okay?"

After I'd hung up with Sara, I speed-dialed Rob's direct line, feeling slightly smug that I had access to one of the best civil rights attorneys in the city. Ironic, considering I was breaking the rules of my agreement every day by working for his wife.

When they'd first started dating, Emilia had wanted me to ask him about the deal I'd signed, thinking he might be able to renegotiate the terms. But all I could think of was having to live through all that again, and how, once the can of worms was back open, all those worms would come wiggling out and make everything even worse.

So, because I'd sworn her to secrecy, Emilia never told him the specifics. And, out of respect for him and their relationship, I'd met them for coffee one day and let her hint a lot. Eventually, he'd stopped her and said that he didn't need to know because he wasn't marrying *me*. I kind of loved him for saying that. Plus, I'd paid for his cup of coffee, which he claimed put him on retainer. So, as my lawyer, he wasn't breaking any laws or ethical codes by not reporting me for something he knew nothing about. That made my daily dose of illegal activity over the past year much easier to rationalize, believe me.

Granted, he'd also rolled his eyes and vaguely wondered out loud why people signed things without a lawyer present. My excuse was that I'd been young and terrified and stupid. No better excuse than that, right?

"Hey," he said with a sigh of relief as soon as he answered. "Thanks for calling."

"No problem. Sara said you wanted to talk to me about something?"

"Yeah...um...This is so hard for me to say."

"Well, if it would make it any easier, you could try saying it in Spanish. But only if you don't care if I understand it or not." Bad joke to cover my sudden anxiety—no good news had ever started with 'This is so hard to say.' Things like: 'I think we should see other people' start with 'This is so hard to say.' Obviously, he wasn't going to say that. Was he going to tell me that something horrific had happened to Emilia? Or that he was gay? Or pregnant? Thank God I didn't watch reality television—I didn't need more fodder for my imagination.

I cleared my throat. "Try closing your eyes while you say it." It always helped me.

"In my first year out of law school, I wanted to impress the firm's partners, show them I was worth my paycheck, so I...."

Is there anything worse than hearing someone struggle to tell you something? Keeping you waiting and giving you lots of time to guess what absolutely horrible thing they were about to admit? Flipping from one terrible reaction to another because they don't just—

"Spit it out, Rob!"

"The opposing side was lying—outright lying—and we all knew it. But there was no proof. Then someone who I thought was a friend came to me with some incriminating documents. At the time, I was so happy to get them, it didn't even occur to me that they might have been forged." He sighed. "That's not true. It occurred to me, but I didn't *want* that to be the case, so I ignored it. I submitted the documents as evidence, and we won the case. The guilty party paid for what they did, and justice was served. Except what I'd done was wrong. I knew it was wrong, but I did it anyway."

Huh. The thing about someone beginning a confession with 'This is so hard to say,' is that once they actually admit what it is, it's always a letdown. Something I should remember the next time I do something tragically stupid.

But, at least, Rob hadn't ruined anyone's life or killed anyone. It was a surprise, obviously, because he was a great guy—honest, hard-working, thoughtful. But everyone could screw up—I was sadly-living proof of that.

"That wasn't too smart."

"You think?" He sighed. "It was idiotic, but it woke me up, made me realize that wasn't the way I wanted to live. Unfortunately, the past doesn't always stay in the past, and now I need your help."

"Anything. You know that."

"I wouldn't ask you if I had any other options. I'm not even sure you can help, but..."

Oh, boy, here we go again. "Rob, spit it out before you have to explain to your wife why my brain exploded while you were on the phone with me."

"The guy who helped me, who came forward with the fake documents, now works for the Conure Group."

Oh.

"He contacted me after finding out that Emilia's agency works with a few people over there. He could've even suggested her to the human resources department, I don't know."

"So...he wants me to put in a good word for him?" I asked hopefully.

"He knew one of you was working with Hayden Bennett, and wanted to know who. When I asked Sara about it, she told me it was you. This guy wants information on what Bennett is working on—a contract bid for Inspects or something."

Inspex. Hayden's important, super-secret proposal that only he and I had worked on.

"He's blackmailing you?" No doubt the thieving bastard would release the info on Robert without implicating himself, 'cause criminals are forward-thinking that way. "What does Emilia think?"

"I can't...I can't tell her, Andi. It'll destroy everything. It'll destroy *her*. It's more than me getting fired or even disbarred." If it had been anyone else, it would've been a selfish move, but I knew how much Rob loved Emilia, and I knew how lost she'd be without him. "I'm not asking you to break the law."

"Really?" I snapped. "Because from everything you've said and all the awkward pauses between those things, it sounds an awful lot like you are." I couldn't. I just couldn't.

"I don't know what to do, Andi. I thought maybe you could give me something to tell him that wouldn't really..."

Hurt anyone? Ruin anything? Too late.

"...matter," he finished lamely.

I closed my eyes and thought of Emilia—how much she loved her life, how happy she was. She'd been there for me a hundred times, helped me when my heart was broken and my future gone. I couldn't let that happen to her. I had to find a way to keep her from falling, even if that meant *I* did.

"I'll figure something out," I said without opening my eyes. But this time, it wasn't because I was lying. It was because I wished I could.

He sighed deeply. "Thank you, Andi. You don't know how much this means to me."

Maybe not, but I knew what it meant for me.

After I'd hung up, I slumped onto the couch and saw that while I'd been on the phone, Hayden had called. Twice. I replied via the chat feature I'd just helped him set up.

I couldn't be Hayden's friend, after all. Because friends didn't stab each other in the back.

10

HAYDEN

NOTHING HAD CHANGED. I'd told Sira about Clare, that was all. Public record, and not something I'd ever tried to hide. But it felt as if everything had changed. When I'd called her back, she hadn't answered. A bit later, she finally responding via the chat box, claiming she wanted to verify the feature had been set up properly. I didn't try calling her again. I did, however, spend the rest of the day thinking about her and what her presence in my life had done. What I wanted from her.

I finally decided it didn't matter what I wanted from her. The only thing that mattered was what was possible—she was an excellent employee who was also a great conversationalist. Inasmuch as a chat box allowed. And I'd have to be happy with that. Inasmuch as I could be happy with anything.

Clare said a quick goodbye when the building's concierge arrived at the door for her bags. She'd only be gone for five days, but had packed for five months.

"Aspen is always freezing," she said, as if that explained it. "You have to dress in layers."

"Of suitcases? Then I guess you'll have enough." I accepted

her answer, even knowing she planned to meet a 'friend' there, and probably wouldn't be spending too much time outside.

Funny thing was, her affairs didn't even bother me anymore. We were never happy together, so it made sense for her to look for happiness elsewhere. For the last few years, I'd convinced myself that my career and being part of the Bennett Foundation made me happy. But while I still believed in their value and importance, they didn't make me happy.

I'd never thought I *could* be happy, that I had the capability. My mother used to tell people I was born with the weight of the world on my shoulders. When I was old enough to understand what Renee meant by that, I thought it was just another one of her lies. A bit after that, I wondered if she really believed it, and actually didn't understand why I never smiled or played like other kids.

When your father smacks you as many times as mine did, you stay as quiet as possible, knowing any move could be the one that sets him off. It sometimes worked. But when your father hates you as much as mine did, you stay as still as possible, so he would forget you were alive.

I met Carson and Laney at a brewery on the Embarcadero. With my brother's innate-yet-puzzling charisma, a few large bills, or both, he'd gotten us the best table in the outdoor seating area. It had a great view that I wouldn't see, especially because Carson had claimed that side of the table. That's what Carson did—claimed things. As an executive, commanding a room and attention, inspiring trust and strength, was required of me. I understood that and used it to my advantage when necessary. My little brother had spent the better part of his life avoiding leadership and responsibility, yet that power came to him naturally. I'd always admired that about him, even before he'd met Laney and she'd finally turned him into a man.

It hadn't been easy for either of them, but once Carson had finally understood what he would lose if he did the same stupid shit he'd always done, he turned it around.

Laney smiled and waved me over as soon as she saw me. As much as I liked her, as great as I thought she was for my brother, being with the two of them always left me feeling a little...lonely. I'd never been able to define it before, but there it was: I was lonely. Envious of what they had.

The metal chair screeched when I dragged it to the side so my back wasn't toward the street. I kissed Laney hello, ignoring the "Break it up, you two," Carson grumbled.

"Fair warning, Hayden," she said, still holding my arm. "If he ever says anything that stupid again, I'm going to have to lay a sloppy one on you."

"Duly warned." I couldn't help but love her.

"Brother," Carson said.

"Brother," I repeated, taking the beer he pushed toward me. "So, what's going on?" We rarely met up for anything other than family emergencies. When Carson didn't speak, I looked at Laney, who was fidgeting in her chair with excitement.

"I'm..." She rubbed her lips together.

"Oh!" I looked down at her belly, then the beer sitting in front of her, then at her belly again. "Are you—"

"No!" Carson yelled, ignoring the heads that turned our direction. "No, she's not." Then he swallowed and the only color left on him was the ink on his skin. "You're not, are you, babe?"

She glared at him and tossed her hands up.

"See?" he said on an exhale. "She's not." Then he looked at her again, to make sure.

"Okay, fine. Sure, Carson, I'm pregnant. But don't worry—it's not yours. Geez. As if I'd just forget to mention that." She smacked him lightly on the shoulder. "Don't you know how this stuff works? You bought me tampons like two days ago."

He held his beer in front of his mouth and mumbled, "You're not supposed to say that in front of other people, babe."

Laney sighed. "Man, Carson, way to ruin my big news. If you'd just told him like a normal person, he wouldn't have had to guess." She looked at me. "You guessed wrong, by the way. And just in case it's still not clear—I'm not pregnant, and won't be for a very, *veeery* long time."

"Clear," I said. When I looked back at my brother, I stopped smiling. Because, as terrified as he was to have children, I think he was also a little disappointed by Laney's emphasis on 'very.' He caught me staring and brushed off the expression that had given him away, and we both refocused on what Laney was saying.

"My lily pad tables are finally all done! For the piece I started eons ago. Remember?"

I nodded as the memory came back to me. Laney was an artist, and had been commissioned to do multiple pieces inside the enormous lobby of a building downtown.

"It took so long to find the right wood pieces for each table." Right, she'd only wanted to use wood that had been salvaged from the bay. "You can't see them yet, not until they're in place. And who knows how long that will take. The building manager keeps nagging me for a date, but it's art. You can't rush that shit." She smiled. "Just kidding. I have to set a date so they can plan their big unveiling thing for the new lobby with a fancy party and all that crap. But I want you to be there. Clare, too."

"Do *I* have to go?" Carson asked, smiling.

"Don't make me kiss your brother," she warned.

"Hey," both of us said at the same time.

"I'm not sure how comfortable I am with that threat," I said.

"I'm *definitely* not comfortable with that threat," my brother added.

She laughed at our mutual dissatisfaction and then kissed her boyfriend. "Yes, you absolutely have to be there. The whole thing is *about* you." They kissed again. I focused on my beer.

"You'll go, Hayden? Please, I need someone to control your brother," she teased.

"I wouldn't miss it." When she threw her arms around me, I found myself thinking that Sira would really like her.

"Who's Sira?" Laney asked.

I flinched when I heard her name. "What?"

"You said Sira would like Lane," Carson said slowly. "Who's Sira?"

"Sira is...um..." I wiped a hand over my mouth, cursing its stupidity.

"Where is Clare, Hayden?" he asked even more slowly.

With only a momentary glance, I saw his eyes widen. Not exactly the same look as Laney—hers held no suspicion—but their intensity came from the same place. Both of them knew something was going on, but they didn't know what. Which made a lot of sense since *I* didn't know what was going on either.

"Clare is in Colorado with a friend. And Sira is...someone I work with."

Carson's eyes didn't move. "Lane? Can you get us a couple more beers?"

She loudly blew out her breath. "Gee, Carson. I don't actually need a hint to be that obvious. You could've just said, 'Can I talk to my brother alone for a sec?' I know we're together, but that doesn't mean we aren't allowed to talk to people, you know?"

Carson finally looked away from me and toward her. "Actually, I wasn't trying to fool you, babe. I was trying to fool *him*. So he wouldn't figure out that I was about to call him on some shit he might not want you to hear. But thanks for the relationship clarification."

"Oops." Laney stammered for a second then nodded once. "I'm going to go get us...some fresh beers." She grabbed Carson's wallet and walked into the restaurant toward the bar.

As soon as she was out of earshot, I threw my hands up. "What do you want to know, little brother?"

"I want to know what the fuck is going on with my big brother. So talk. Who is she?"

"She's no one."

"She's obviously someone."

I paused, looking for a quick way out of the conversation, not sure if I wanted a way out. Carson was as close to a confidante as I'd ever had. Until Laney had come along, I would never have thought to discuss women with him, primarily because Carson's only experience with them was sexual. For the past few years, my only experience with them was...*not* sexual. Wow, I needed help.

"Waiting. Impatiently."

"Okay." I took a deep breath. "Yes, Sira is someone. She's someone I...I see everywhere."

"Fuck, man." He ran a hand through his hair. "What about Clare? You just gonna give that up?"

"Wait a minute. Now you've decided you can judge me? You've been fucking up for twenty-five years, doing whatever you want whenever you want to."

"Exactly," he said, nodding. "I was fucking up. Now that I have something good, I would never do anything that could blow it."

"That's the thing, little brother. I don't have anything good. I've *never* had anything good."

He grimaced but didn't argue. We had the same father, the same mother, and we'd kept the same secrets growing up.

But I had one even he didn't know about. I'd been there when our father died. I was there, and I could've stopped it from happening. But I hadn't. Every day since, I'd played by the rules, did the right thing, lived a life I didn't want, all to make up for that one moment.

"And you think this thing with Sira is good?" Carson asked.

"There is no 'thing with Sira.' I've never even met her. And I never will." I laughed at myself. "But it's as if I see her everywhere."

"So she's what? A webcam girl?" He misunderstood my shocked silence as a need for clarification. "You know, the women who strip and pretend they like having a bunch of hairy, old men jerking off to them."

"I know what a webcam girl is, Carson. I was just trying to figure out why you'd think I'd be that delusional." Then again, I guess it wasn't that much of a stretch. I sighed. "I don't even know what Sira looks like, but every time I hear a woman laugh, I look over and wonder if it's her."

He glanced in the direction Laney had gone. "Look, Hay, I don't want to judge."

"You mean any more than you already are?"

"Right," he said emotionless. "But honestly, on my list of things I'd rather never do, imagining my brother getting naked with anyone is pretty close to the top."

"Above or below imagining me jerking off to a webcam girl?"

"Below, but just barely." He shook his head as if to get rid of any and all images that might have appeared. "I don't know the details, but it's hard to miss how weird you and Clare's relationship is. You act more like brother and sister, but not in the inbred, freaky, 'I'm my own grandpa' kind of way."

"Good, because I was really worried about that," I grumbled. "Do you have a point, Carson?"

"Get a divorce."

It was my turn to grimace. "I can't do that. Clare needs..."
She didn't need me, but she needed someone.

"Clare's a beautiful girl with a big trust fund. She'll be just
fine. And you're a big boy, although *how* big I don't want to
know." He clenched his eyes and growled, shaking his fist.
"Okay, I did it to myself that time. Eww. Seriously, tell me you
don't have a dick so I can picture you as a Ken doll."

"I worry about you." When he didn't open his eyes, I said,
"Fine. I'm—" No, I couldn't do it. "Carson, I have a penis. A big
one. So get over it."

"No way! Ken doll. You're a Ken doll. Okay, I got it." He
opened one eye and smiled, looking exactly as he had when he
was a little kid before I'd been sent off to boarding school. When
things were simple and easy, and the only unpredictable thing in
our lives was our father's temper.

"Are you going to judge me or not?"

"Yes! I mean, no. I mean... Aw, shit. You said something to
me, not too long ago, when I was being an idiot. Now I'm going
to say the same thing to you, only with more finesse, and
possibly a dirty joke."

"Can you at least wait until I've had another drink before
you massacre whatever wisdom I shared with you?"

"No. I gotta say this before Laney gets back. You ready?" He
bounced his shoulders up and down a few times. "Here
it comes."

"I don't think I'll ever be ready."

"Someday, someone's gonna come along who you never saw
coming. She's going to throw you a rope and, if you don't catch it,
she's gonna go full-on cowgirl and hogtie your ass."

I cracked up. "I really can't imagine myself saying anything
like that."

"Shut up and listen for a second, will you?"

I flinched at the anger in his tone.

"Just..." He paused, his gaze pleading. "I was there too, Hay. With Dad. I felt it, all of it, and it fucking hurt. *Still* hurts sometimes."

"I'm sorry." Guilt raised its giant foot over my head and stamped down as hard as it could. I wondered if anyone else felt the earth shake. "I should've been there for you, little brother."

"No, you shouldn't have," he scoffed. "You should've stayed the hell away and not come home during school breaks. *I* wouldn't have. You weren't responsible for me. You weren't responsible for any of it. Fuck, *I* was the one who said no when you turned eighteen and asked me to come live with you. *I* was the one dumb enough to think I could 'fix' Renee. So stop thinking that shit. Yesterday." He took a well-deserved breath. "Now, where was I before you ruined my big moment?"

I'd forgotten how good he was at finding something to make fun of no matter how bad the situation. "It still hurts."

"Right, okay, give me a sec to get my dramatic mojo back." Another breath. "Okay, got it. Yeah, our home life sucked ass, and we both dealt with it in our own way. I watched you, Hayden." Any hint of humor was gone from his voice. "It took me a while, but I finally figured out that the only way you could make it stop hurting was to turn everything off—all your feelings and hopes and..."

He swallowed. "I get all that. But the bastard has been gone for a decade, and you still haven't come back, still haven't woken up. It's like you're doing the eternal sleep thing with him, and who the fuck would want to sleep next to that prick?" He took a breath and smiled. I couldn't breathe, but I did start to process what he'd said. And every word rang true.

It had been easier to stop feeling anything, and it still was. Except, after the pain I'd been trying to control no longer existed, a life built from it *did*. My way of coping was to slowly suffocate my chance at happiness.

"If this woman—Sira?" Carson waited until I made eye contact and nodded. "If Sira can make you feel something again, don't let her get away. Let her *in*. Because if you don't, if you play dead and just pretend to be alive, I don't know if you'll *ever* come back."

It was getting late, which meant the bar was filling and the noise was growing, but my brother and I sat there in silence for a little while.

"Wow." I cleared my throat. "I'm a lot smarter than I give myself credit for. You sure I said that?"

"No, yours wasn't nearly that impressive," he said, his grin growing. "But the general idea was the same."

"Did I make a weird face afterward like you're doing right now?"

"What weird face?" he asked, brushing his hair back. "Screw you. I don't have a weird face. I have a great face."

"You're right. Mine is just greater."

We laughed and lobbed insults until we saw Laney watching us intently through the restaurant window. Carson held out his hand toward her. "She's incredible, isn't she?"

"Absolutely."

"I hope she and Sira get along well. Because it would suck if they didn't, brother." That simple statement, said by a man who'd fought so hard not to fall in love but who'd ended up there anyway, was more powerful than anything I could ever tell myself or deny.

Whatever could or couldn't happen between Sira and me, she was the only one who'd made me feeling anything in a long time—annoying brother and his endearing girlfriend aside. Without even trying, she'd given me something to hope for. So I'd be stupid not to take the gift.

When I got home, the house was as quiet as normal, but it had never bothered me before. Carson's words had been bouncing around in my mind since I'd left the happy couple. Everything he'd said made perfect sense. Unfortunately, I was still no closer to knowing what to do about it.

But as one of my grad school professors used to say... 'Those who refuse to go to the table before they've come up with a fool-proof plan are the fools who come to an empty table.'

I got a drink before sitting down on the couch and texting Sira. *'I'd like to meet you. In person.'*

Her response took a while. *'What for?'*

Because... *'Because I'd like to meet you outside of work.'*

'That's not a good idea.'

'Why not?'

'I'd rather not go into it.' Her next message had popped up before I had a chance to respond. *'How about we discuss something different? Something work related.'*

'Did I offend you?'

'Oh please. You're going to have to try a lot harder than that if you want to offend me.'

'I don't.' I typed.

'Don't what?'

Don't want to talk about work. Don't want to pretend. Don't want this to stop, whatever it is and no matter how wrong. *'Don't want to offend you. But I'd still like to know why you don't want to meet.'*

...

I watched the gray bubbles that signaled she was typing. Then they stopped, but no new text appeared. So I waited as long as I had the patience for—probably close to thirty seconds. *'Sira?'*

'Because you're very married and very nice, and I am very not married and not nearly as nice.'

Oh. That wasn't what I was hoping those bubbles meant. *'You're much nicer than I am.'*

'Is there anything else you need from me tonight?'

'To meet you.' Then I added, *'Although, it doesn't have to be tonight.'*

Wow, the bubbles kept going and going. Again, I was disappointed by their efforts.

'Maybe I'm not explaining myself clearly enough. If we met, there's a good chance I would embarrass myself. There's another chance, albeit a much, much smaller one, that you would do something you'd regret. Either way, meeting each other would be bad. Do you understand?'

No. And yes. I understood, but I couldn't accept it. *'Meeting=bad. Talking still good?'*

'Even though you type like a first grader, I suppose so.'

'Good.' Not good *enough*, but I'd give it time.

'Do you have anything else you need me to work on?'

I sat back in my chair and sighed. "Help me find a way out of my marriage."

11

HAYDEN

I HAD a lot of other things I should have been doing, but then, I *always* had a lot of things I should be doing. And I did them—days, nights, weekends. Not a day went by without doing those damn things I was supposed to do. Except today.

Today, I was busy with something else. Since I'd arrived at the office at eight this morning, I'd done nothing but stare at my desktop computer, wondering what the hell was wrong with me. The thing was almost a year old and had only been used a half-dozen times until three weeks ago. Any day now, the letters were going to start fading off the keys from too much use. And there was only one reason. Because I couldn't control myself.

I clicked the little chat icon and selected the only name it contained, noting the tiny green dot that indicated that she was at her computer. I was running out of work for her. She was fast and thorough, as if she did nothing else. That would be unfortunate. Just because *I* did it, didn't mean anyone else should. Although, I hoped for her sake that she accomplished more than I was currently capable of.

'Am I giving you too much to do?' I sat back and waited. Maybe she'd just left her computer on and wasn't there.

'*No. Why do you ask?*' she answered instantly. Did she sleep next to it?

'*I don't want to overburden you.*'

'*Bring it on, Hayden.*'

I smiled as I typed, '*You've just asked for a challenge I'm not sure you're up to facing.*'

'*I think I can take it.*'

But could I? '*No one else ever has.*'

'*What happened to your old assistant?*'

'*I buried her in the backyard.*' I pressed send and then typed, '*Only kidding—I don't have a backyard.*'

'*Are you amusing yourself right now?*'

'*Absolutely.*' In a way new to me. Hayden Bennett didn't 'chat' or smile or enjoy much of anything. He worked. Everything else was either secondary or nonexistent. And the thinking in third person thing needed to stop yesterday. What was wrong with him...me...? Oh, Christ. This was rapidly approaching stupid, if it wasn't already there.

'*Are you going to answer my question?*' Her question? Oh right, my previous assistant.

'*Natasha is on maternity leave. And because I know you'll ask— the baby's not mine.*' I sat back again, wondering why I'd written that. Another thing that I didn't do was worry about what others thought of me. It was a useless pastime that only encouraged a person's confidence to slip. But now I cared about what a person I'd never actually met or seen thought of me. And I wanted her to care about what *I* thought of her. The idea bothered me. But instead of pushing it away like I should've, I considered it. Wanted to explore its cause and ramifications, if only to understand the dynamics. In a business sense...primarily.

Definitely stupid.

'*Ha. That's not what I was going to ask.*'

I swallowed, understanding what she wanted to know. *'I have no intention of getting rid of you, Sira. In the backyard or otherwise.'*

'Thanks.'

'Not necessary. I enjoy your work almost as much as I enjoy our chats.'

'Me too.'

I felt my heart start to beat faster, felt the muscles of my chest tighten. It was a foreign, but also welcome, sensation. Carson's advice rang in my ears, along with his bizarre cowgirl analogy.

'But we probably shouldn't chat so much.'

I blinked, then re-read the words. Our chats were the best part of my days. I didn't want them to end. *'If it's a matter of your time, I'll compensate you.'*

'Doesn't it seem a little insincere if you pay me to chat with you?'

'You forgot to add 'fairly pathetic.'' Thankfully, it was possible to laugh and type at the same time. *'But I don't want to take up time you would otherwise use to earn an income.'*

'You could always pay me more for the time I work for you.'

I laughed. *'Excellent idea! How much am I paying you now? Whatever it is, increase it.'*

'Wow. I'm surprised you've gotten so successful if you'll trust someone you barely know to set the price.'

'Do I barely know you, Sira?'

I waited for her response. When it didn't come immediately —as it usually did—I wondered if I'd pushed too far. So I typed, *'Plus I have great lawyers who will hunt you down if your next check is written out for a million and change. Although, by then, I suppose you could've fled to a country with no extradition.'*

'I pick Bora Bora.'

Of all places, why that one? Clare and I had gone to Bora Bora for our honeymoon. I'd chosen it because the sound of the island's name had a certain humor to it, and it was far away from our regular lives. Back then, I was naive enough to think the distance would allow us to have an honest and open conversation, even after the point of no return. It didn't happen. Clare had been even more reserved, and there was nothing I could do about it. Our marriage was a legal confirmation that she'd never have what she truly wanted, could never be who she truly was. I understood her disappointment, although it was still hard not to take a little personally.

So we'd spent a week in paradise thousands of miles away from our families, and still thousands of miles away from who we were. Neither of us where we wanted to be or with the person we were meant to be with. Not that I'd ever actually thought there *was* someone I was meant to be with.

'*Have you been to Bora Bora?*' I asked.

'*No. But I like the name. It's fun to say.*'

'*It's also beautiful. Peaceful.*' And with the right person, probably extremely romantic. '*You should go.*'

'*As soon as I get that million dollar check.*'

'*But I would know where you'd gone and could find you.*'

'*True. I'll have to check on their extradition laws. I think I'll take off early so I can plan my escape.*' Escape. That sounded perfect.

I paused, wanting to say something I shouldn't even think. But I still had no idea what she looked like, only knowing her voice, her wit, and her intelligence. I really wanted to see her smile.

Because she was so comfortable with technology, I imagined her to be young, a bit younger than me. But apart from that, I couldn't imagine. Well, yes I *could* imagine. I imagined all the time. Another new occurrence in my life —daydreaming.

In my mind, she was pretty but not beautiful, average height, not particularly thin or particularly large. Yes, I wanted to meet her. Very much. If only to see if I was right. Right. If that were the sole reason, I might have been able to stop myself from typing what I did next.

'I really need to meet you in person.'

She could've lived anywhere on earth, but she lived here, in the same city I did. I didn't know what part of San Francisco she lived or worked in, but she'd mentioned enough local businesses and events to let me know she was inside the city or somewhere just over a bridge from here.

'I thought we'd gone over this. Besides, you'd have to contact my boss, and she'd probably say no. Nothing personal. It's company policy. Too much danger of one of the people thinking it's not a work-related meeting, or of both people knowing it's not a work-related meeting, if you know what I mean.'

Damn it. *'Does that sort of thing happen frequently?'*

'Not a lot. Just a few times.'

'Has it ever happened to you?' Did I really just ask her that?

'No.'

'Would you' Shit. What was I doing? *'Sorry. Finger slip.'*

'What were you going to ask?'

Something I shouldn't. *'Forgot what we were discussing.'*

'Scroll up and reread our conversation.'

'It wasn't important.' I pressed send and immediately started typing again. *'Okay, it was.'*

'You're a confusing man.'

I smiled. *'Very true.'* My fingers tapped the keys rapidly, but not hard enough to make any words appear. Because I didn't know what to write. Screw it. *'I'd really like to meet you. No strings, no bosses. Maybe tomorrow?'*

I waited a while for her to respond. Enough time to sit back in my chair and worry I'd crossed the line again.

'Why?'

Good question. Simple answer—because I was an idiot. Harder answer—because I needed to know if what I was feeling was real or just an illusion, something brought about by a smart, charismatic woman who would have absolutely no interest in me whatsoever. This was all so foreign to me, but I couldn't deny it was happening.

Why? Because if we met, maybe I would get an answer. I would know if our chemistry was only an effect of our anonymity or if it was something more. Because I had to know if what my brother had said was possible.

I picked up my phone and dialed her number before I could convince myself not to.

"Hello?" I don't know why she sounded so different—she hadn't changed, I had. My perceptions, at least.

"Sira?"

"Yeah." Her voice was hesitant, which it probably should be. We'd only spoken a few times and the last time had ended with me admitting I was married. It made sense for her to be a little battle shy.

"I know there are lines, boundaries to a working relationship, and I've always stayed within them. Always. I want you to tell me if I ever step too far across them or make you feel uncomfortable in any way. Because I would like our relationship to continue in whatever manner it can."

"Wow," she said after a moment. "You speak a lot faster than you type."

I sat up in my chair. "I'm about to say something that could be grossly inappropriate. Therefore, I want to be absolutely sure before I start that, if you were to feel uncomfortable—in any way —you would tell me. At that point, I would immediately stop the discussion and promise to never mention it again."

Her silence wasn't encouraging, but I would wait, living with a mind full of turmoil and doubt, for as long as was necessary.

"Okay."

I let out a breath. "You asked me why I wanted to meet you.

And my answer is because I don't type well enough, and I want to get to know you more than is possible with chat boxes and emails and phones."

"You're my client, Hayden."

"I realize that, and I've come to the conclusion that I don't care."

"You're married."

"I realize that too, and I do care about that." Which was the reason I was currently feeling nauseous. Because of a contract built on nothing but respect—no love, no passion, just respect. "My marriage is complicated. It's not something I've ever wanted to hide from you, but maybe I should have brought it up sooner, or at least before I started having feelings for you." I heard a long sigh.

"What kind of feelings?"

"I'm not sure, which is why I want to meet." My heart hadn't pounded like this since my father was alive. Fear. This was outright fear because this was something I couldn't control, couldn't maneuver or affect. This was another person having control over me, her thoughts more important than my own.

"How *many* feelings for me?" she asked.

"I'm hesitant to put a number to them because I'm not sure how that would be done. But I'm comfortable with saying 'some.'"

"'Some' isn't good. Neither is 'any' or 'one.' Those aren't good either."

"I know, but knowing that doesn't make them any less real. Or less confusing." I released my grip on the arm of my chair, stretching my fingers just so I had something to focus on other than waiting for her response. It didn't work—my fingers' movement had no effect on my anxiety level. "If we met, just once, I'd be able to understand them better. Maybe they'd turn out to be nothing. But if we never meet, then I'll never know.

And I would really, really like to know." To get past the wondering, hoping, fantasizing stage. Just end it without anyone getting hurt.

"What if they don't turn out to be nothing? What then, Hayden? I'm not going to break up your marriage."

"You don't need to. It's already irreparably broken. If it weren't, I wouldn't be asking you for anything."

"It's still not good."

"For what reason?" I kept my voice calm, even though it was a struggle. She hadn't said no yet. She'd said a lot of other things, but not 'no.' What if there was a chance that she felt the same? That I wasn't alone in this. That I wasn't imagining it.

She cleared her throat. "I like my job and would enjoy keeping it."

"So if we were to meet in a social environment, you would lose your job?"

"It depends."

"On...?" I understood her hesitancy but wished it wasn't there. I was putting myself on the line, admitting to something that shouldn't be, and all I wanted was for her to be honest, as well. Whatever the answer.

"If you were to make a complaint..."

"No matter what happens, I'll never complain about you."

"Even if you don't, I wouldn't be able to work with you anymore."

"What if I hired you full-time and kept my mouth shut?"

"Then you'd be a liar," she snapped. "And I'd be a whore."

I flinched back in my chair. "Whoa! That's not at all what I meant. Not even a tiny bit. All I'm trying to do is find a solution. I'm not asking for more than a meeting." *Right now.* After a moment, I asked, "Do you believe me?"

"Yes," she said quietly. "But I still don't think it's a good idea."

"What if we'd met somewhere else, in one of those chat

rooms or something and you didn't work for me? Would you agree to meet me for dinner?"

"In this scenario, are you married?"

"Barely." In this scenario or not. "We've both admitted that it's over, but it's still not public record. Would you say yes to dinner?"

"Yes." It came out as a whisper, like a secret she didn't want to share or admit to. So I knew neither of us was speaking hypothetically anymore.

I sighed, feeling unbelievably selfish, and unbelievably happy, and unbelievably guilty all at the same time.

"I never want to hurt you or create any problems for you."

"Too late."

"Have I hurt you?"

"No, but you've created a lot of problems."

"Ah, well then, I—"

"Because I want to meet you, too. And that's not good."

I couldn't have disagreed more. It was *very* good. All I had to do now was find a way to make the hypothetical into something real.

"I'd like to meet you, talk to you in person. That's all. I have zero intention of doing anything else. We would just be two people who get along, getting along face-to-face. Is that possible?"

"No."

I sighed. I was so used to getting my way, being able to logically argue my point until the other person had no choice but to agree. This wasn't business, though. This was more personal, more... me. That's what made it so different and so frightening.

"How would meeting me be any worse than autocorrect and typos?"

"To err is human, Hayden," she said wistfully.

So is to love.

12

ANDI

"Are we there yet?" I asked Emilia about two minutes into our jog. By 'jog,' I mean twenty feet of traditional jogging followed by thirty feet of dragging my feet while we power-walked. And by 'power-walk,' I mean walk slowly with bent elbows and fisted hands.

"Not even close. So you gonna tell me what happened or what?"

"Nothing, why?" Oh, shit. Rob must have told her about being blackmailed and that I was supposed to get him out of it. I still hadn't decided what to do. Every time Hayden sent me something about Inspex, I felt like I needed to throw up. What information could I possibly give Rob that wouldn't do massive damage to Hayden's project?

Or maybe Emilia had spoken to Hayden, and he'd told her he was feeling uncomfortable or that he needed to switch to a more professional assistant, a smart one. Totally logical, because right now, I didn't qualify.

"Well, *something* happened, because up until two seconds ago, your smile was huge. And don't blame the sunlight again."

Oh. I blew out a breath, even heavier than the last few. I

hated keeping things from her, but I knew how badly she would freak out if I told her about the conversation I'd had with her husband. Plus, that wasn't what I'd been smiling about. "Runner's high just wore off."

"We've gone about five hundred feet." True, but early in the morning in Golden Gate Park, weaving in and out and around all the other runners tripled the actual distance traveled.

I stalled until I knew she wasn't going to let me out of it. "Someone messaged me." And I shouldn't be thinking about it or re-reading it in my mind obsessively.

"Are you sexting with someone? I can't get Rob to do that with me. He claims it's something about getting a hard-on at work, but what's the point of having your own firm if you can't get a hard-on whenever you want, right?" Her smile was tight from the effort we were putting into our twice-a-week torture run.

"I agree with Rob. Not because of the hard-on thing, but because I know how easy it is for other people to find that stuff online." I thought of Hayden's last message—*Just looked up how much I pay you an hour. To save money and time, from now on, I'm going to leave all the vowels out of my texts. Thx :)*' Then the next: *'Btw yr gttng mr mny nw.'* It had taken me a minute to try all the possible vowel combinations. Once I'd figured it out, I thanked him for the raise.

"This one was a regular message," I said. "But it was...cute."

"What the hell? Cute? Andi Clark used the word 'cute.' Definite sign of the apocalypse."

"I seriously hope you're wrong. No way could we outrun a zombie yet." I wiped my hands over my face—hiding and trying to wipe off any sign of happiness that might be on there. "Ugh. I'm stupid-smiling about someone I have no right to stupid-smile over."

"Why not?"

"I have a confession."

"Say two Hail Marys and call me in the morning."

"I'd rather have two Bloody Marys and call you in the morning." I slowed down and stepped off the path so we wouldn't get trampled by other runners—not that I'd really consider us runners, of course. But we were trying.

She followed me, taking her water bottle out of the clip at her waist. "Confess quickly, before my heart rate goes back to sitting-on-the-couch level."

"I should've told you right away, but I wasn't sure what it meant or if it meant anything."

"Yikes, Andi is wearing her serious face today. What's up?"

We rested while I considered how to tell her about Hayden. "I think I screwed up again."

Emilia's body tightened. "In what way?" I couldn't blame her for being suspicious. She had every reason to be. When I screwed up, I screwed up big. And she always felt obligated to find a solution. It wasn't what I wanted, and I'd told Emilia countless times not to do it, but it always happened anyway. Which might be one of the reasons why I waited so long to tell her anything. But this one could affect her business, so I had to come clean. At least partially. Kind of like when you take a shower but don't wash your hair—*that* kind of coming clean.

"A line may have been crossed with one of my clients."

"What kind of line?" she asked after a long sigh. Probably more from needing oxygen after our attempted run than from frustration with me, but I wouldn't put money on it.

"Nothing physical, but we get along a bit too well. Professionally speaking."

"Well, is it harmless workplace-type flirting, men-and-women-can't-ever-be-friends kind of thing, or something more serious?"

I shrugged. "I don't know about his side, but on mine, it's like flirting-with-intent."

"And he flirts back?"

"Yeah, but probably without intent. Or at least not the *same* intent." Although in our last actual conversation, he'd pretty much put it out there—he had 'some' feelings for me. But he didn't specify that they were romantic, so I'd convinced myself they were more curious than anything else. Like how I wondered what having a penis would be like—I didn't actually want to *have* one because there were way too many downsides, but I was still curious and would want to play with it a little. Ugh. Bad example.

"Which client are we talking about?"

"I don't want to tell you. Not until I've figured it out."

"How long is that going to take? Because patience isn't my thing."

"I've noticed. But I don't want to get him in trouble, and you need the challenge."

"I drank a kale and avocado smoothie for breakfast this morning—there's no greater challenge than that." She nodded toward the path and, after I grudgingly agreed, we started running again. "Just tell me if it's the sex toy salesman."

"It's not the sex toy salesman. Happy?"

"Not as happy as you'd be if it *was* the sex toy salesman, but whatever." She laughed. "Okay, before I take the mystery man off your book, you should ask him if whatever you're thinking is reciprocated."

I stopped again, but not because I was trying to get out of the run. "Ask him? That's the worst idea ever." Especially because I'd be thinking about playing with his penis.

"Not outright, but not like we're in junior high either. We're adults, and adults can deal with this stuff honestly yet tactfully." She grabbed my arm and pulled me to continue. "Look, you need as many clients as possible. So unless you're absolutely sure one or both of you can't handle it, then you should figure out how to deal with it. Then the question becomes: If he's not romantically interested in you, can you keep your hands on your keyboard and out of your pants?" She laughed.

"This isn't funny, Em!"

"Yes, it is. Because I've never seen you like this before, and it's making my day."

I smacked her shoulder.

"Come on, this is *you*, Andi. You're smart and a great person. You'd never do anything horribly inappropriate. But since I don't know him, if you find out for sure that he's flirting-with-intent back, then I'll assign him to another VA. But I don't want to if it's all in your head."

Was it? Was it all in my head? Maybe. Possibly. Probably. Even if it weren't, nothing would happen other than me feeling a little uncomfortable while I worked with him. If we could continue working together.

"Second confession," I said. "He wants to meet. He knows we're not allowed unless he goes through you. But he didn't ask you—he asked me. So that implies it's social, right?"

She glanced at me quickly before refocusing on the path ahead. "Well, the good news is that just because a guy wants to see a woman socially, she isn't actually required to say yes. We won that right a couple years ago. If *he* hasn't realized that and takes it badly, then I'll take him off your book and everyone else's. We don't need those kinds of clients."

"He's not like that. I don't think he would take it badly. He'd probably do the opposite—apologize and be all noble and stuff. That's the problem...or one of them."

I couldn't even refer to our jog as power-walking anymore. It was more like slow-motion walking. Until Emilia figured it out and yanked my arm to make me speed up.

"I changed my mind. He sounds awesome, and you just stupid-smiled about him. So right after you fill Sara in on whatever work you've been doing for him, I'll take him off your book and put him on hers. And then you'll be free to go and get him."

"I can't do that! Because of the third thing, which is actually the thing I should've started with because it's the biggest, most important, and the reason I'm a horrible person for even thinking about him in that way." I paused, concentrating on taking in the air I'd missed during my rant. Plus, admitting you're a terrible person and admitting *why* you're a terrible person are two entirely different things—one takes a lot more courage than the other. "He's married."

"Wait." She stopped running and looked at me with wide eyes. "Have we been talking about Hayden Bennett this whole time?"

I grabbed her arm and pulled her off the path before she got us run over. "Maybe."

"It is! Oh man, can you imagine Hayden Bennett selling sex toys?"

"*Now* I can," I muttered. "Thanks a lot."

"Flirting with intent, huh?" Emilia took a sip of water, studying me. "Yes, Hayden is married, but I don't think it's going to last much longer. According to some gossip I may or may not have overheard at the club the other day, they haven't been seen out together in about a year, and I don't think they've *ever* been seen together smiling. Not that you should move on it, of course. Not until they're 100% split up."

I stopped panting, then stopped breathing entirely. "Are you suggesting that I camp out on his doorstep, hoping his wife leaves him?"

"God, no. You'd freeze your ass off." She laughed. "Stop being so serious, Andi. You barely know each other, and you've never met. Obviously, I don't think you should mess with a married man. And I know you would never do that, so what's the big deal?"

"It's not a big deal. It's a medium-sized deal." Why did anything with the word "deal" in it make me hungry?

I started jogging again, a little faster so we could finish this run and conversation, and I could go home to do some emotional eating. "It's entirely possible that our conversations would look completely harmless to an outsider and mean nothing to him. But for me, they're not. That's the problem. *My* problem. Do I try to ignore the way I feel and keep working with him, or do I just give up now?"

"Okay. So we're just discussing whether or not you should keep working for him?"

"Yes." For my sanity. For all the time I waste imagining about how we might meet, what he would say, what I would say—which in my head is always really smart sounding, but in reality, would be the exact opposite. But all that fantasizing was becoming a full-time job. And reality isn't patient.

"But," Emilia said, "if he were to split with his wife—which would have nothing to do with you because I know you'd never do that—then whatever happens happens."

I knew she just wanted me to be happy, to find someone who was as good to me and for me as Rob was to her.

"Just because it happened for you, doesn't mean it will for everyone."

"I know," she said. "And it would never have happened if Rob had been married. Most relationships born in the office are like tall, dry grass. They catch fire really easily, but then it gets so out of control all you can do is run like hell. Which is why I have the policies I do about interaction with clients." She smirked. "But it would be so great, wouldn't it?"

"Give it up, Em. It's not going to happen." With Hayden or

with anyone. I had way too many problems and too many examples of my truly horrible judgment.

"It's strange, though. Rob and I share a lot of the same friends with Hayden and Clare. And a lot of them *share* share, if you know what I mean."

I did—without her wink and weird facial expression. Rich people were easily bored, and bored people would do almost anything to stop being bored, including activities that might be considered risky or stupid. From what I could tell, Hayden worked all the time. So did that mean he didn't have time to be bored, or that he was trying to avoid the kinds of activities boredom encouraged?

"That's why it took me so long to figure out we were talking about Hayden," Emilia said. "Everything I've ever heard about him is that he's a workaholic who hates social drama and never steps out on his wife."

Why did the idea that he had integrity and was faithful disappoint me? "Well then, I guess that means he's happy with her, doesn't it?" My gaze didn't leave the ground in front of us, not until we reached Emilia's car. I couldn't deal with this. With him. It was causing more stress on my heart than the torture Emilia had just put us through.

"I need a Bloody Mary." Maybe then I'd gather up enough courage to go fire my amazingly noble billionaire client. Actually, firing him would kill two birds with one stone—I couldn't exactly leak information about Inspex if I wasn't working on it, could I?

Perfect solution. Of course, if it was so perfect, why did I suddenly feel the need to throw up? Oh, right. I always felt the need to throw up after doing anything that made my under-boobs sweat.

13

HAYDEN

I READ HER COMMENT AGAIN. I didn't expect it to have changed—I was just hoping I'd read it wrong.

'I'm going to be handing some of your work over to a colleague, Hayden.'

Nope. Still pretty much the same. *'Some?'*

'All.'

Great. The first time I get fired, and it's by my assistant. I felt a dull pain in my head—probably the bruise to my ego. Too bad my assistant couldn't get me an aspirin. Too bad I no longer had an assistant. Because she'd just fired me.

No, hurt psyche or not, I had no intention of being fired, especially without a logical reason. Granted, logic and reason didn't seem to be coming as naturally as they once did.

Damn it, I needed something a lot stronger than aspirin.

I considered asking her why but knew she'd have an excuse ready, one that had nothing to do with the truth. So why bother demanding she lie?

'Whatever I've done or said to made you uncomfortable was wrong. If you tell me what it was, I won't do it again.' There. To the point. Open-ended. And much harder to lie about.

'Nothing.'

'But...?' "Don't leave it like that, Sira. Come on." *'If I'm being fired, at least tell me why.'*

'You're married.' Well, she definitely hadn't lied. She must just think I'm a dirty old man or something. I wasn't sure how many bruises my ego could take in one day from this particular woman.

'You can't fire someone for being married. It's illegal.'

'Don't make me say it.'

Say it? We weren't *saying* anything. We were tap-dancing with words. *'Can we please discuss this on the telephone?'*

'Definitely no.'

I hated this. Hated having to be careful with my word choice, of not only trying to translate what I was feeling—something I was already confused about—into words on a screen. With no inflection, no emotion, they were just letters strung together that were too easily misunderstood.

'I'll make sure you get the best assistant we have. The second best, anyway. :)'

No. That was unacceptable. I wanted the best. I wanted her. *'We don't have a traditional marriage.'* Shit. Why did I write that? What was I suggesting?

'Are you swingers? Like, an open marriage?'

I blew out a breath. I'd never had to explain it. Never discussed it with anyone, including Clare until very recently. So what could I say to make Sira understand? Clare and I had more of a one-way door marriage. And until now, I'd been fine with it. I had a job that kept me overly occupied and a nice home. And when that wasn't enough, I had my right hand and lots of long showers. Not exactly what dreams were made of, but no one could say every aspect of their life was perfect. Cosmically speaking, I was still way ahead. I had more success than I had a right to.

On second thought, it was probably better that we not meet in person. If we did and it wasn't absolutely horrible, the world would probably collapse or start turning in the other direction.

'*Our marriage is complicated.*' In many ways. '*But I won't betray my vows.*' I'd signed a contract that I would never break, regardless of what, or whom, Clare did. '*That's not what I'm asking you for. This has absolutely nothing to do with my marriage.*' Although it wasn't totally off in left field, if I were honest with myself. Which I used to believe I always was.

'*I'm SO embarrassed right now. I didn't mean to suggest that you would or that you were even thinking of me in that way.*'

'*There's no need to feel embarrassed.*' Because I *was* thinking of her in that way. Knowing it was wrong for everyone and doing it anyway. '*My fault for not expressing myself clearly. Which is why I wanted to speak on the phone.*'

'*I hate talking on the phone.*'

I ran my hands over my face. This was useless.

A few seconds later, my cell phone rang. Damn it. I answered without looking, still staring at the screen, wondering if there was another way to convince her.

"Bennett," I grumbled.

"It's...Sira."

"Oh!" I looked up, obviously forgetting how the telephone worked, as well. I'd turned back into a teenage boy—complete brain malfunction as soon as a pretty girl started speaking to me. "I... How..." Could I have forgotten how to talk on the telephone?

"Should I call you back on your office line?"

"It's fine. I'm..." *Christ. Really?* When was the last time I'd felt this inept? This ridiculous? I'd asked if we could speak on the phone, and now I was proving myself incapable of doing it. I cleared my throat. "Wow. Please forgive me if I've ever said anything that made you feel as awkward as I do right now."

"You're feeling awkward?" Thankfully, her laugh was light and not anything more humiliating.

"I'm glad someone's enjoying it."

"You're a lot different than you seem on your LinkedIn profile. You might consider updating it."

"To say what?"

"That you're human. Not always sure of yourself."

"I usually am. Luckily, you're the only one who brings this out of me."

Her laugh stopped. "About that...Hayden, look."

I've seen enough movies to know the next thing she said wouldn't be good.

"I think it'd be better if we stop working together. I was joking about that 'second best' thing. I can find you someone else, someone just as good as me."

"I don't want anyone else. I want you." I'd like to think my comment only created the silence it did because she misunderstood it, because she'd thought I was referring to something other than just the way she worked. I'd like to think that. But I couldn't. Because it wasn't true.

"I can't...I can't do this, Hayden," she said finally. "It's not even about your marriage. It's more that......I'm incredibly tempted to do something I shouldn't."

"If you understood my situation—"

"Your situation doesn't matter. It's *our* situation that's the problem. For *me*. And the best way to deal with that is to remove myself from it."

"I don't want you to."

"Good thing I do, then."

I paused, wanting to tell her about Clare, to explain why I *needed* to keep feeling this way about someone. That it had never happened to me before, and I was terrified it would never happen again. That I'd go back to sleep and forget how to be alive. But I didn't know what words to use without betraying someone I respected and cared about. So I didn't say anything.

"The office will let you know as soon as they've found my replacement. Take care, Hayden. I...enjoyed getting to know you."

"Sira, don't!" But I was yelling at an empty line.

14

ANDI

"WHICH LEVEL OF HELL IS THIS?" I asked Emilia on our way into the country club. She didn't answer.

Today's torture was 'spinning.' Seriously, who comes up with this shit? Twenty-five sweaty women who pay good money to ride fake bikes while horrible music blares and a man in tight spandex shorts yells at us for being lazy. And we do this by choice? Even worse, we actually had to sign up in advance for this crap, just to get a spot.

"Do you want to press charges?" Emilia asked about a mile in. At least, I'm assuming we'd gone a mile. I wouldn't be sweating this much otherwise, right?

"What are you talking about?" I yelled back. Thankfully— and I use the word in the most ironic way—we'd gotten to the class early enough to snag two bikes next to each other. But even so, screaming was necessary.

"Hayden Bennett."

"Hayden?" My guess was that she'd waited until now so that I'd have no more oxygen flow to my brain and wouldn't be able to understand what she was talking about. Well, boy was she wrong—I wouldn't have known what she was talking about five minutes ago. Did that mean we could stop now?

"I'm not sure how we'll do it without your name coming up, Andi. But if you want to press charges, I'll support you."

"You have no idea how confused I am right now." And I couldn't blame a runner's high because we were biking to nowhere. Plus, I didn't actually know what a runner's high felt like. It was supposed to make this easier, wasn't it? And not so excruciating? "Why would I press charges against anyone, let alone Hayden?"

"Sexual harassment doesn't have to be physical, Andi. It can be verbal, too."

I stopped spinning and waited for her to follow. Because, obviously, I wasn't the one with impeded oxygen flow. "He didn't sexually harass me physically or verbally, Emilia. Why would you think that?"

The instructor yelled at me, his voice the only sound that was more piercing than the music. "Don't stop now! We got a long way to go!"

He was kidding, right? We weren't *going* anywhere. But, as evidenced by the number of glares I saw in the room, everyone else seemed to think I was holding back our journey or some-thing, so I started pedaling again.

Emilia wiped her hair from her face. "First, you tell me to reassign him because you think you might have crossed a line— I totally didn't believe that, by the way—which is why I tried so hard and so unsuccessfully to talk you out of it." She puffed out a few breaths as if she were in labor. No irony there. "But if my advice pushed you into something harassment-ish, I'll never forgive myself."

"There's only one thing you should never forgive yourself for, and that's making me do this class. But you didn't miss anything where Hayden is concerned. Or *was* concerned. Promise." I crossed my heart, holding it an extra moment to make sure it wouldn't explode. I swear someone told me exercise was supposed to be healthy. Liars.

"I figured, but I had to ask." Her non-pause made me wonder about the honesty of our relationship. Before I could call her on it, she started talking again. Well, huffing and puffing and talking again. "Especially after he called and practically begged me to convince you to work for him again. For more money, too."

"He begged you? Are you sure you're not getting him mixed up with one of the other men who can't live without me?" At least, that's what I *tried* to say—my wheezing probably made some of the words incomprehensible. "I don't think Hayden has needed to beg for anything in his entire life."

"Okay, 'beg' is too strong a word, but he did say that he'd never had anyone better, and he doesn't want anyone else."

"Maybe he should talk to his wife about that," I mumbled.

"So did he do something obnoxious or what?"

"No. Not in the tiniest bit. He never did or said anything close to harassment. He's a nice guy, and I would never complain about him. If anything, I should complain about myself."

"You *do* complain about yourself. All the time." She smiled, even after I reached out to smack her on the shoulder.

"Come on, ladies!" the torturer yelled. "We're halfway there!"

In desperation, I glanced at Emilia, who had obviously lost her mind—she was laughing. "I just can't work with him anymore. I'm uncomfortable, he's uncomfortable, and it's a total mess."

"Has he actually said he wants a physical relationship with you?"

"Not in those words."

"Well, are you absolutely sure the words he *is* using mean what you think they do? I know he's hot, and he has every reason on earth to fall for you because you're amazing, but could it be that you're putting more into what he's saying than is actually there?"

"Yes!" I hadn't meant to scream it, but luckily the torturer and his happy *torturees* thought I'd meant it in a cultish kind of way, so they all echoed my call.

"Yes," I said to Emilia quietly. "It totally could be that! In fact, I'm ninety-nine percent sure it *is* that! But I can't stop thinking about it, reading into things, hoping he's hinting at something he probably isn't hinting at. It's me. It's *totally* me. And I don't know what to do to stop myself from doing it. So the best thing for me to do is run away."

"You never run away."

"I always run away." I sat back so I could throw up my hands. "You just happen to only see it on Mondays and Thursdays."

"Speaking of, can you run away tomorrow instead of Thursday? I have an appointment that afternoon."

"Ladies," the instructor yelled, "if you can talk, you're not working hard enough."

I hated that man. And his tight little ass, too.

"This was a mistake—the class, I mean." I slowed down, crossed my arms, and glared at the torturer, daring him to say something.

I stayed in that position for the rest of the class, ignoring his not-at-all-subtle attempts to encourage me. He might be able to control the twenty-four other women, but no man in tights was ever going to intimidate me into exercise or anything else. Eventually, he gave up and, probably to prove his virility, started making comments like, "Looking good, ladies!" and winking at everyone but me. His insincerity was incredible, as was the way the exhausted women bought into it and lapped it up.

Seriously, no one looks good with boob-sweat rings and shiny, red faces. No one.

As soon as class was over, we all dismounted our bikes and walked bow-legged into the locker room. Emilia opened her assigned members-only locker and stood back as I grabbed the crap I'd stuffed into it.

"Spinning is awful, isn't it?" she said. "Running is terrible too, but not *as* terrible."

"Why don't we call it a tie?" I rubbed a hand over my ass gently. "I think they deliberately make those bike seats as painful as possible."

"If you'd been following the instructor, you wouldn't have been sitting long enough to worry about it."

"Wrong. If I'd been following the instructor, I wouldn't have been *alive* long enough to worry about it."

We put on our flip-flops—foot fungus was all about equality and didn't care how much money someone had—and headed for the showers. I'd gotten over my fear of naked people when I'd seen the club's shower set-up. If not for the pain one had to go through to *need* the shower, I'd be here every day. Each stall was as big as my entire bathroom, and the shampoo and conditioner they provided could actually tame my hair. Plus, their towels were incredibly poufy. It was like drying yourself with a stuffed teddy bear. Eww—disturbing image. I take it back.

Emilia started talking as soon as we were done hosing ourselves off. "I'm surprised you're letting whatever it is between the two of you stop you from doing the best client you've ever— Wrong word choice. Stop you from *keeping* the best client you've ever had." She didn't flinch when her towel fell. Since she'd lost all that weight and worked us both so hard to keep it off, she had no problem talking to me while topless. "He has a ton of work for you, right? He pays a higher wage than any other client, and your schedule would be a whole lot emptier without him. Can't you just find a way to ignore everything else?"

"I'm not sure." I pulled my shirt over my head one-handed, the other one clutching my towel to avoid an accidental nip slip.

"Andi, you are the strongest person I know. And probably the most focused. So let's run through a few different scenarios." She continued after I nodded warily. "Number one—this whole romantic entanglement thing with Hayden is all in your head. The answer to that is to suck it up and deal with it. You're not sitting next to him all day—you're across town from him. At night, you can dream about him sweeping you off to some secluded destination and banging your brains out, but during the day, you stay focused on your job and ignore the inclination to over-examine his every comment. Because they don't mean anything. He's married, and you're a good person. Therefore, it's not going to happen."

"You're right."

"Of course I am, but I'm not done."

I wiggled into my undies, the towel securely tucked around my waist. Emilia had no such trouble since her towel was already in the bin. So she just watched me struggle with an amused grin on her face. Where did she buy her confidence?

"Scenario number two," she continued, "he totally has the hots for you and wants to screw you on your desk until you have keyboard shaped dents on your ass."

"Thanks for the image which will never leave my brain." Granted, the screwing-on-the-desk one was ruined by the dents-in-my-ass one—'cause I don't need any more of those, thanks very much—but that was probably for the best.

"You're welcome. Now back to the scenario. Here's the flaw in it: As much as I love you, and as beautiful as I think you are inside and out, the guy barely knows you. So we're not talking about true love here."

We weren't? No, of course we weren't. If anything, we were talking about two people liking each other a lot, who hadn't been exposed to the dangers of getting sex mixed up with love. Who hadn't gotten confused and decided that great sexual compatibility meant they should be together. If anything, Hayden and I were just two people who'd gotten to know who each of us really were without the games and pressures of a physical relationship.

Shit. Was I talking myself *out* of it being real or *into* it?

Emilia went on, totally unaware of my screwed-up internal argument. "We're talking about a man who may not fully understand the parameters of your working relationship. Who might be lonely, have a terrible marriage, and think his respect for you and your work means more than it does. Now, I don't think Hayden Bennett is a stupid man. If you told him what's up, he should be smart enough to deal with it. If he can't, then that's on him, and you walk away with your head held high."

"You're right again." I tossed my wet towel into the bin and buttoned my pants.

"Of course, I am." She grabbed a fresh bottle of water from the club's members-only fridge, cracked it open, and downed at least half of it. "So, as we've just learned from both scenarios, this is not an insurmountable problem. I think you should consider giving him one more shot. I'm not going to force you into anything, but if you sit down with him and tell him what is and is *not* going to happen, it might clear things up between the two of you."

"Maybe. But you're not talking about *sitting down*, sitting down, are you? Because I don't think I'll be able to sit for a couple of days." I rubbed my butt again to increase circulation.

"Fine. You both talk standing up and in different places." She slammed her locker and spun the lock. "Oh, quick change of topic before you get back to worrying about things you can't control. Are you helping Rob with something? I'm guessing it's computer related because my help isn't good enough. Anyway, he mentioned that you've been hard to get a hold of."

"You mean you're okay with your hot husband getting a hold of me? Thank you! Rob will really help me forget about Hayden." Actually, thanks to caller ID and the fact that very few people knew my number to begin with, it had been easy to avoid her husband. I had nothing to tell him anyway.

She glared at me. "Just for that, I'm going to sign us up for another spin class and make sure we get two spots in the front line." Laughing at her own joke, she tucked her water bottle into her oversized purse. "I am now going to focus on my desperate hobble to the car and leave you to think about my incredible advice."

I did think about it. All the way to the car, on the drive home, and through four hours of Netflix binging. Oh man, if the zombie apocalypse doesn't seem all that bad compared to real life, you have serious issues.

Emilia was right—Hayden was probably just a bit confused. If I sat him down—metaphorically speaking, because sitting was out of the question for at least a few days and meeting him was out forever—and set some rules, maybe we could continue working together. After an unknown amount of time playing it straight, I'd be able to think of him as just another client. He'd be a paycheck, not a friend, and definitely not anything beyond that.

Plus, as was the case in Emilia's first scenario, I was probably just being an idiot and reading too much into everything. He had no interest in me, apart from me being an employee. It wasn't as if no boss had ever befriended an employee before. So maybe we could be friends, and I could figure out another way to handle the blackmail issue.

Right, because things always worked out the way I wanted them to.

15

HAYDEN

I WAS on my third cup of coffee, feeling jittery but no less exhausted. I'd spent the previous night working, but was so distracted by thoughts of Sira, everything had taken three times as long to go through. It was my own fault. She had every right to be upset. I'd never been fired before, but if I'd ever deserved it, now was the time. Eventually, the tang of disappointment would go away.

When my phone rang, I hesitated before answering, sure it was whomever the agency had chosen to replace Sira. "Bennett."

"We need to talk." *Her* voice. Not angry, not weak. Strong, like she was about to put me in my place. And, for once, for her, I would allow it.

"I'm listening."

"I really liked working with you, and I appreciate the complimentary things you said to my boss about my work." She took a breath. "I may have reacted badly, or misinterpreted certain things, and for that, I apologize."

"If an apology is necessary, it should be from me. Your reaction was completely appropriate."

"Thanks, but I don't agree. That being said, for whatever

reason—real or imagined—things may have gotten a bit...out of hand and, while I'm not exactly sure how or why, I'm hoping that if guidelines are set up, it won't happen again."

"What sort of guidelines?" I would agree to almost anything that would end with us speaking.

"Well, for one, meeting in person—even if you ask my boss —won't be happening. Our conversations, as much as I enjoy them, should be kept to a minimum to avoid any misunderstandings. And...um...there was a third one, but I forgot what it was."

"Something about me not being allowed to think about how much I'd like to buy you dinner, perhaps?"

"You think of— Um... No, that wasn't it. But now I think we should add a fourth—you're not allowed to say things like that."

"I'll do my best," I said, smiling. "But it's like handing someone a sealed envelope and telling them not to look inside. Can't be done."

I knew there was a line, and I knew I'd crossed it. In for a penny... Why not just stalk the poor woman? Who was only trying to do her job in a professional manner. The problem was that I never gave up. On anything.

Not since my father had beaten me unconscious after little league. Final game of the season, and an eight-year-old, hyper-competitive Hayden got pissed off at the ref's call, threw his mitt down, and stomped off the field. The memory of the injuries that had followed my outburst and a whole bunch of other paternal lessons still drove me. Had gotten me far. At least, in terms of money and shit I didn't give a shit about. Far enough to where I was seriously contemplating ruining a woman's life on the off chance our flirtation could be more than that.

Fuck you, Dad. Thanks a lot.

"You need to understand that certain...ideas have entered my consciousness," she said. "And I need them to go away. If you—

even in jest—play on those ideas, I'm going to have to permanently separate myself from you."

I should walk away now before I got in any deeper. Yes, I could find another assistant. No, I didn't want to. Sira understood me, read between my lines and gave me what I wanted before I knew what that was. But that was work, not life. Why did I think one would bleed into the other? Because they did in every other way. Work *was* my life.

Maybe I was in need of some serious therapy. Maybe I should just leave her alone. Maybe.

But the world didn't run on maybe. The world was made up of yes's and no's. And if you didn't pick one, someone chose for you. Another lesson I'd learned from my father. And from watching him die right in front of me.

"Do you understand, Hayden?"

"Yes," I said slowly, forcing the word out. "Yes, I understand." As much as I didn't want to.

16

HAYDEN

JUST LIKE ANY OTHER DAY, Clare was sitting on her chair when I came home. But instead of reading, she stared at the floor, her knees tucked into her chest. It was a subtle difference, and if our life together had any variation in it whatsoever, I wouldn't have noticed.

"How was your day?" I asked. Same words, different actions. Instead of just walking by her on my way to the kitchen, I stopped.

"Fine. Yours?" Her voice was strained, hoarse.

"Clare, what's wrong?"

"Nothing."

I waited for a moment, wondering if I should just leave her alone, take her at her word. I probably should. It was what she obviously wanted. But I didn't. "Clare, talk to me."

When her head popped up, I saw her eyes, red from crying, her brow tight with anger. "I said it's nothing!"

"You don't have to tell me if you don't want to, but it's obviously not nothing."

"What the hell do you know?" She vaulted out of the chair and shoved my chest with both hands. I stepped backwards, but she kept coming, shouting uncontrollably. "You don't know anything about me, Hayden. Least of all how I'm feeling."

When she slapped me across the face, I went from stunned to *more* stunned. I pushed her away as gently as I could. "What's wrong with you?" I'd known her for six years and had never seen any violence in her before. I'd barely even seen her angry, other than a short-lived fight with a friend or when the caterer screwed up. But never at me.

She came at me again, raising her hand to strike.

I grabbed her wrist and backed her up. "What the hell?"

Her eyes widened when her back hit the wall, and she yanked to be free, lifting her knee a little too close to my balls for comfort. I slammed into her to keep her still, to not give her room to recoil. I pressed her hands against the wall with mine, our bodies flush. Her breath came fast, heavy, her chest rising and falling in gasps, her jaw shaking.

"Where is this coming from?" I was too close to her, my body against hers, blocking her movement. It had been too long since I'd been in this position, felt a woman's breasts pressed against my chest, her hips pushing into mine. I felt the blood rush to my cock, felt it press into her belly.

Right then it could have been anyone. I was so confused, so frustrated. All I wanted was to feel good. To feel *something*. Relief. Release. Wanted.

She leaned forward as if to kiss me, her lips separated. I shied back, letting go of her. Her hands immediately dove to my belt, opening up my pants, gripping my erection. It had been so long since someone had touched me, wanted to be with me. Clare was my wife. So what was stopping me?

I cupped her jaw, unable to keep my eyes off her mouth. I could take it, cover it with mine, lift her skirt and bury myself inside of her. It would be so easy, such a relief.

But this? This was wrong. I wanted her, and it could never happen.

"No," I said, pulling away, prying her off, and stumbling back. "What's wrong with you?"

"What's wrong with *you*?" she spat. "Why can't you just fuck me, Hayden? Just let go for one second, stop over-thinking everything, and take me right here?" Her skirt was tucked up, exposing long beautiful legs and the edge of lace panties.

She was so beautiful and so sexy. And she didn't want me. Not really. All of this had been caused by a level of emotion that she'd never felt for me. And never *would* feel for me.

"You're not thinking clearly." Which made two of us. I swallowed, unable to look at her anymore because my control was paper-thin. I turned away and dragged myself into the kitchen, fastening up my pants on the way. "You're angry. At something or someone. Not me, that's for sure. Because you don't care enough about me to feel that much passion. So, who is it?"

Her voice came from right behind me, still breathy. "I care about you."

"Not like that, you don't." I went around the island so there would be a big chunk of granite between us, protecting both of us from something that shouldn't have even gone this far. "Who is it?"

She slid onto a stool, staring at me, her anger and desire defused and replaced with remorse, regret maybe. Then she looked down as if she couldn't face me and speak at the same time. "No one you know."

"Shannon?"

Her head popped up in surprise. "How did you...?"

"Just because I try to stay out of the drama of our social circle, doesn't mean I don't know what's going on."

A panicked look appeared on her face. "What are people saying about me?"

"Don't worry." I leaned back against the counter. "They don't know."

She fidgeted. "Know what?"

We'd never talked about it, but I never thought it was because she was trying to keep it from me.

"I'll admit to not being the most attentive man in the world, but I'm not stupid."

"I didn't say you were," she said quietly, picking at a fingernail.

"We've been married for three years, known each other for six. Do you really think I've never noticed how you look at her?"

Clare's brows came together. "Maybe *I'm* the inattentive one because I have no idea what you're talking about."

I sighed. Enough. I'd had enough lies and numbness, sleepwalking through my existence with no wonder or excitement, no goal I actually gave a shit about.

I took a bottle out of the wine fridge and filled two glasses, not speaking until we each had one to stare into. "We have a good life, don't we? Security, stability, friends."

"Yeah," she said, swirling her glass gently.

"Do you know the only thing I've ever really wanted and have never had?" And, until recently, never imagined I *could*.

She shook her head.

"For someone to look at me the way you look at Shannon. For someone's eyes to light up when they see me, to warm just because I'm there. To need me that much." I took a sip of wine to ease the ache in my throat. "To love me that much."

"I don't—"

I silenced her with a hand. "We're past ignoring it, Clare. Lying to each other or pretending things aren't what they are."

Her shoulders slumped, her incredible confidence and posturing gone. "How long have you known?"

"Since the beginning."

"That's impossible. We—"

"Since the beginning," I repeated. Since before we'd gotten married. Before we were even engaged, I'd known. When we'd had sex, I'd known, and I'd pretended she actually wanted me, loved me, and wasn't just letting me inside her because of a marriage certificate.

"Why'd you marry me then?"

"For all of the wrong reasons and a few of the right ones."

She shook her head, but she also looked relieved—not to have to hide anymore, to have someone to be honest with. "I'm sorry."

"There's no need to be. It is what it is. I could've done something, said something, so I'm not without fault." I filled her glass after she emptied it.

"Shannon dumped me." She raised her glass in a mock toast. "Said she was too tired of hiding."

That explained her outburst. "Did she ask Frank for a divorce?"

"No." She chuckled sadly. "She's trying to go straight."

"Think it'll last?"

She shrugged. "Not sure. Frank has no idea, so..."

"You thought *I* had no idea. Maybe he already knows."

"Maybe. But he isn't the man you are. Her cheating just makes him feel better about his own. If he knew the other man is actually a woman, he'd probably just keep pretending he didn't know. I guess it'll be easier now that we're not together anymore." She swung off the stool and came around the island, sliding her glass across the counter until she was two feet away from me.

"I should've done a lot of things differently, Hayden." Her voice was soft, sorry.

"Me, too."

"But it feels kind of great to finally talk to you honestly about it."

I smiled. "It does, doesn't it?"

She nodded without speaking for a moment. "So what do we do now?"

"Not sure." I hadn't given it much thought. I'm very good at closing my eyes to what I don't want to think about.

"I still love you. We could try working on things."

I nodded. "We could." But it would never be enough for either of us. Making do for the sake of appearances. I watched her dazedly as she loosened my tie. But I put my hands over hers when she started to unbutton my shirt. "Are you bisexual?"

"I've always known I was gay," she said, shaking her head. "I had boyfriends because it was expected, but I always had a good...*friend* for sleepovers."

I took her hands and brought them to her sides. "Then thanks, but whether we stay together or not, I'd rather you not force yourself to sleep with me."

"I wouldn't be."

"Really? Last time I checked, I had a dick. So if you're not bisexual, I don't have the equipment you want."

She stepped back. "Why did you stay with me all this time if you knew?"

"I told you—some right reasons and some wrong reasons."

"Can you be more specific?"

I took our glasses into the living room, setting them on the coffee table and sitting on the couch. It surprised me when she sat next to me versus on her favorite chair.

"My first reason is your father." Not because he was the head of the company I worked for, though. I'd gotten the job on merit. I'd *taken* the job because it was the expected thing for me to do. "He's—without a doubt—the biggest bigot I've ever met."

She didn't even react, definitely didn't disagree. We'd been through enough family dinners at her father's house to know all about what he called 'The Downfall of San Francisco.' I couldn't count how many times I'd heard his descriptive commentary about other people's kids who'd come out, every time sitting next to Clare, wanting to take her hand or at least reassure her that not everyone felt that way. Instead, having to redirect the conversation to Bart's second favorite topic—money.

"You've stayed with me for years and put yourself through so many Sunday dinners, just so he wouldn't disown me?"

"Honestly, I've never thought that would be a bad thing, but I know it would hurt you." And as much as I hated her father, I loved her more.

"Why else?"

"Because I'm an idiot." I blew out my breath, completely unprepared for this conversation and this moment. It was a rare thing for me to so bluntly admit my shortcomings—both because I couldn't afford to show weakness, and because no one really cared. "I figured by the time I was ready to stop working hundred-hour weeks, you'd come out, we'd get a divorce, and I might be lucky enough to find someone who actually likes me."

"I like you. I just don't like your dick." She smiled.

"Okay, then," I said, totally unoffended. "I'll be sure to put that on my personal ad—'must like dick.'"

"No way!" She backhanded me in the chest. "No husband of mine is posting a personal ad."

"I was kidding, Clare. I'm not looking for anyone."

"Why not?" Turning her body to face me, her expression settled into seriousness. "I can't come out. Not yet. Maybe not ever. But that doesn't mean you can't find someone. Half my friends are having affairs, and *all* of their husbands are."

"I'm not interested in that. Sneaking around, worrying someone we know might see me with someone else?" Reality didn't matter nearly as much as perception. And integrity. As soon as that faltered, regardless of the reason, the whole thing could come tumbling down. I made a promise to myself as much as I did to Clare. "No thanks."

She took a breath. "Then we'll get a divorce. The other half of my friends—the ones not having affairs—are divorced and either dating men ten years younger or are on their second marriage with someone ten years older."

"Maybe," I said slowly. "But before we do anything, we should discuss it more."

"Are you worried my father will convince the board to fire you?"

"It's a concern, yes. Not enough to force you to stay married to me, but it's a concern."

"Please, Hayden." Her eye-roll was so dramatic, her entire head got involved. "My dad likes you more than he likes me. If, or when, I come out, he'll like you *way* more than he likes me. Plus, you'd get a lot of pitying slaps on the back because you were both duped by his daughter, the lesbo." She slapped her hands onto her thighs. "That's settled. We're getting a divorce. I want the China." She smiled, happier than I'd seen her in a long time. But I couldn't help but think we were rushing things.

"Think about it first, Clare. There's no hurry. Big decisions need more than fifteen minutes of consideration."

Her brow furrowed. "Yesterday I didn't know there was another way to have the life I wanted without hurting you. Today I do. So if I wait for tomorrow, I'll just be wasting time. Yours and mine. Plus, we need to get you laid ASAP. Seriously, Hayden, two years? I didn't think that was possible."

I wouldn't have either, if I didn't know firsthand—pun intended.

I didn't know what to say. Sure, sex would be highly appreciated, but acting before you'd given an idea time to brew, thought about possible scenarios, ramifications, benefits and—

"Wake up, Hayden." She waved her hand in front of my face. "You have that look on your face, like you're so lost in your own head you've forgotten anything else exists. So, back to you getting laid. I have a ton of friends who would kill to hook up with you. Seriously, you'd be horrified to know how many comments they make. All the time. Don't freak out if they start swarming as soon as I tell them that we've split."

"Your friends would do that to you?"

"It's the way we are." And exactly why I would never want any of them.

"Can't you just tell them I'm gay?"

"Jerk." Her laugh was open, more honest than I'd ever known. "Come on, there's really not even one of them you'd want to do? Damn, Hayden. So many gym memberships, juice fasts, and boob jobs gone to waste. Okay, fine, we'll find you someone else. There isn't anyone you're even attracted to?"

I must have taken too long to speak because she suddenly bounced up and said, "I knew it. Who is she? Do you know her from work?"

"I... It's complicated."

"Is she married or with someone?"

"I don't know."

"Well, then, the first thing you need to do is find out."

I shook my head. "It won't matter. She knows I'm married, and she's not really happy with me right now."

"Then we tell her you're not married and figure out how to make her fall in love with you." As if it were that easy. I didn't even know what love felt like and had never wanted anyone to love me before. So how would I be able to make someone?

"Come on, Hayden. I thought you never gave up. Don't be an ass and let this be the first time."

17

HAYDEN

I MET Bart near the Ferry building, slightly confused by both his need to meet and the venue he'd chosen. When I saw him standing with another man whose back was to me, that confusion turned into suspicion.

"Hayden," my father-in-law called. "Thanks for coming on such short notice."

When I reached out my hand, the other man turned around. "Hey, Bennett. I was just telling Bart how you could use the vitamin D."

"Tim." Since when did Bart need a sidekick, let alone a salaried one? I shook hands with both men and waited for an explanation.

"Do you know why I asked you to meet me here?" Bart turned and walked away, Tim right on his heels, me following warily. When Tim glanced back at me, and the old man slowed a bit, I assumed that meant the question was directed at me.

"I have no idea." But I can't say I was looking forward to finding out.

"What we're standing on right now is man-made. *American* made. A hundred and fifty years ago, this was all part of the Bay.

When space got tight, the founders of this great city sold parcels of water. Called them 'water lots.' It was the owner's responsibility to fill them in."

Growing up in a San Francisco family that had built its fortune in shipping meant I knew the Bay's history, but I let the old man enjoy giving his lecture.

"Quickest way to do that was to bring in all the ships nobody wanted anymore and sink them." His speech was as slow as his gait.

And right now, I had a lot more work to do than patience. "Because people were only concerned with looking for gold. Yeah, I know the story. What does it have to do with me?"

"I'll tell you what it has to do with you." He swung around to face me, his eyes showing an anger that wasn't apparent in his voice. "I'm not a ship that can be sunk, you understand?" Not in the slightest. Good thing he didn't seem overly concerned with what I thought. "Your father and I built this company from nothing, Hayden. We put everything we had into it. Gave up everything."

That wasn't even a little bit true. Both men had come from old money. Both men had also made sure their business didn't cut into their womanizing and drinking time. The only thing they'd truly excelled at was hiring competent employees whose hard work made Conure one of the largest cargo shipping companies in the United States. The only thing they'd sacrificed had been their families.

"When your father—God rest his soul—passed away, I took you in, gave you the tools you needed to someday run the whole thing. Just like he'd have wanted."

Yes, my father had wanted a son to take over his share of the business, but not the two he'd provided DNA for. No, we were too weak, too stupid to run Conure. So neither he nor Bart had given me anything. I'd had to work my way up the ladder, despite sharing a last name with one of the company's founders.

"I've watched you grow, my boy." Is there anything more condescending than calling a twenty-nine-year-old man 'boy?' "And, for the most part, I'm proud of what you've done."

"For the most part?" No longer able to stand there and listen to Bart's bullshit or watch Tim obediently nodding and kissing ass, I started walking again. Unfortunately, the two men took that to mean I wanted to continue this little tour of Christmas-Never-Happened and followed me.

"Now, I've always left you to do your own thing, Hayden. You're a good man, from good stock."

Now he was comparing me to livestock?

"You're not one of those flakey liberals who care more about themselves than this city and the people who built it. You don't need a parade or any of that bullshit. But now I'm hearing whispers of a deal you're putting together..."

That's when I starting caring about the conversation. "What kind of whispers? From whom?" Obviously, people talk. I'd be stupid to believe that word hadn't gotten around about some aspects of the Inspex deal. My concern was how many aspects and what Bart was being deliberately vague about.

"Can't say where it's coming from," the old man said.

"Really? You brought me and the head of the marketing department down here just to enjoy the waterfront and our stroll down memory lane?"

Tim shrugged when I looked at him. "You know how the business world is, Bennett. We're like a pack of teenage girls."

"Actually, I don't give a lot of thought to teenage girls, Tim." It was his flippancy that set me off, this bizarre meeting, and the men's obvious knowledge of my business and unwillingness to share their source. "But I do know how business works. And seeing as the three of us use the same letterhead, if either of you heard anything that would affect my deal, I'd like to think you'd share that information even without the dramatic view."

"You mean because you've been so forthcoming with us about Inspex, right?" Tim's comment oozed sarcasm.

"Why the hell would I share sensitive information with anyone who compares themselves to a teenage girl?"

"Enough!" Scowling, Bart raised his hand. "I didn't bring you down here to listen to you squabble."

"Then what *did* you bring us down here for?" I snapped.

"To tell you that I will not be forced out of my own company," he growled. "I'm not going to stand by while you sink everything I've built." Suddenly, I remembered who I was dealing with—my father's equal in too many ways, a tyrant to his employees and his daughter, a man who'd never faced a foe he couldn't crush. But I wasn't his foe.

"I'd never try to force you out, Bart, even if I had the power to." The board of directors was the only one who could force his retirement, and they still believed he was in charge. "The Inspex deal will benefit all of us. Even him." I flicked my head toward Tim. "But I'm not going to compromise the entire project by sharing it before all the pieces are in place." I sighed, knowing I had to give him something. "In about a month, the federal government will be announcing a new project."

Even saying that much was more than I'd wanted to share. Recognizing the signs of something big coming down the pipeline and asking the kinds of vague, theoretical questions politicians would answer wasn't enough. I had to wait for the bidding process to open, just like everyone else. My only advantage was being able to line up the manufacturers and get them to sign exclusivity contracts before the news broke.

"Whoever wins that contract," I said, "has to come in with a bid that offers higher quality at a lower price than everyone else. Down to the penny."

"He's right, Bart," Tim added, as if he actually knew what he was talking about. "Down to the bolt."

"I don't need your help on this, Tim." No way could either man miss my anger. "I need your silence, now and the next time you hear a rumor you want to spread." I ran a hand over my mouth. "Thank you for the tour of the ship graveyard, Bart, but I have to get back to work. When I have news to share, I'll share it."

"With Brecken Shipping?" Bart growled. Brecken Shipping was one of our major US competitors.

"What are you talking about?"

"Who do you think we heard about Inspex from, Hayden? Because, like you said, it sure wasn't you."

This was the worst possible news. If Brecken knew about Inspex, the only ace I had left was the work I'd already done. All that work... How the hell had Brecken found out? And who else knew?

Damn it. "I need to go." I paused, considering my next words. "I have no desire to fight with anyone. I'm only doing what I think is best for Conure. Just like my father would've wanted."

18

ANDI

GETTING a phone call from a guy shouldn't make a twenty-three-year-old woman feel like she was thirteen. Or even more embarrassingly—*act* like it. Especially when the guy who was calling had no interest in her, no matter how old she was. Not to mention that I'd just set some pretty firm restrictions on what our relationship was and wasn't. Sadly, those restrictions had very little to do with what I wanted and didn't want. Proven by my prepubescent reaction to seeing his name on my Caller ID.

Oh yeah, and there was still that sentence screwing around in my head: 'I'll figure something out.' What the fuck was wrong with me? So far I'd been able to dodge Rob's calls, but I was tired of getting the same voicemail message asking how it was going. How did he think it was going? It was shit. This whole thing was shit.

So I stopped squealing, sat back down, ran my hands over my smile, and put on a grown-up expression. He was a man... who I worked for...who obviously needed to talk to his very professional assistant, so maybe I should pick up the damn phone already.

"Hi," I squeaked. Oh yeah, that was professional. And lots of points for originality, too. Ugh.

"Who else do you work for?" Hayden's voice was flat, expressionless, and that put me on an uncomfortable edge. He hadn't used that tone of voice with me since our very first phone call, back when he didn't know me at all. So...

"What's wrong, Hayden?"

"Tell me who your other clients are." The order was more growled than spoken.

"Why? Do you need a new butt plug?" I snapped. "Because whatever you have up your ass right now seems to be working just fine."

"I'm glad you're amused because I sure as hell am not. I want the names of any of my competitors that you work with."

What the hell? I hadn't even figured out how to screw him over without screwing him—physically or professionally—so what was he talking about? "I can't tell you that. And you know I can't tell you that because it was on the contract you signed with the agency." So why was he asking? "We don't share information on our clients."

"Even when someone offers you enough money to do so?"

Whoa. Maybe my paranoia was misdirected. Maybe everyone in business was a crook, and Hayden was no different. "Are you...are you trying to bribe me?"

"I'm not into sloppy seconds. And I don't cheat to get what I want. All I want to know is who you gave it up to and how much it cost him."

"I'm sorry—all I heard was the incredibly offensive parts of that statement. Was there anything else to it? Anything that *didn't* make you sound like a complete asshole?"

"Tell me who it was, Sara." He hadn't called me that since our very first conversation. And, weirdly, it made everything more real.

"No one bribed me." I was pretty sure I was in an intellectual sort of shock—the type where your brain comes up with a bunch of scenarios but, since none of them make any sense whatsoever, everything just kind of shuts down and plays dead and the only thing left is bitchiness.

I took a deep breath. "What's this about?" I should've just hung up, maybe yelled a couple of curse words before I did. But this was such a huge departure from the Hayden I'd gotten to know, and I really needed something to help my brain sort this shit out.

"It happens sometimes—a competitor playing the game well, making a lower bid, calling my bluff—and I suck it up."

I had no idea where he was going with this, but it didn't sound like he was going to break into song anytime soon.

"When you play for high stakes, you accept that you'll lose a few. But I can't lose this one. So I made a few calls, spoke to some of the people I've been negotiating with..." He paused. "Damn it, I can't lose Inspex! I can't. It would ruin everything."

This was about Inspex? "You know what would be great, Bennett? If you told me what the hell you're talking about and what it has to do with me."

"I'm going to ask you this once. And your answer had better be the truth." He paused for a moment. "Have you been leaking information about Inspex to my competitors?"

"What? No!" I jumped out of my chair. "No, I didn't do anything like that. You send me something, I work on it, and then I send it right back to you. I don't print out anything, I don't talk to anyone else. I swear." This was bad. I couldn't prove a negative. If he accused me publicly, Emilia would have no choice but to fire me. And if he decided to push it, I'd have to come clean to protect Emilia's business. And then I could be brought up on charges. Again. "I swear, Hayden. I didn't share anything with anyone. If someone leaked stuff, it wasn't me."

Not for lack of trying, though. My anger was so incredibly hypocritical. I had intended to give something to Rob's blackmailer. I just hadn't decided what would satisfy a criminal but not ruin two good men. Which meant that I was innocent of whatever Hayden was talking about. Being accused of something I didn't do felt worse than being accused of all the awful things I *did*.

"I want to believe you, Sira," he said, sounding defeated. "I want to trust you. But this is business. This is beyond my trust issues or even my livelihood. This kind of thing affects everyone involved, all the way down to the person who repairs the copier. If I don't close this deal, my people don't get paid. I can't hide this—it's already gone too far."

"I can find out who did it. Please, give me a chance to find out what happened before you say anything to anyone."

"How do you propose to do that?"

By breaking the law, my plea agreement, and my promise to myself that I would never hack anything ever again. It didn't matter that I would be doing it while trying to help because that was the same excuse I'd given myself last time. Trying to help one person always seemed to hurt someone else. And in this case, I wasn't even sure I was concerned with helping Hayden or Rob. I think I was more concerned with helping myself.

"There's always a trail left behind," I said. "You just have to know how to find it."

"Then find it. Prove I was right to trust you, Sira. Please." It was the hardest 'please' I'd ever heard, as if he'd squeezed it out through a locked jaw. It was also the most desperate. Only Hayden could pull off those two inside one word.

I kept my questions focused—what had been leaked and to whom. His tone was flat as he told me about his conversation with the senator, how Conure's biggest US competitor had been sniffing around for information he hadn't shared with anyone else. Then Hayden had called the owner of a small parts manu-facturer who Hayden had discovered and no one had ever heard of. Whoever leaked the information had obviously known exactly what was in the deal Hayden was about to propose, probably down to the page number it was on.

"I didn't do this," I said when he was done. "But I'll find out who did. Promise."

"I hope so, Sira. I really hope so. I'll be spending the weekend figuring out if there's a way to salvage this, to have *something* to present to the board so they don't fire me. I'll need to tell them who screwed us over, and I really hope I won't have to use your name."

"Me, too," I whispered too late.

After he'd hung up on me—not that I was doing anything but pretending to be an empty line anyway—I slumped down into my chair. He'd given me a chance to find out, which meant that he hadn't already convicted me, but he didn't sound hopeful either. I knew he'd hated making that call as much as I'd hated getting it. But he'd given me a chance. And despite the fact that it meant breaking the law again, a chance was more than I deserved.

So far, I'd been putting off doing anything about Rob's situa-tion. Now, with this chance—fingers crossed—I would do the right thing for the right reasons and wouldn't ruin anyone's life who didn't deserve it.

It took a while to hack into Conure's mainframe. The fire-walls were old-school and easy to get through, but there were a lot of them. Hopped up on caffeine and nervousness, I kept checking over my shoulder as if a S.W.A.T team would barge in any second. Thankfully, besides being paranoid about all the wrong things, I'd somehow gotten in a few of the right things, too.

The second I'd stripped down and reconfigured the new

computer Hayden bought me, I set up a complicated routing system for my IP address and a much better security system than Hayden's multimillion-dollar company had. First, the cops would need to know to look, and then they'd need to know *where* to look. And since this was my first hack since I'd gotten busted—yay me, where's the cake?—I was probably way down on their list of interesting people.

Once inside the mainframe, I could basically go wherever I wanted to. Every email, every document was accessible. Nowadays, even the copiers left a trail of everything that had gone through them. For ease of use and speed of copies, documents were scanned onto the hard drive and then printed from the digital version. Convenient for everyone—including people who shouldn't be looking. People who weren't allowed to.

People like me.

19

HAYDEN

I SLAMMED the door and threw my briefcase on the floor. I wasn't going to get any work done tonight. I wasn't going to do anything but fume. I'd been duped. All I could hope for now was that it hadn't been by Sira. I'd given her far more sensitive information than I should've, allowing a person I barely knew access to secrets that could ruin the biggest contract Conure had ever bid on and make a US senator add me to the list of people *not* to do business with.

Stupid-stupid-stupid. Sira could be working out of a prison for all I knew. Maybe that's why she couldn't meet me in person —visiting hours were only for family or conjugal visits.

This was, without a doubt, the biggest screw-up I'd ever made in my professional life. It could end with me being forced out of my job, losing my stake of the company, even being black-balled in the business world. I'd be exactly who my father always thought I'd be.

Damn it, I hoped I was wrong and that she hadn't just been stalling when she'd asked for time to investigate. If I hadn't wanted to trust her so badly, I would've hired an outsider to look into it, but she'd seemed so afraid of me telling anyone. I didn't want her to lose her job if she wasn't to blame. And I wanted so badly to not have been wrong to trust her. To care about her.

Stupid. She'd probably be in Bora Bora by tomorrow, and I'd be left to pick up the pieces red-faced and feeling like an idiot. Because I was one.

Too tired to go through our normal bullshit, I passed right by Clare and headed for the wet bar. A glass of bourbon would help. If it didn't, I'd have another. And another. Until all thoughts of Sira and this mess disappeared from my mind. Then I'd flop onto the bed with my shoes still on and be blissfully numb until morning. So at 7:00am, I'd be ready to pick myself up, take a very long, stress-relieving shower, and prepare myself for damage control.

In the time it had taken to set up that brilliant and complicated plan, I'd finished my first drink, the bourbon-flavored ice falling onto my lips. So I poured number two.

"What's wrong?" Clare asked from behind me.

I spun around, the bourbon splashing onto my hand. I was surprised she'd even noticed. Even looked up from her book to see me. Even though we'd stopped pretending we wanted to be married to each other, my life was the same.

The only thing constant is change. Nope, not in my world. In my world, the only thing constant was everything. Everything plodding forward, and me asleep with my eyes open, wondering when it would end but doing nothing to slow it down or hurry it up.

As I wiped my hand off, I said, "Why would you think anything is wrong?"

"Because you are having two more drinks than you usually do."

"I'm surprised you notice how much I usually drink or don't drink."

"Wow." She stepped back at my tone. "Well, I buy the liquor, and I'm usually the only one who drinks it. Is that an acceptable answer?"

When I looked at her, I saw that her brow was furrowed as if I'd hurt her. Shit, I didn't want to hurt anyone. "I'm sorry, Clare. Yes, I had a terrible day. I didn't mean to take it out on you."

"Was it my dad's fault?"

"No. Today, for once, it wasn't his fault. Of course, if I head straight for the bottle when I come home on Monday unemployed, then yes, it will be your father's fault." I put up my hand. "I take that back. If I get fired, it will be entirely *my* fault." For trusting someone too much.

"I doubt that, Hayden," she said, taking the drink from me and topping it off. "You're pretty great, but my dad is an ass. So whatever happened today was probably his doing. Not that he'd admit it."

We didn't speak about Bart very much, but she was absolutely right about him being an ass. Or worse. He was also my employer, Clare's father, and the reason we'd gotten married. While Clare and I had known *of* each other years before we met, Bart had set it up perfectly as soon as he could—his beautiful daughter shoved into the arms of his favorite employee, who also happened to be the son of one of the only men he'd ever considered his peer. The years since my father's death had only made Bart more certain he wanted me in his family—what with the shares of the company I still held.

Our relationship had been expected, and both of us had met those expectations, our long courtship a subtle indication that neither of us wanted to get married. I think we were both waiting for the other to back out. Truthfully, it was my lack of courage that had brought us to the altar, not any noble idea of chivalry or to help her get away from an overbearing and bigoted father. I didn't know Clare's reasons, other than trying to be someone she wasn't. All of that healthy reasoning had been topped off by an enormously ostentatious ceremony and reception neither of us had wanted.

"I wouldn't worry. He knows how lucky he is to have you." Clare made herself a drink and went back into the living room. "I do, too."

I didn't ask what she meant by that—if she was referring to my value to her father or to her. I hoped for both. I'd worked my ass off for years, and I was damn good at my job. And even though our relationship held no romantic love, I *did* love her. Respected her as a friend and as a woman.

I excused myself to my office, taking the bottle with me. I closed the door and spent a long time staring at the computer without turning it on, remembering the day Sira had helped me set it up, and I'd pestered her into revealing more about herself than she was comfortable sharing.

I'd never tried coaxing personal information out of someone who I had no right to ask, but I seemed to be good at it. I'd never tried because I'd never really cared to know—if people wanted you to know them, they spoke. If they didn't, they kept their mouths shut. Hell, I'd watched Clare stay silent for years. But I'd wanted to know more about Sira, and so I pushed. I pushed when I shouldn't have, on a person I shouldn't have. Because I cared about a person I shouldn't.

I hoped I was wrong, that she'd be able to clear up this mess and have a name I could give the board. If she couldn't, my only recourse would be to hire an investigator to look into the leak and her.

After my sixth or seventh drink, I picked up my phone and located her number in my contact list. 'Drunk dialing' I think it's called. Supposedly, it never ended well. I'm not sure how much more bad shit I could handle. In the only smart move I'd made all day, I turned off the phone, tossed it onto my desk, and refilled my glass.

How many more until I was too incoherent to remember how to use the damn phone?

The next morning, I woke up face down on my bed, naked, the pounding in my head comparable to hammering a nail into something. Like my forehead. I didn't remember taking my clothes off. I blinked when I saw my shoes in my closet, and my suit and shirt in the dry cleaning bin. I definitely didn't do that. After brushing the horrible taste off my teeth and slipping on some briefs, I slowly walked into the kitchen and found Clare.

"Thank you," I said, squinting in the bright overhead lights.

"For what?" She put a piece of cantaloupe into her mouth and slid the tray across the island toward me.

I shook my head, afraid to eat anything because it might not stay down for long. "My clothes. Putting me to bed. I didn't... Did I do anything awful?" The last thing I remembered was tipping the bottle of bourbon over and watching the last few drops fall into my glass.

Her jaw dropped. "I can't believe you don't remember one of the best nights of my life, Hayden. It was incredible. You were awe-inspiring."

My eyes grew wide until I had no choice but to close them in reaction to the light. From what I remembered, I was an attentive lover, but it had been a while, and I'd been very drunk last night. So I assumed she was joking. But if we... "Did we...?"

Her laugh was small, almost a giggle. "No, we didn't, but your expression is priceless. I'm sure you would've been awe-inspiring if we had. You know, after you'd finished throwing up and I got you cleaned up in the shower."

I cringed. "That last part actually happened, didn't it?"

"Yep. But don't worry. You were a perfect gentleman almost all night."

"Almost?" I swallowed.

"You got a little grabby-grabby in the shower. I had to beat you off with the loofah." I stood there, speechless while she ate some more cantaloupe. "Not that kind of beating off, Hayden, don't worry. No harm was done and no pleasure was had. I was barely even offended when you called me by someone else's name."

"No. No, I couldn't have. Please tell me you're kidding." I watched her face for signs of internal laughter, hoping beyond hope that they'd appear soon. They didn't appear. "I don't know what to say. I was obviously inebriated and said things I didn't mean."

"I think you meant it. It was really romantic, even if it *was* meant for someone else's ears."

I didn't ask who. It was better that we pretend it hadn't happened. It could've been anyone really—I might have thought I was a pirate gathering my spoils for all I knew. "Can we talk about something else?"

"Sure," she said, poking her fork into another piece of fruit. "Who's Sira?"

Oh shit. "I think I'm going to be sick."

20

ANDI

By 3:00 am that morning, I couldn't keep my eyes open long enough to read anything. So I'd climbed into bed and set my alarm for 5:30. Running on coffee and fear, I'd worked all day, my eyes drawn to the bottom right corner of the computer screen whenever I wasn't looking over my shoulder. Not my proudest moment.

The chat window never popped up, the red dot next to Hayden's name never changed to green, and I missed him. Aside from some weekends or when he was out of town, we chatted at least a few times every day. Knowing that he *could,* but was unwilling to, stung.

The worst part was that I had no right to be angry. Not only did it make sense to suspect the person he'd shared the information with, but he was also right—I *was* lying to him. About everything but this.

No matter how logical, his distrust still hurt. Hypocrisy ain't just a river in Egypt...or whatever that saying was. Shit, you know you're exhausted when you can't even get a cliché right.

If I could figure this mess out for him, not only would I be off the hook, but I might be able to help Rob out of *his* mess without hurting anyone.

Of course, as the hours slipped by, so did my ability to lie to myself, and that was a huge problem. It became more and more obvious that all my good reasons to keep working had become secondary to Hayden's opinion of me. So as ridiculous and twisted as it was, I couldn't blow this, couldn't screw it up, because if he kept hating me, I'd have nothing left to hope for.

As unrealistic as they were, my delusional daydreams about Hayden had made me realize how badly I wanted a relationship. Not a one-night stand or friends with benefits. Someone to come into my life and want to be with me, to make me laugh, to challenge me and make me feel special. As much as I'd like it to be, it couldn't be Hayden. But my attraction to him helped me remember what it was like to feel something for someone else. He got me dreaming again and made me stop living in the past. I could have a future, a happy one. Maybe.

I'd worked hard to repair the damage I'd caused. And maybe, just maybe, once I'd accomplished that, I could set my sights on something else. Some*one* else. Someone more possible than Hayden. Someone almost as good.

No problem. I'd fix this and see the chat box pop up again with a snide comment asking what took me so long. Yeah, right. Positive thinking only worked when you could believe your own lies.

By Saturday night, I was so tired of staring at the screen, I'd believe anything. The Chinese take-out guy was my soulmate? Definitely—he knew exactly what I wanted, as if he could read my mind. Or, at least, he could read the order I'd placed a half hour ago. I could be a Michelin-star chef? Yep, if Michelin was the brand of my coffeemaker. The world had ended? Of course, it had—why else would there be no hot water? Oh, would you look at that—my shower has a knob marked with a big fucking 'H.' Might want to try turning that one next time.

I'd blown off all the work I'd planned to do for my other clients this weekend, but it had taken twenty-four hours to find absolutely *nothing* about Inspex. Hayden was the only one in his office who was working on it, so I'd had to search for the name Inspex in a billion different locations. I was trespassing, poking my nose into a whole bunch of innocent people's hard drives, innocent people's lives just like I'd done to the people I'd helped defraud. So I took a lot of deep breaths and tried not to read too closely, just skimming for a capital 'I.'

Then my only remaining brain cell came through, a tiny lifeline mixed into a lot of useless garbage:

"I'd like to phone a friend, Meredith." Yep, I think I even said it out loud as I grabbed my cell phone.

"Andi? It's one in the morning." Rob's voice was groggy, and I could hear Emilia's panicked voice in the background. "Is everything okay?"

"Yeah, I'm fine. Sorry to wake you. I didn't realize what time it was."

"She's fine," he told his wife. A few times. Then I heard her grumble, "Then tell her to go to sleep like a normal person."

"I wanted to ask you something, Rob. About that favor…"

"Sure, okay," he said quickly. "Hang on." He covered his phone and said something like 'Be right back' to Emilia. A few seconds later, he sounded completely awake. "I'm listening, Andi. What's up?"

"I need you to tell me who is blackmailing you. What's his name?" Conure was a huge company, but whoever it was had to be greedy and unethical, as well as ambitious, which probably meant we could scratch off the guy who sorts mail.

"Tim Carpenter. Did you get something for him?"

"Not yet. But with any luck, he got impatient and went after something himself. With even more luck, I'll be able to find something that will take care of all our problems. Cross your fingers for me. And your toes. And anything else you got. Oh, but do it while you're sleeping because I don't want Emilia to be mad at me."

"You're a good person, Andi. I shouldn't have asked you—"

"Stop." I didn't deserve his praise or his misguided belief in me, but I added, "When I call back with good news, then you can thank me, okay?"

We said good night, and I got back to work—this time, with a name to focus my search on.

And boy did I find something. It took some work to get through Tim's security—criminals really value security when it's theirs. Once I did, it was like taking candy from a baby, a baby who would be screaming and crying as soon as I handed his jerk-ass over to Hayden.

"Hallelujah." With an instantly clear mind, I read more and then went through other documents in the same location. In some of them, I recognized my own voice, having tinkered with things until Hayden thought it 'sounded right.' Others I'd typed up—except I'd put Hayden's name at the bottom.

Somehow, Hayden's personal notes had been slightly doctored and then had left the company's system from Tim's IP address. "Oops, now how'd that happen, Timmy?" Probably a computer glitch that kept happening every time he pressed 'send.' Damn computers.

When I came across the fifty-something-th draft of a Power-Point presentation that I'd spent hours and hours on, I knew I had him. All I had to do now was hand the proof over to Hayden and convince him that I hadn't planted it. Hopefully, Tim wasn't his best and most trusted friend. Good thing Hayden didn't like people.

That afternoon, with the incriminating name written on my finest post-it, I called Hayden on his cell phone.

"Yes?" He normally answered with his last name, so the fact that he hadn't made me think he was having as bad a day as I was.

"I found something."

"Talk." It was as if everything we'd ever said to each other had disappeared. There was no familiarity in his tone, nothing that let me know he was smiling. Everything had changed, and I hated it. This was out of my control, something I'd had nothing to do with, and it had destroyed everything good that had come before it.

"I found some drafts of contracts and emails regarding Inspex," I said quickly. "It was only you, right? You're the only one who should have them?"

"And you."

I closed my eyes. "I didn't do anything wrong, Hayden. I wouldn't." In a global sense, that was a complete lie—everything about my life was wrong. Everything I'd spent the last few days doing to get this proof was illegal. But I would never betray him, never take money for anything that would hurt people.

"What were they, and who stole them?"

"I found a lot of stuff, but the most recent was the Power-Point presentation you keep changing around. This one was a few drafts ago, though. Someone named T. Carpenter must have hacked into your email account and downloaded them to his or her computer." I felt even worse for having to pretend I'd never heard the name Tim Carpenter before, after the faith Hayden had shown me. Once a liar...

"From there," I continued, wondering if my babbling was due to the lie or my excitement, "they were encrypted and went out to a few addresses I have here. They are—"

"T. Carpenter?"

"Yeah. Do you know him or her?"

"Him." He paused for a second. "Yeah, I know exactly who he is. Before I confront him, I need what you've found, and I need to know how you found it."

You don't want to know how I found it. "I would email you the details, but your account has been seriously compromised. You should set up another password. A really difficult password."

"Good thing I got you that printer, isn't it?" Finally. His voice seemed more relaxed. Still angry, but more relaxed.

"I guess it is." The sense of relief felt better than sex...I think. "Wow, I don't know if I'll remember how to do it." Print something out *or* have sex.

"I'm sure it'll come back to you," he said. "Personally, I've always needed to really hold something to know it's safe. Otherwise, I never know if it's real." He cleared his throat. "If Tim got into my email, then he had access to every email you've sent me and the reverse, correct?"

"Yes."

"Could he have found all of our chats, as well?"

"Yes, but I don't think we used the chat feature to discuss details for the PowerPoint too much, so..." My words slowed down as I started to understand what he was talking about. Would he get fired for our flirting? Or was he just concerned that I might get in trouble? "Not the text conversations, but... I could set something up, to block people from accessing your computer or the messages you send. But it will take time and"— I blew out a breath—"you'd have to trust me to remotely log on to your computer."

"It has nothing to do with trust. There's nothing on it that you haven't already seen, including our chats. If you want to use that information against me, you could."

"I never would." I couldn't stop a small whimper from leaving my throat. All I could do was hope he didn't hear it.

"One last time," he said. "Just so that I know. Just so I can hear you say it. Please don't make me regret trusting you. If you're lying, I'll find out as soon as I speak to Carpenter. So—"

"I didn't have anything to do with him getting the information, and I would never, ever do that to you."

He sighed. "Thank you, Sira. Send everything you found to my office by messenger. Put it on my account."

"Hayden?" I asked quietly.

"Yes?"

"Are we okay?"

After a pause, he said, "We're fine."

21

HAYDEN

WE WEREN'T FINE. 'FINE' was a nothing word. It had no meaning, no commitment. The world ran on yes and no, good and bad. There was no reason to use 'fine' to describe anything but dishes. Or my life.

I got to the office even earlier than normal Monday morning. As soon as Tim came in—two hours later—I confronted him in his office, proof in hand. It didn't take long until the truth came out. Not from Tim's mouth, of course. He spattered and sputtered and made a mess of himself while denying everything, demanding to know where I'd gotten the information and loudly declaring it fraudulent.

"This isn't an argument, Tim," I said calmly. "Or even a discussion. This is me holding something in my hand that proves what a dishonest asshole you are. It's not news to anyone but, until now, it's just been a communal opinion. Now, it's fact."

His eyes darted around the room, looking for either an excuse or an escape route. "You made that shit up to cover your own ass, Bennett. Just so you could blame someone else when the board decides to fire you."

"You know how good I am with computers, Tim. In fact,

that's what makes you feel superior to me, isn't it? So how would I have made this up?"

"As if you can't find a dozen people who would gladly do the great Hayden Bennett a favor."

There had never been a great Hayden Bennett. Hayden Bennett was just someone with a powerful last name who'd spent his entire life hobbled by that moniker's weight and responsibilities.

"Stop the bullshit, Tim," I said. "All the denial in the world can't change the truth." I should know.

He followed me out of his office to his secretary's desk. Rosie looked up at me with big, glossy eyes that begged not to be brought into it. Unfortunately, that wasn't possible.

I hated threatening people but, occasionally, it was necessary. And it always worked. I didn't waterboard them, shine bright lights in their faces, or keep them awake for days at a time. All I did was ask them for the truth. As long as I stayed calm and told them what they might lose by lying, that was usually enough to encourage a mostly honest person to act like a *completely* honest person.

"I didn't steal any of those documents, Mr. Bennett," Rosie said, her lower lip trembling. "I didn't know why Mr. Carpenter had them or where they'd come from. But I knew they were there. On his computer. I assumed you'd sent them to him. You or your assistant."

"You lying bitch," Tim yelled. Her quivering jaw turned into overflowing eyes and loud crying.

I spun toward Tim. "Say another word to her, and I'll stop being civil. Trust me, it's already a challenge."

He shut his mouth so fast I wondered if he'd be able to open it again to answer my next question.

"How did you get them?" I hated asking, fearing the answer, but I had to know if Sira had had any part in it. Maybe it had been an accident. Maybe Tim had approached her with a few smiley faces and told her I wanted her to send him everything she had on Inspex.

Tim glared at the woman sobbing at her desk for a minute, then looked at me. "Are you worried about your girlfriend, Bennett?"

His one last-ditch effort to take control of the situation smacked me in the center of the chest. Aside from the incredibly inaccurate word choice, yes, that's exactly what I was worried about. Not for any public fall-out or amusement a nice scandal would provide people. All I wanted now was proof I hadn't been wrong to trust her, to not find out she'd used me, and I'd missed it because of a screwed-up emotional state. One I had no business having to begin with.

When someone invades your life, takes over your thoughts, and secretly steals whatever they want from you, you want to know how. And why.

"Seriously, pal," Tim said smugly, "I couldn't give a shit what you got going on the side. Of course, your wife's daddy might." And there was the threat. A threat that had no effect on me because the man I was glaring at had only partially answered my question. Until that was done, I didn't really care what else happened.

"He might," I said calmly.

Tim sneered. "Although, you really should get your girl-friend to teach you not to use such fucking stupid passwords before Bart fires your ass and you can't afford to keep her anymore."

"My password," I said through a stiff jaw. "You figured out my password."

"In about four tries."

That was it? It was that simple? It was my own fault. I bit down hard, my teeth grinding together. I'd accused Sira of being involved, insulted her, threatened her. I hadn't trusted her enough to even consider the possibility that *I* was the reason the information got out. Damn it.

"Why did you steal from your own people, Tim? What did it get you?"

"Nothing I'd enjoy more than to see you fall off your high horse. To prove your daddy's money and a fancy education doesn't make you any better than the rest of us."

"Spite? I don't buy it. Did Brecken make you an offer after you pawned off my work as your own?"

He laughed. "*Nǐ zài xiǎng tài xiǎole*, Bennett."

So it really was just to see me fall. "Too bad you won't be able to take that job offer—your Mandarin needs work." But his meaning was clear—why would he care about this company, or its biggest US competitor, when he already had something going on with a larger, foreign one? What a spiteful jackass.

"Your proof is bullshit, and you know it. No way it'll stand up in court."

"That may be true, but you know how the business world is, Tim. We gossip like teenage girls, even in China."

Tim turned to Rosie, who was sobbing apology after apology. "Would you shut up, you old bitch? We're trying to talk here."

I would probably never know exactly why I did it. Why, at that exact moment, my control cracked open and my rage slipped through. Actually, 'poured out' was more accurate. Maybe it was in defense of the woman weeping, maybe it was to punish a thief, or maybe it was just to vent my anger at myself. Whatever the reason, my fist met the side of Tim's jaw without any decision being made.

The bastard stumbled onto Rosie's desk and then fell backwards onto the floor near her feet, taking most of her desk accessories with him.

Someone must have called security when they heard Tim

yelling. Two guards were moving toward us quickly with their hands on their belts. I briefly wondered if I was about to get tased and thought how much that would make Sira laugh. I may have even smiled, at least until Tim spoke.

"The second you say anything to Bart or the board"—the words came out from only one side of his mouth while he stabilized the other side with his hand—"is the second I tell him all about your after-hours assistant."

I nodded. "Which will be followed shortly thereafter by him patting me on the back for stopping a thief and juggling two women at the same time."

Tim's face soured as he realized the truth of my comment— no one ever knew which way Bart would go on an issue. Although, I was confident my father-in-law would go whichever way proved hurtful to the most people and most beneficial to him.

I bent down and spoke quietly. "You have a choice here, Tim. You come clean and walk away with what you have at this moment, or you pretend you didn't do anything wrong and walk away with nothing."

"Bennett, listen, I—"

I shushed him with a hand. "Don't tell me. I'll hear it from the lawyers."

After the two security guards had pulled him off the floor, Rosie stopped sobbing and got me some ice for my hand.

All in all, a very productive day. And it was only 9:30 am.

"Thank you for your help, Rosie." I went back to my office, closing the door on the countless stares from those in cubicles or offices who were pretending not to gawk. I sat down at my desk and took out my cell phone. Sira didn't answer. It didn't feel right to leave a message, so I booted up my computer.

'I'm sorry.' I pressed send and sat back in my chair, waiting for her response. It came about a minute later.

'Don't be. I understand why you were suspicious.'

I didn't. *'Are we okay?'*

'We're fine.'

Fine. Why did a word I could use to describe every part of my existence sound so horrible coming from her? I didn't want 'fine' anymore. I wanted great, perfect, amazing—all the words other people used to express the good in their lives. Sira was the best part of my day, just the idea that she might be thinking about me made me smile, feel grateful.

I didn't want a single part of her life to be fine. I wanted her to have so much more than fine.

I waited, trying to think of what to say. How to make it up to her, to show how sorry I was for doubting her and how much she'd helped me. Before I could come up with anything, another comment appeared.

'I'm bored. Got anything for me to do?' A great sign we'd gone back to normal. Somewhere I wasn't content to be anymore. But now wasn't the time to deal with that.

'Lots. Beginning with setting up that block on my computer.'

'Okay. Did you set up a new password? Make sure it has numbers and punctuation.'

Yeah, can't forget that. *'Hang on.'* I logged onto my email account and went through the required steps, surprised at how quickly I'd learned a very simple task that I'd never bothered to learn before I met her. When I typed in the new password, I smiled. At least it would be something I'd never forget.

When I heard my door open, I turned around to see Bart, red-faced, storming into my office as if his name were on the door instead of mine.

"Tell me what happened."

I held up a finger, knowing it was going to piss the man off, but only slightly caring. He certainly deserved it after believing in a thief more than me. He sat down in the chair his daughter had bought me as a wedding gift. Beautiful chair. You couldn't tell by looking at it, but it was insanely uncomfortable, for me at least. My legs are too long. How many things in my life could I say the same thing about—looks perfect but doesn't fit me.

'I need to go. Do what you have to do for the security.' I signed off and spun my chair around to face my boss. I explained what had happened, leaving only Sira's involvement out—my suspicions and her retrieval of the information.

Unfortunately, Bart didn't get to be who he was by having a good nature or being slow. "How'd you find out what the cock-sucker did?" Initially, I'd considered it a sign of trust that Bart felt comfortable using his more colorful expressions around me. It turned out trust had nothing to do with it. Bart simply behaved the way he wanted to and people let him. *I* let him.

Some would look down in discomfort or even blush, but they would never say anything aloud. Very similar to how people had reacted to my father. As if I needed another reason to dislike the man.

"I have a friend who's good with computers and followed the trail back to Tim." I should've said 'my assistant.' It would've been nice to give Sira credit for what she'd done, at least. Before I could correct myself, Bart spoke.

"Well, you owe him a drink." Of course, he would assume my friend was male—she was far too competent to be a woman. "A *couple* drinks, because that computer shit ain't your forte. Or mine."

"Great idea. I'll do that as soon as possible." Take her out for a drink under the guise of a celebration for a job well-done.

"I thought you were slipping, Bennett. Heard a few things that...disturbed me, and thought you were slipping. I'm glad I was wrong." That was as close to an apology as I'd ever heard him say.

"As much as I appreciate you saying that"—and was uncomfortable that he had—"unfortunately, you weren't entirely wrong. I neglected the security on my email account and let Tim walk right in. It's been changed since, and I'm having my friend upgrade everything."

"Hmm...I hate this computer shit. It doesn't make any sense —information gets turned into numbers and sent through wires to be put back together? How the fuck does that make any sense?" He shook his head. "Maybe I'm just too old, a relic of the past." He may have paused to give me time to disagree. I always disagreed with him, except for comments like that. So I looked at him pleasantly and waited for him to leave.

Bart cleared his throat. "We can't have anybody sneaking around in those computers, and it's happening more and more often. Today is the first time it's happened in *my* company, but then, maybe there's somebody out there who has already gotten in and seen everything. The bastard could just be waiting for the right time. Or the right offer. Get your buddy to take a look at the whole system, see what he thinks we need. Tell him he can bid for the contract, and we'll put him high on the list."

That was the best offer Sira would ever get from him —'Thanks for uncovering a thief and possibly saving us millions, but you're still not getting shit.'

"I'll pass along the offer."

"Tim, huh?" he asked in wonder, putting his hands behind his head and leaning back in the chair until the front two legs lifted off the ground. "Would've never thought he'd do some- thing like that. Didn't think he'd have the balls to. Never trust a faggot, Hayden. Especially the ones who don't own up to what they are. They're used to lying."

I clenched my eyes at the slur. Over the years, I could prob- ably count how many conversations I'd had with Bart in which he *didn't* use that word, or another equally derogatory one. Bart was of the mind that as long as he didn't say them in front of 'the little queers who were overly sensitive and had teams of lawyers on speed-dial,' then he was being respectful of their 'girlie' sensibilities. That he could speak his hate freely in front of his friends and family bothered me even more than his belief that I was in both of those groups. And Clare? Well, Clare was family and surely felt the same way he did about everything and everyone.

"Tim isn't gay," I said. "He's a dishonest asshole."

"Same thing."

"Not the same thing, Bart," I snapped. "Completely different things."

Bart lifted his head, his eyes wide. Then he cocked his head to the side. "You say potatoes, I say po-ta-toes," he sang...badly. "You say..."

I smiled at the reference, not at the man who'd used it. For once, I agreed with him. I would do anything to call this whole thing off.

22

ANDI

WHEN I TOLD Rob the news about Tim, and that I'd found a way to prove Tim was a dickhead without bringing Rob or me into it at all, the gratitude in his voice was palpable. Then Emilia grabbed his phone and put it on speaker, so I got to hear him explain the entire thing to her and then listen to her verbally beat him up for being stupid, not telling her earlier, and dragging me into it. Eventually, I hung up to give them some privacy. When Rob called me back a while later, they both apologized and thanked me.

The last thing I deserved was their gratitude. I mean, it wasn't as if I hadn't gotten something out of it. Plus, I'd broken a whole bunch of promises and laws to do it, so I put a quick end to their undeserved appreciation, said goodbye, and went to bed.

'Power and money make men do awful things.'

'True,' I typed. 'Although, you have a ton of power and money. So why aren't you a douchebag?'

'Oh, I am. Not sure how you missed it.'

I laughed. 'I miss a lot of stuff.'

'You mean like me not being a bird-loving dead man?'

Oh shit. *'You had to bring that up, didn't you?'*

'Of course. I'm a douchebag, remember?'

It had only taken a day for Hayden and me to slip back into our normal working relationship. It had taken two more days for us to start a different kind of relationship, one where he felt obligated to check in with me regularly for no apparent reason other than boredom. A week and a half later, I couldn't get rid of him. Not that I'd tried very hard, of course.

I tried. *'Unless you really start paying me to giggle, I should get back to work.'*

'Am I annoying you?'

'Yes.' No. If anything, it was annoying that I *didn't* get annoyed by his constant interruptions.

'Then I'll try to stop. But I'm fairly sure I'll fail.'

I chewed on my lip for a second. *'You annoy me because you're impossible to understand.'*

'Am I? I feel like a very simple man to understand. You must be confusing me with someone else.'

Yeah, right. *'That's probably it. People like you are a dime a dozen.'*

When I heard a knock on the door, I quickly typed, *'Gotta go,'* and went to answer it without waiting for his response. My stomach dropped when I saw who was standing there.

Flashback moment of the worst kind. Same detective, same nondescript clothing, but now his hair was a little grayer and his wrinkles a little deeper. Unfortunately, he probably wasn't here for a social call.

"Hello, detective. Long time, no see." Long time no *want* to see. Or talk to. Or think about. Detective Williams reminded me of a huge chunk of my life I'd love to forget. Not that I could, but boy would it be great.

"How have you been, Andrea?" Hearing my full name again

after so long killed any pleasant nostalgia I had left. I imagined a bunch of suitcases with tags that read: Andrea. The name I hated because it only reminded me of the ex-boyfriend who'd left me with all that baggage to begin with.

My suddenly clammy hand slipped on the knob of the door I was partially hiding behind. "Why are you here?"

"I'm investigating a case," he said without expression, without giving anything away.

"And you want my help with it?" It was possible. When the police tech people couldn't figure something out, they used outside resources. They'd never used *me,* and I never thought they would, but it could happen.

"I'm here to talk to you about your possible involvement, Andrea."

"I wasn't—" I swallowed, fear moving down from my mind to the rest of my body. "I haven't done anything. Not since I got in trouble. I swear."

He had a cop-face, one that wasn't easily read, but throughout the investigation and trial, I'd learned how to recognize certain things about him. For instance, his hands were in his pockets—a sign of trust. He looked at the ground instead of watching my every move—a sign he wasn't on guard like he'd been with my ex-boyfriend and the other two guys who'd set up the scam.

"I really hope that's true," he said, "but I'm going to need to speak with you about it."

Speak with me. Oh. Okay, that wasn't good.

"Right now? I'm kind of busy." Freaking out. Plus, we were standing about thirty feet away from tech paraphernalia I could get in trouble for having.

"Are you working right now, Andrea?"

"I go by Andi. And I'm just doing odd jobs and that sort of thing for pocket money." He knew about the money I'd inherited from my grandmother, along with this house. He just didn't know that instead of living off it, I'd used it to repay all the people I'd hurt.

"With technology?"

"No," I lied. It was just one word—one word didn't matter. *Aaand* there was another one. They always travel in packs.

Lies *always* mattered—to the person being lied to and the person doing the lying.

"Then what are you busy with?"

I sighed, giving myself a little time to come up with something. "My boyfriend is here...in the bedroom. We were getting... busy, you know?" Hopefully, that would embarrass the interrogation right out of the detective.

He nodded slowly. "What were you busy with two nights ago around 8:30?"

"I'm not sure." I looked up as if trying to recall where I was. Knowing there was a 99.9% chance I was sitting in front of my computer working. "What day is it today?"

"Tell me what were you doing on Wednesday night."

"I was with a friend," I blurted before logic had time to rear its ugly head. Then sighed. It was actually impressive how quickly I could screw something up. It wasn't a lie—I had been with Emilia, but the last thing I wanted to do was drag her into any more of my trouble.

"The same friend who's currently in your bedroom?"

Could imaginary friends testify against you in a court of law?

"No, I was out with a girlfriend. Do you need her name?"

He pulled out a pad of paper and a wooden pencil. A bizarre homage to the olden days for a detective who investigated computer crimes. "And her number." Great. I was going to owe Emilia big time. But it wouldn't be for long. They'd find out who was doing something they shouldn't have been doing on Wednesday night and forget all about me.

I gave him Emilia's information, making a mental note to warn her that he'd be calling.

"And what about the previous day?" he asked. "That would be last Tuesday."

Shit. "Um...I'm not sure. I'd have to think about it."

"I tell you what," he said, sliding his notebook back into his pocket. "Why don't you come down to the station and let me know as soon as you can."

"I didn't do anything wrong, detective."

His eyes warmed a little bit as if he believed me. "Like I said, I hope not. But somebody got into a computer system they shouldn't have, and they had help doing it, which means the tech guys will be going through a long list of known hackers in the area. And while you were never prosecuted, your name is still on that list. So, eventually, they're going to get to it. To *you*, Andrea."

"Andi," I corrected stupidly. As if that changed anything.

"Right." He looked away for a moment. When he refocused on me, he spoke quietly. "I know the last time was a stupid mistake made by a naive kid. That was clear from the first conversation I had with you. When you finally stopped believing that shithead of a boyfriend, you did the right thing. But this one is... This one isn't that simple. Multiple enforcement agencies and departments are in on it. Right now, they're working off the assumption that two people were involved—one who knew how to get into the building and another with computer expertise. I suggest you talk to a lawyer."

"I can't afford a lawyer."

"Then you'll get one assigned to you by the state if you're arrested."

"Wait! Arrested? But I didn't do anything." My heartbeat picked up, and my throat closed down. "Why would I be arrested?"

"Like I said, this one is a lot worse than the last." He scratched the back of his neck. "A security guard was killed during the break-in."

I couldn't find my breath. Didn't remember *how* to breathe. "I'd never kill anyone, detective. You know that! I mean, besides the whole morality thing, I couldn't. Just look at me." I held out my arms as proof. "Do you really think these wimpy things could overpower a security guard?"

"Just..." He put up his hands, as if that would somehow calm me down. "Talk to a lawyer."

"But I didn't do anything," I whimpered.

He blew out a breath. "I'm not stupid, Andi."

"I never thought you were."

"Then why did you tell me you're not working with computers anymore?"

Oh shit. I held onto the door to keep myself standing.

"I don't care about the little crap you've been doing. In fact, I've always thought that part of your agreement was bullshit. But I do care about *you*. Understand?" He waited for me to nod. It was a struggle. "I'm here to give you a heads up. I wouldn't do that if I really thought you were involved. But if *I* know you've been going into places you're not allowed to go, and this case becomes the shitstorm I think it will, there's a chance someone else will figure it out, too. I just hope you're not working on anything even remotely connected to this case."

Me, too.

"Now, like I said, there are a lot of names higher on that list than yours, and we're just getting started. So you have time." He glanced at his watch. "I gotta go. Just...talk to a lawyer, Andi. A good one."

After I shut the door, I stumbled into the living room and slumped down on the couch, pulling my grandma's quilt over me. Everything had been going so well. Of course, something

had to ruin it. I'd been piling up bad karma for a while now—
lying for my job, working with computers, doing shit I shouldn't.
But murder? I couldn't even fathom that. It just didn't compute.

Although, I didn't exactly have a right to feel persecuted.
Detective Williams *should* be suspicious of me. I'm a suspicious
person. When was the last time I'd been honest about anything
important?

It's so easy to tell yourself that you're not doing anything too
wrong or that your lies aren't hurting anyone but you. So easy to
forget that you want to change when you're living every day
separately—morning to night, plodding along, no clear goal
ahead. So easy to veer off course and ignore what you're doing to
survive.

'I'll just do it today, only today.' Lying to myself is an
addiction.

Dazedly, I heard my cell phone ring. I slowly turned my head
toward the side table, then watched the phone vibrate on the
wood for a second. I picked it up and answered, knowing whatever it was couldn't be worse news than I'd just received.
"Hello?"

"I'm bored," Sara said. "Wanna do something tonight?"

I should call Emilia and tell her I'd given the detective her
name. She wouldn't have to lie to him—on Wednesday night,
she'd dragged me to an evening Pilates class. I'd blocked most of
the experience out, but it had to have ended later than 8:30.
Didn't it? Oh god, what if it hadn't? What if I didn't have an alibi
for either night in question? If only I'd gone out with Sara and
gone home with some guy the police would believe because he
would have no reason to lie. Maybe I needed to start covering
more of my ass. Maybe I needed to stop *being* such an ass.
Tomorrow.

"Hell yeah," I said. "It's Friday night! I want to go out, get so wasted I can barely walk, and screw some lucky bastard so hard he won't be able to stand till Monday."

"Yay!" Sara yelled. "The old Andi is back!"

Was she? That wasn't a good thing. Not a good thing at all.

I focused on getting ready to go out, breaking out my trampiest clothes from where they'd been tucked away the last time I was thinking clearly. I turned the radio on full blast and sang along with every song, whether or not I knew the actual words. Anything was better than thinking.

Thankfully, the dress was so tight, all the wrinkles were ironed out naturally. I tried the same thing with my hair— slicking it back into a bun that was so tight I even got a mini facelift out of it. I may have gone a bit overboard, but when your life seems to be barreling downhill uncontrollably, being mistaken for a hooker doesn't seem like such a big deal. In fact, tonight's plan involved keeping my goals and my standards equally low.

Before I left, I went to shut down my stupid computer and saw that Hayden had responded earlier. I stared at the words, my heart pounding so hard, my dress almost split open.

It wasn't important. Whatever Hayden and I were doing— not important. That he thought I was someone else—not important. So until I reported to the police station in a few days without a lawyer, forgetting all of my lies seemed *very* important. Just for a little while, I'd forget.

So I shut it all down and walked away. Unfortunately, his comment wasn't as easy to turn off.

'I don't think I could get you confused with anyone else, Sira. You're probably the most singular person I've ever met.'

Little did he know.

"ANDI!" Sara whispered. At least, it *sounded* like a whisper compared to all the noise around us. She nudged me, hard, in the boob. I think she was aiming for my arm, but we'd had enough cocktails, I couldn't be absolutely sure what she was trying to do. "There is a super-hot guy at your 6:00 who can't stop staring at you. Wait. He's at your 7:00. Nope. 8:30. 9:00 or 9:15 now." Great, he was circling. Like a shark. Or maybe he was just on his way to the bar, which was somewhere around here. I think.

"He's probably a music producer who was so amazed by my karaoke performance that he wants me to sign with his record label."

Sara laughed. "Our bad karaoke was at the last bar. Or two ago."

"It was?" Well, would you look at that? Nope! Nope, don't look at that—looking at that made me dizzy. "You're right. This place is a lot blurrier than the last place we were in. Where are we again?" I could've asked '*when* are we' because I didn't know the answer to that question either. Actually, between the guy at my 9:00 or 9:15 or wherever he was, and the darkness inside the bar, I knew exactly what time it was—one drink past too many.

"Hotel bar," Sara said. "Super hot, super rich guys." She was super rich and had no interest in a guy for more than one night, so I wasn't sure why that was a big deal.

"I shouldn't be here. I already have one more super hot, super rich guy than I can handle."

I felt someone tap me on the shoulder—with a hand, not a boob—and then saw Sara's expression turn to confusion. *More* confusion. When I turned around, a guy wearing a black jacket, white shirt, and tie looked down at me.

"Thank you," I said. "But I don't need any more drunks. I mean drinks." My liver must really hate me right now.

He nodded. "That's a very good idea, but not why I'm here. Are you Sara Antonopoulos?"

"No," I said, pointing to Sara. "She is."

"Sorry." He faced Sara. "A guest requested that you meet them in the lobby."

She glanced at me, her mouth in the shape of a donut. I need a donut.

"Who?" she asked the guy.

"A gentleman."

"I told you this place is awesome." Sara looked at me again, made another 'O' face, and we both busted up laughing. "A gentleman wants to meet me in the lobby," she parodied.

The hotel employee looked at us as if trying to figure out why the 'gentleman' wanted to meet us at all.

"Wait." I tried my best to focus. "Who is he really? Does he have a name, this gentleman caller?"

"Of course, he has a name," Sara slurred. "And I will find out what it is just as soon as I can."

"Hayden Bennett," the guy said.

My gasp didn't make it all the way out, so I started coughing, grabbing at Sara blindly before she got away.

"Don't go. Please don't go." I had to think. Something that was virtually impossible, unless I wanted to think of dirty stuff about him, which I did amazingly well, even while sober. Unfortunately, that wasn't what the moment called for. It called for logic and...something else. Clear-headedness! That's what it called for.

Oh shit, was I in trouble.

Obviously, Hayden wasn't here trying to pick up random women because he'd asked for me by name, or by my fake name, or Sara's name, or... But how did he know I was here? And did he look as good in person as he did in pictures?

Oh shit. I thanked the judgmental hotel employee so he would go away. I had serious sobering up to do.

I leaned in close to Sara, steadying myself on the table next to us. "Sara, it's him. It's *him* him."

"Him who?"

"Him, my client. My...my whatever he is. Hayden Bennett. He asked for me. Well, he asked for you, but that's because I use your name." Damn it. I shouldn't have sent the hotel guy away. I should have told him to tell Hayden that he'd made a mistake and that no one named Sara Antonopoulos was here. "Whatever you do—don't go out there."

Sara's cheeks filled with air, and she slowly blew it out. "You're totally right."

"Thank you."

"*You* should." Sara pushed me toward the lobby. We caught up with the hotel guy easily, because he was bigger and not rudely shoving his way through the crowd like Sara was.

"Hey," she called out when we were close enough for him to hear. "We were kidding. She's Sara. Can you take her out? She's a bit wobbly."

"No," I begged. "I can't. I can't."

The guy took me firmly by the arm—probably hoping I wouldn't fall down and take him down with me, or just vomit on him—and dragged me away. I stared back at Sara, shaking my head.

Sara's only response was to mouth, 'You're welcome,' and smile. Then she turned her attention to a guy she'd been chatting with earlier.

Worst. Friend. Ever.

The hotel guy dragged me out of the loud bar and into the very, very quiet main lobby. It was like we'd entered a library. I shook him off, not wanting any more of his 'help.'

"Be aware that all of my Facebook friends will hear about the way guests are treated in this hotel. All four of them, mister. Got it?"

"Got it," he said, walking away while gesturing to my 6:30 or 7:00 where—

"Oh shit!" I covered my face. One, so Hayden wouldn't see me being this drunk. And two, so I wouldn't see him being that gorgeous.

Life was so unfair. Here I was drunk and wearing hooker clothes, and there he was with his perfect hair and his perfect clothes that his perfect chest probably wouldn't bust out of the first chance it got. Although, in his case, I doubted anyone would mind. In *my* case...

Quick boob check. Hands still over my face because yeah, that made so much sense. At least my boobs were where they belonged.

"Hi." Even his voice was perfect. Bastard. "I promise, being here is a totally innocent coincidence."

"Doesn't matter. Because I'm going to pretend you aren't here at all, and that this is just another fantasy—" Never drinking again. "Yep, I just said that, didn't I?"

"Yeah. Fairly loudly, too."

One of these days, I'd master the 'think before you speak' technique. Unfortunately, today was not that day. "Wow. Okay. Um...looks like you got your meeting after all." And I bet he was feeling *really* fortunate about that right now. "*Aaaand* step one is now complete."

"Remind me what step one is."

"Step one: I embarrass myself."

"I'm not sure you've completed it then," he said, sounding a little closer than he'd been, but I couldn't look. "You're loud in a quiet place. I wouldn't have thought you embarrass so easily."

"Damn, you're hard to impress. But I'm sure I'll come up with something even more delightfully embarrassing soon." Not exactly sure what that would be. Except—

Boob check.

"Am I so hideously ugly that you can't even look at me?" he asked. "Or do you want to play peek-a-boo?"

I laughed under the safety of my hands for a second and then came out from behind them. "How terrifying is it that you're not the first man who's asked me that?"

"I think he was referring to a much less innocent game than I am."

Innocent. Right. Bummer.

Hayden had the kind of face you could stare at every day and never quite figure out. If you took any of his features and stuck them onto someone else's face, that person would instantly become ten times more attractive. So with all those parts on *one* face, it was kind of surreal, almost too—

Oh crap, how long had I been staring at him?

"Well, um...this is...awkward," I babbled. "But, then again, you *did* say you wanted to see me drunk. You should really be more careful what you wish for."

"Actually, I said I wanted to see you *ugly* drunk. And now I know that's never going to be possible."

I mumbled a quick thanks because I wasn't actually sure it was a compliment. I think it was. I think it was a really good one. But the shock of this meeting had only just started sobering me up, and I had a long way to go yet before I could judge sarcasm or irony.

He nodded toward the hotel's reception area. "Can we...*talk* a little?"

I paused, my sanity winning out over my incredible desire to scream, '*God, yes! Get us a damn room already! What took you so long to ask?*' Because that would be wrong, and I would wake up tomorrow with bigger problems than a hangover.

I spoke each word slowly, making sure 'take me, take me now,' didn't slip in there accidentally. "That might make it a lot harder for you to make sure step two doesn't happen."

He leaned forward slightly. "Remind me what step two is."

"Do you *ever* listen?"

His mouth opened, but no sound came out. I waited, desperately trying not to sway too far over in my heels. I could use a sit-down, but not near a bed. All kinds of wrong could happen if I sat down with him on a bed.

"For some reason, I've been distracted lately." His gaze slid slowly down my body before he caught himself and snapped his focus back to my face. "Do you have a little time to fill me in on everything I may have missed?"

I swallowed. "Step two—that you'll leave our meeting regretting something."

"I think I would have more to regret if I left right now." He nodded to the center of the hotel again. "Just for a little while. Then I'll call you a cab or take you home myself."

"Wow, Hayden," I mocked. "You're going to get us a room and not even let me stay in it? How chivalrous of you. Why don't you just save some cash and do me in the elevator?"

His eyes widened, and he laughed. "I didn't mean— There's another bar at the other end of the lobby, a quieter one. I thought we could have coffee together. No room. No elevator. And, if it's what you prefer, absolutely no chivalry."

"Coffee." I wondered if he could hear the disappointment in my voice. "That's it?"

"That's it."

It was a bad idea. I was drunk and horny—he was gorgeous and off-limits. For a number of reasons. "I can't. I'm here with someone."

His expression fell. "Oh, of course you are. I'm..." He ran a hand through his hair, ruffling it and making it look even better, less tamed. "My timing is bad. Perhaps another time."

"Let me think about it when I'm sober."

"I hope I didn't overstep my bounds." He looked lost for a moment. It didn't last long, but I'd seen it. Through the confident, controlled mask I knew he wore when he was with other people. I could see all the way to who I knew he really was— funny, charming, and...yeah, a bit lost.

"No lasting damage," I said. "But I should go get my friend."

"Your friend. Yeah, you should." He'd said 'friend' like someone would say, 'I have to clean the bathroom of the YMCA. With my tongue.'

I didn't know why I felt the need to explain, because what, or who, he thought I was doing shouldn't matter. But it did. And *he* did. And I needed to deal with the facts. "If I leave her alone too long, her terrible taste in men will get her in trouble."

"Does she have long straight hair?"

"Yeah."

"Was she wearing some kind of sparkly green shirt?"

"Why?"

"She left while you were playing peek-a-boo."

"Oh shit." I spun around, looking for her, my unsober mind figuring a *quick* glance around the lobby would help me see a few minutes ago. Duh. Sure it could. "Where was she headed?"

"They went to the valet line."

"They." Great. I reached for my wallet/phone case and found myself out of luck. "Damn it." Sara had used my phone to take a picture of me and must have stuck it in her purse, so I had no phone and no money. "Damn it, damn it, damn it."

Hayden stepped forward cautiously, like I was a panicked animal, which I actually was—a drunk and panicked animal. "She's not allowed to do that?"

I shook my head. I shouldn't have left her alone. "I have to find out where she went."

"It seemed like she went willingly."

"Of course, she did. She always does. That's why I need to find her."

"Can I help?"

"You could let me borrow your phone."

He handed it to me, and the first thing I saw was my fake name in a very short list of favorites. I ignored that and dialed Sara's number. No answer. So I tried mine. No answer on that one either.

Sara would never take a guy to her place, so it was useless to go there. I needed my computer. So, if I could bum bus fare from Hayden and be home in an hour and a half or find a ride and be home in fifteen minutes. And the only person who could give me a ride was...

Damn it. "I need a ride home."

"My car is just a few blocks away."

I looked at him. "Normally I would ask to see your ID and a major credit card, but I already have access to that information."

His passwords, account numbers, home and office addresses, and pretty much everything else there was to know about him. If he was an ax murderer, he didn't use his credit cards for duct tape and shovels. But taking him to my house? That would bring him into my life, and I wasn't sure I was ready for that to ever happen.

"Can I trust you, Hayden?"

"You know me better than 99% of the people in my life. So you tell me."

"Yeah, I can." The bigger question was: Could I trust myself?

24

ANDI

I PUT the cup of coffee Hayden had bought me on the way out of the hotel into a cup holder, careful not to spill it all over his very expensive, very pristine car, and then dialed Sara's number again from his phone. There was probably no reason to panic, but the reaction was visceral for me.

I was still pretty tipsy and needed to pay close attention to what exactly I said. Or did. So I didn't say anything else to Hayden. I could tell he was watching me out of the corner of his eye while he drove. Every time I checked, his face would turn slightly but not all the way, and his lips would separate as if he was about to speak. Then they'd clamp together tightly.

"Hayden, maybe things would be less awkward if you just said what you want to say."

"I was just wondering why you're trying to rescue a friend who probably doesn't want to be rescued."

That was an explanation I owed him. One of many. "Sara doesn't always think things through. I know because I used to be the same way." And guess how well that had turned out. "Back then, she took care of me." Then, overnight, our roles switched and I became the responsible one.

The most troubling part was knowing why I'd been like that —I'd been punishing myself. Sara knew all about my screw-up, but I still didn't know her reasons. Anything that turned a happy and hopeful person into someone who couldn't go a weekend without getting into trouble wasn't good.

"All I can do is make sure she's safe, you know?"

Hayden nodded, probably wondering what any of that actually meant, but thankfully not asking. "Doesn't it get confusing with both of you named Sara?"

I looked out the window to hide my I'm-such-a-terrible-liar expression. I really should limit the time I spent in public...to none. "Well, I don't speak in the third person, so if I say 'Sara,' people usually know I'm referring to her."

"Right." He laughed, his smile showing off perfect teeth and a small dimple in his cheek. No one should be allowed to look that good—it was bad for everyone else's self-esteem.

"Can you drive faster?" I asked. Having a big freak-out about being so close to a disgustingly gorgeous man should wait until after I'd made sure Sara was okay. Since there wasn't much I could do about it on the way home, I might as well bide my time with a *medium-sized* freak-out. "How did you know I was at the bar?"

"On my way back from a dinner meeting, I passed you and Other-Sara on the street. You-Sara said something truly obnoxious very loudly, and I recognized your voice. So I followed you in a completely non-stalkerish way, just to see if I was right."

"What did I say?"

"I'm not sure it should be repeated." He winked. "Ever."

I grimaced. "See? I embarrassed myself, and you are completely un-intimidated by me now."

"Actually," he said softly, "sitting next to you, I find myself quite intimidated."

"You're just saying that to be nice."

"I'm saying that because it's true. I've wanted to meet you for a long time."

"And now you have. Impressive, ain't I?" I'd considered pulling down the visor to see what three bars and no-idea-how-many drinks had left behind, but what would that do besides make me feel even worse about this whole situation?

"Very." He smiled, keeping his eyes on the road as we got closer to my neighborhood.

This was a seriously lousy time to confront him, but unfortunately, all that liquor still hadn't blurred out the detective's visit. "Hayden, did you tell anyone how I found out who was stealing your shit."

"My shit?" He laughed. "No, I thought you didn't want me to, but I'd be happy to give you credit."

"No," I said quickly. "I don't really want anyone to know. I don't like getting mixed up in that kind of thing." Wasn't that the truth. "Plus, you know how it is—as soon as someone finds out you do something well, they're constantly asking for favors."

"People never ask me for favors. Do you think that means no one thinks I do anything well?"

I grimaced. "Yeah, I'm sure you've brought horrible shame onto your family, what with all your incredible successes. They've gotta be so embarrassed."

"If you ever meet any of them, don't mention you know me. It'll just get uncomfortable."

I called Sara again to avoid constantly staring at him and wondering if the heat I felt was from being so close to him or being so filled with cheap booze.

"Still no answer."

"Maybe she's not answering because she doesn't recognize the number," he said.

"Possible. It's the third on the left," I said as we turned on to my street. Little boxes of single-family homes lined each side.

They all looked alike, and they all held middle-income, happy families. Except for mine. Someday I'd get around to fixing up my place, but it wouldn't hold a family until after I was long gone.

He pulled into my driveway. "It's lovely. Yours?"

I nodded. "My grandmother's really. She left it to me when she died. It's not what you're probably used to, but it has a roof... mostly." I slipped out of the car and stumbled only once, which was impressive. He followed me up to the porch.

I took a breath before I opened the door, making peace with what I was about to do. Nope. No peace here. My mind seemed pretty well ravaged by war, actually. Letting a client into my home was against every rule Emilia had set. But more than that, it was against every rule *I* had set. And Hayden wasn't just another client.

So many things could go wrong as soon as I opened the door. How weird would it be to have him wait on the porch? The swing would squeak, but it would hold him.

I turned toward him, the door still locked behind me. He was maybe a foot and a half away, looking at me with an expression that might actually be very similar to the one I wore, both of which were highly dangerous. "I'm giving you an out now."

He cocked his head to the side. "Clarify."

"You're allowed to leave now."

"If it's alright with you, I'd rather stay a bit longer."

Was it alright with me? Yeah, way more than it should be. For all the wrong reasons.

When I hesitated, he added, "You might need another ride somewhere tonight."

Although, if I had to pick Sara up somewhere, I could take a cab. And pay a ton of money to hear the driver complain and drive me around the city searching for her.

"That's an excellent point." I nodded gratefully.

This kind of crap was why I'd stopped drinking, why this night should've never happened, and why I really needed a car. If Sara needed help or a ride, I couldn't give her one. So, logically—and having nothing to do with the fact that I really, really, really wanted him to stay—it made sense for him to stick around a while.

Plus, I wasn't going to give in to my baser urges, no matter how much power they currently held over me. Especially while my friend might need me. And I would *never* go to bed with a married man. So as far as I was concerned—Hayden was safe from me.

"I'm not sleeping with you, Hayden," I said, still facing the door. "So if that's what you're thinking is going to happen, you're totally wrong." Well said. And not even a little bit slurred.

"I'm not going to sleep with you either."

"You're not?" Not as well said. There was a bit too much disappointment in it.

"No, I'm not. I'm here to assist in whatever way I can, not to take advantage of a beautiful woman who's been drinking."

Beautiful? I kind of got stuck on the word, unable to move past it for a moment. But then all the others hit me and made much more sense. "Right. Okay, then… That settles it. Neither of us is sleeping with anyone— I mean, each other. Neither of us is sleeping—" I scratched my head. "I'm going to switch topics now."

I heard him chuckle as I unlocked the door and went inside. "Whatever you see in here is classified."

He shut the door behind us. "Lights?"

Right. I flicked on a lamp in the living room. "Don't touch anything, move anything, or lay down on anything." That last one was so that I didn't get distracted.

He crossed his arms over his chest, his fingers denting his biceps. Very distracting biceps.

Focus, damn it. But not on him.

I didn't turn on too many lights, just in case there was anything incriminating lying around, like a piece of mail with my real name on it. As long as he didn't know who I was, then he wouldn't know the computer setup he'd bought me could put me in prison. And he wouldn't get in trouble for knowing. *Great. Lies were so useful.*

Now was not the time to go into it. I wasn't sure when that time was, but it definitely wasn't after drinking heavily. If I started talking about it now, we'd probably end the night with me sobbing onto his shoulder, confessing about that pack of gum I'd stolen when I was nine. Or the time—yesterday—I'd hidden Emilia's keys so we were late for spin class, and by the time we got there, only one bike was left so I generously said she could take it and then went home and finished off a pint of Ben and Jerry's.

I shook my head and led him to the kitchen. "Help yourself to whatever's in the fridge." Nothing in there had 'Andi' written on it. "I'll...um...be back in a few minutes."

He looked at me strangely but didn't say anything. I went straight to my office and booted up my computer. Halfway through the boot, I realized that while the fridge might not have anything with my name on it, there could be any number of condemning things in the room I'd just left him in. Better to keep him close.

"Hayden, can you come here?" Thank God my computer wasn't in my bedroom. I quickly shoved my bills into a drawer, hearing the click of his shoes on the wooden floors. When he came inside the office, I dove into my chair.

"Nice." He came up behind me and rested his arm right above my head. "So this is where the magic happens, huh?"

"Nah, the real magic happens next door in my bed—" I bit my tongue. Literally. "Never mind."

"Is that...?" He blinked and tilted his head, looking at my desktop computer—using the word loosely.

"The system you bought me?" I tilted my head too—nope, didn't make it any better. "Um...I did a little customization, that sort of thing, but yeah, it is."

I'd salvaged what I could from my last computer and combined it with the one he'd given me. It looked a bit Frankenstein-ish but worked like a miracle. Plus, if I ever got in trouble with the law—which would never happen to sweet, innocent, never-screw-up-anything me—well, it was a hell of a lot easier to hide than the original set-up.

"Think of it like this: Computers are like people—what's going on inside is more important than the way it looks outside."

"Huh." He shook his head after a little more staring. "So what happens now?"

"Now I track her phone," I said quietly.

"You what?"

I spun my chair around. "I'm going to track her phone, but please don't tell anyone because I could get in trouble, beyond just making Sara mad."

"My mouth is shut about anything that happens tonight. Anything."

I was sure he hadn't meant that to sound so seductive. I spun back to the keyboard, hearing him back up and lean against the wall. My heart was beating triple-time as I worked—once for staying alive, once for Hayden being in my house, and the last for my Sara-induced anxiety. It only took a few minutes to get into the phone company's system and then a few more to triangulate Sara's phone. When I heard Hayden sigh, I knew I had to explain, at least a little.

"If I had my phone, I could just use the app that tracks the chip in Sara's phone. It's usually used by parents who want to know where their teenager is, but it's also handy for paranoid friends." I'd set up the tracking on Sara's and Emilia's phones without them knowing. I was hiding so much from so many people, sometimes I couldn't keep it all straight. A perfect example of that was the man standing behind me, leaning against the wall and not even knowing my real name or anything about me.

"Why are you paranoid?"

"Long story. No laugh-out-loud parts." He was silent, maybe waiting for me to go on. But I wouldn't. "Actually, it's not really something I can share." Even if I knew exactly what had happened to Sara, why her behavior had changed from one night to the next, I couldn't tell Hayden.

"Maybe you could install one of those tracker things on my phone, too. I'm always losing the damn thing."

I whipped my head toward him, needing to see his expression to know if he was making fun of me. Damn, he had a great smile, dark, intelligent eyes, and just a shadow of stubble softening his jaw.

I think I sighed.

"I'd be happy to, Hayden. But then I would know exactly where you are at all times."

"Where I *am*, not where I want to be, correct?" His tone was bittersweet—humorous but sad at the same time. I didn't look too long, though, because if I saw what I hoped I might, my priorities would change. And my judgment might get even worse.

Just as the dot appeared over a map of the city, Hayden's phone rang. "Bennett." Then a pause. "This is Hayden Bennett, a friend of the other Sara's."

I jumped out of my chair. "Give me the phone." As soon as he handed it to me, I said, "Sara, are you okay?"

"Yeah," she grumbled. "That guy was a total loser. He took me to this gorgeous house and then told me he lived over the garage. So I'm thinking, 'Okay, he works for the owners, and they give him a place.' Right? But no, his parents own it and support him. Obviously, I'm not looking for a boyfriend so I could overlook that because, whatever, times are tough right now. But you should've seen his room. No, actually, no one should ever have to see that. There was no way I was laying down on that bed. No way. Seriously, it was *so* disgusting, Andi."

I covered the phone up as if Hayden could hear Sara call me by name, but he'd turned away and was looking at the books on my shelf. I tried not to think about a couple that were up there. I was a single woman who didn't date or leave the house very often, and who liked to read. So yeah, there might be a few titles I wouldn't want my mother, or my boss, or whatever Hayden was, to know I had. I refocused on what Sara was blabbing on about.

"I don't think he'd washed his sheets since high school. You know how men are, so you know what's on those sheets. Eww. *Soooo* I took a cab home and was about to turn off my phone when I saw that I'd gotten a call. Or four. I called the number back because I thought it was sticky-sheet boy, but it turned out to be your boyfriend."

"He's not my—" I shut my mouth because the last thing I needed was for Hayden to hear that word anywhere close to this situation. "I'm glad you're okay. Let's meet tomorrow so I can get my phone back. And don't ever leave without telling me where you're going again, got it?"

"Okay, Mom. Got it. Oh, and Andi? Don't do anything I wouldn't."

"There *is* nothing you wouldn't do." I hung up on her giggle and handed Hayden his phone back.

"So, all is well?" he asked.

"Yeah, false alarm." I shut down my computer and led him

into the living room. "Sorry I made you come over here for nothing."

"I'm not over here for nothing. I'm over here for you."

"Me?" Maybe it was because I wasn't worried about Sara anymore, or maybe the alcohol had worn off and my brain could function again. But all of a sudden, it hit me—holy-mother-board, I was standing three feet away from Hayden Bennett. Hayden Bennett was... *Aaaand*, there went the brain function.

"Um..." Yep. Three years of college, student loans I'll be paying off until the end of time, and the only thing I could think of to say was, 'um.'

"It's nice that you care about someone that much."

"Uh-huh." My command of the English language was so impressive he'd probably ask me to speak at his next board meeting.

He stepped closer to me. "Is there anyone else you care about that much? Or more?"

I got what he was asking—did I have a friend I spent a lot of time naked with—but the closer Hayden got, the harder it was to move...anything. Including my mouth.

"Nuh-uh." See? No mouth movement at all.

"That's...good news."

I can't even describe the sound I made. It was like an affirmative sigh with a little fear tossed in somehow.

"I'm still processing that I'm finally in the same room with you," he said quietly. "But it's late, so..."

Okay, this was just awkward for everyone within a three-mile radius. Us standing about two feet from each other. Staring at each other.

Why did he keep glancing at my lips? I hoped it wasn't because he was anxious for me to say something. He'd be seriously disappointed unless he wanted to hear another 'um' or 'uh-huh.'

"Could I have a glass of water before I go?"

"Go?" I shook the stupid out of my mind. "Yeah, of course. Of course, you're going to leave. And hydration is important." I slammed my lips together and headed for the kitchen, brushing his shoulder slightly as I walked by. The tingly feeling was completely gone by the time I got to the sink. I'd be fine. I filled up two glasses and downed mine while handing the other to him.

He took a sip before setting it down on the counter. A sip? That's it?

"I thought you were thirsty."

He shook his head. "The water was just an excuse to give me a chance to think of another excuse to stay longer. But it's delicious. Thank you."

"I only serve the finest of tap waters."

"Then I'd hate to waste it. It's only polite to stick around until I've finished it and thought of the next excuse, don't you think?"

"Definitely." Thank God I hadn't put it in a to-go cup.

He pointed to one of the kitchen chairs, waiting until I nodded for him to sit down. My kitchen was the least romantic place on earth—designed by an eighty-year-old woman that the twenty-three-year-old woman who lived here now hadn't gotten around to redecorating.

"How did you know it was Sara who left?" I asked. "How did you know she was my friend when she walked by?"

"I saw her with you, and then, while you two were standing in the bar, Other-Sara saw me through the doorway. Probably because she'd caught me staring at you."

"How did you know what I looked like?"

"I didn't. I recognized your voice but didn't expect you to look like you do. So I stared. And when she saw me staring at you, she stared at me. And frankly, Other-Sara has a way of staring that makes a man feel a bit...objectified."

"And I'm sure that's never happened to you before." I laughed until the look on his face drained all the humor away, leaving only feelings that shouldn't be there. "How were you staring at me before she started staring at you, Hayden?"

He smirked. "Remember, I didn't expect you to look like you do. So I stared in a mostly bewildered and"—he looked away guiltily—"possibly objectifying manner. But only slightly objectifying."

"I don't believe for a minute that you aren't used to people looking at you."

"I'm completely used to it. It happens all the time. I have one of those faces, common faces, that everyone thinks they recognize." If he thought his face was common, he needed to replace all the mirrors in his house with ones that actually worked.

"Do you actually think that's why people stare at you?"

"I hope it's not because I have something between my teeth." He shrugged. "Although, even if I did, I don't spend much time smiling, so how would anyone know?"

"Something between your teeth? Sure. It couldn't be because you're ridiculously attractive and seem to be important in certain circles?"

"You think I'm attractive?"

I laughed. "Don't get overly excited, Hayden. Everyone else thinks you're attractive, too."

"I'm not concerned with what everyone *else* thinks of me."

I took a deep breath. Then another. Then another, until I remembered that's how people hyperventilate. And that would just suck.

"You're married."

He leaned back in the chair and took a long swig of his water. Almost finishing it. Probably wanting to go. "We keep coming back to this point, don't we?"

"Are you surprised? It's kind of a deal breaker."

"No, I'm not surprised. Disappointed, yes. Surprised, no." He finished his water and got up to put it in the sink. I was a millisecond away from asking him to stay when he turned on the tap, filled his glass back up, and spun around to face me. "I understand why you don't believe me when I tell you Clare and I are getting a divorce. I understand because you don't know me as well as I wish you did, as well as I wish *I* knew you. So I'm not asking for anything more than that chance—to get to know each other."

"I think you've had enough water for one night." I took it from him and dumped it into the sink. "Come back when your divorce is official." I put out my hand, like that would fool either of us into thinking this was a business relationship. Maybe I was trying to remind both of us.

"I will. I will come back. And you're going to have to come up with another reason to not see what this could become." He took my hand and lifted it to his lips.

I swallowed when I felt my girlie insides melt. "Where do you get your moves, Mr. Bennett?"

"I watch a lot of black and white movies." Made sense. Men didn't behave like this anymore. Men didn't behave period.

I stared at him, frozen in thought. "I believe you. Maybe I'm an idiot, but I believe you're getting divorced. Because you believed me when I told you I didn't leak that information to your competitor."

"I didn't, though," he said sadly. "Not until you showed me proof."

"Well..." I sighed. "I guess that means I'm either a better person or a bigger idiot than you are."

"Definitely the former."

I should've added 'better liar' to those options. But I think this was the proof I needed. Proof that I could trust him, that he was the man I hoped he was. If I knew that for sure, then I could tell him who I was. But I couldn't go first. Blind trust had ruined my life and my future, so it was a little tough to muster more up.

"I'm going to ask you this once," I said. "Please, don't make me regret trusting you." The words that mirrored his own held the same amount of meaning. This was about trust, and this was for good. "Are you really getting a divorce?"

"Yes."

"But not because of..." It would be the height of arrogance to think it had anything to do with me.

"Are you asking if my interest in you was part of the reason?" Thankfully, he answered without waiting for a response. "Splitting up is the right thing for both of us. Your involvement is limited to the fact that I never imagined anything better was possible for me. Now, when I talk to you or...look at you, I think there might be. But you get a small say in that part of it, I suppose."

"Gee, thanks." I ducked my head. "There are a lot of things I haven't told you about me yet. Maybe you'll change your mind once you know."

"Are you married?"

I popped my head up. "No."

"In a monogamous relationship with anyone? Let's not count me for right now because our monogamous and incredibly passionate relationship hasn't begun yet."

Damn, I wished he hadn't said that. "No."

"Then the only thing left is for you to give me your ID and a major credit card."

"What?"

He smiled. "Like you said, if you give them to me, then I know you're not a serial killer or a rapist. Anything other than that I can deal with."

Man, I hoped that was true.

25

HAYDEN

WHAT WAS HAPPENING TO ME? I'd met a woman for the first time and was already falling for her. Granted, we'd known each other a while, but things like this didn't happen. Not to me, or anyone else. The love-at-first-sight phenomenon could be easily explained away by hormones and other chemical reactions. But this was the reverse. Maybe the fact that I liked her so much was actually making her more attractive. Love *before* first sight.

"You are very beautiful," I said, sitting down at her kitchen table again, determined to stay as long as possible. "Very drunk, but very beautiful."

"I'm not drunk anymore." She stood behind a chair, gripping the back tightly. As if that chair would keep us apart more than half a second if I tried to get to her. But I could control myself...for now.

"I'm glad you didn't try to refute the other part."

"If I'd been listening, I might have. But I didn't hear what I could be refuting. Was it anything good?"

I laughed. "Very, very beautiful."

"I can't hear you," she mocked, pointing to her ears in the silent room. "It's loud in here."

"And so different from what I imagined." Which would have been perfect, too. "I didn't think you would look like you do."

"What? You imagined me sitting in front of my computer all day, combing my mullet and covered in cat hair?"

"Of course, not." I'd imagined her pretty, not stunning. "I knew you wouldn't be covered in cat hair. It would be dog hair from the pack of wolves who raised you."

"Ah." She sat down, a very wicked, probably slightly drunken smile lighting up her face. "Well then, you're exactly right. But Mom and Dad don't shed this time of year, so fur isn't a big issue. You should probably avoid me in the spring, though."

"You don't look at all Greek."

"Greek?"

"Your last name is Greek, isn't it? I thought—"

"Yeah, Greek," she said quickly. "I'm adopted."

I couldn't stop glancing at her lips. The ones that teased me, challenged me, controlled me. Punished me when they would say goodbye. The ones I would give anything for just one taste of.

"You need to stop looking at me like that, Hayden."

I blinked, but every time I opened my eyes, they moved right back to that mouth. "I apologize." I tucked my head down to break the hold she had over me. But nothing could stop me from reaching for her chair, slipping my hand in between her legs and curling my fingers under the edge of the seat, sliding her and the chair closer to me.

"Because if you keep looking at me like that, option two is going to happen whether you want it to or not."

I whipped my head up, held still for one moment, and then reached my hand out to touch her. After all this time, we'd never been close enough to touch.

We were far from knowing everything about each other, but

what I knew, I adored. And wanted. I couldn't walk away without touching her, making sure she was real and not just something I'd made up in my mind.

My fingertips traced her jaw lightly, then moved to her lower lip. My cock swelled the moment she unconsciously moved her tongue to where I'd just touched. Somehow we'd closed the gap between us, and if I moved my thumb out of the way, I could easily replace it with my lips.

When she scooted forward, I moved my hand from her chair to her leg. Her skin was warm, soft. She inhaled sharply as her thighs closed, her hand covering mine to...

Oh shit, she wasn't trying to stop me. She was directing me, guiding my touch.

"This is a really bad idea, Hayden."

"Why?"

"I work for you. You're married. And I don't think I'll be able to turn this off if it starts."

"Hasn't it already started?" Not the physical—that hadn't gone nearly far enough. But we couldn't claim this was just a working relationship anymore. Not after being in the same room, feeling the pull between us.

"We could still stop now and pretend nothing happened."

"I don't want to pretend anymore."

"Hayden, please. You know this isn't right."

Actually, all I knew was that fighting this desire was useless, more proof of its danger.

My lips hovered over hers, shaking with anticipation and fear, while I wondered how big of a mistake I was making. Because this was definitely a mistake. Things like this didn't happen to me, so something was obviously about to go horribly wrong. Therefore, it became simply the degree of which this was wrong that was important. And how much each of us was willing to trust. To risk.

"I shouldn't be doing this," I whispered. "Not tonight." With each consonant, our lips met, lightly, gently. Our words bringing us together. Like always.

"I warned you."

"I guess I wasn't listening." Damn it. "I should really go."

She'd been drinking, and I was in no frame of mind to make a good decision. Plus, I'd promised her I had no intention of sleeping with her, which was now a total lie—I would happily rip off all her clothing and sink my tongue into her, taste her everywhere, take out years of sexual frustration on her body. Why did I promise her I wouldn't?

"I wish—" she mumbled against my lips. "Yeah, you should go." Neither of us moved away, holding the line between denial and admission, honesty and risk, innocence and desire.

"I don't think I can." I felt the air move as the corners of her mouth curled.

"You're obviously not trying hard enough."

"Am I taking advantage of you?" I asked, not sure what I would do if she said yes.

"Yes."

Damn it. "Sorry about that." But not enough to move away.

"No, you're not."

"No I'm not," I repeated. "But I should be. So let's move that apology to me being sorry I'm not sorry about that."

"You should've asked me if I minded. I don't. Plus, when you think about it, I could be taking advantage of you."

"Then I'm begging you to continue."

"Hayden," she tapped my chest. "I think one of us should move away now."

Right. "I'll do it."

"Take one for the team."

"You have no idea how much I wish I could," I grumbled. "Okay, I'm leaving now." No. I couldn't. Not without tasting her, feeling her mouth. "Right after I kiss you. With your permission."

"Did you seriously just ask for my permission?" As she laughed, she straightened. It was only slight, but I had a sudden panic attack that she'd pull away completely. I wrapped my hand around the nape of her neck and pulled her back toward me. Not into me, just *to* me.

"I guess that proves that you don't do this all the time," she finished, not laughing at all.

I blinked and released her. Did she really think that everything I'd said was just a line? Something I'd used before on other women? "I told you I didn't."

She grabbed me by the shirt. "Did you? Maybe you misspelled it so badly I couldn't make it out." She scooted even closer, her knees passing mine. "But let's get back to you leaving. And what you needed to do before you left. What was that again? Finish your water and...?"

"Kiss you."

"Oh yeah. That. Just once?"

"Just once." *Tonight.* "But it will be a long one."

"I'm going to refrain from commenting on the length of anything right now, and ask you a question instead."

"Okay, but make it a quick one."

"I'm going to refrain from commenting on that as well, because I really don't think what's in my mind right now would be quick."

I groaned. "Ask your damn question."

"Just for clarification: What we're discussing here is a long kiss and nothing else. Is that correct?"

Tonight. Nothing else *tonight.* "Correct."

"And then a) we forget it ever happened and b) you don't fire me and we go on working together, right?"

"I won't fire you. Promise. Anything else that needs clarification?"

"Nope." She grabbed my tie and yanked me toward her.

Thankfully, I hadn't sworn to the other condition. Because nothing on earth could make me forget this ever happened.

I slipped my arms behind her back and pulled her closer until she had to part her legs around mine and settle on top of my lap. Every time our mouths parted and then came together again, so did our hips, her core sliding against the erection tenting my pants. I kept my arms tensed, holding her hips, allowing her only the smallest of movements against me. Because honestly, if I let her have her way, there was an excellent chance I would come in my pants, her scent filling each breath, her taste on my tongue.

After we'd gotten to know each other's mouths pretty damn well, I pulled her dress down from where it had scooted up and was now exposing her beautiful thighs and a peek of black lace. What I *wanted* to do was pick her up, carry her into her bedroom, and spend the rest of the weekend with my lips on her skin. But I disengaged, adjusted myself, and walked to the door. She followed.

"Thank you for the lovely evening," I managed, my body screaming at me, begging my brain to stop being so damn rational for once. "Get some sleep. I'll be contacting you in a few hours."

"A few hours?" She looked at the clock. "But it's Saturday."

"I know. And I'll be contacting you." After one last, more modest but still smoldering kiss, I backed away and went to my car.

It was a miracle I didn't back up into the neighbor's front yard because, for the life of me, I couldn't look away from her. The porch light didn't make her glow, nor did any other light, because *she* glowed. With life and humor and intelligence. I didn't know adults could feel this way. Had always assumed it was all part of a teenager's hormones that gave the feeling of simultaneously being complete and completely empty. Wanting more, *needing* it. Needing her.

But I shifted the car into first and drove away, because she'd been drinking and, regardless of what she said, I wanted her to be one hundred percent sober the first time I took her to bed. I knew there would be a first time, and a second, and a fifth, and a fifty-fifth. Because I never gave up once I decided what I wanted. And I'd never wanted anything as much as I wanted her.

26

ANDI

I DIDN'T EVEN THINK about it until after he'd driven away and I'd closed the door, but he still didn't know my real name. Maybe if he'd called me Sara instead of Sira, I would've remembered to come clean. It wasn't as if call-center people didn't use fake names, so it shouldn't have been a big deal. But as soon as we'd kissed...and kissed......and *kissed*, it had become a big deal.

I woke up to the smell of sweat and sex. Not nearly as exciting when you went to bed by yourself, believe me. When I heard someone knock on the door, I crawled out of bed.

Hayden stood on my front porch, looking like perfection, complete with two cups of coffee. "How often do you see the sun?" I could *so* get used to seeing his smile every day.

"What's the sun?"

"Thought so." He handed me one of the coffee cups. "Come on, Sira, it's time you got out from behind your screen occasionally. Life can be lived without electronics."

"Blasphemy. What are you doing here?"

"I'd like to say I'm here to spend the day getting to know

someone better. But, unfortunately, I have to get some stuff done —less interruptions when no one else is in the office. Oh, one more thing before I go. I don't know what's in your tap water, but can I get a little more?"

"Tap water?" I wish I had a camera or artistic talent or something, anything that could capture the beauty of his teasing smile.

"Yeah. I don't know why, but I woke up in the best mood ever. I feel happy, relaxed, excited. The only thing I can think of is the water you served me last night. I mean, what else could it be?"

"Right. Had to have been the water. Did you bring a bottle for me to fill? Or should I just spray you down with a hose?"

"Thanks to you, I took a cold shower last night." He laughed. "I'll make sure I bring a bottle next time." He turned to go but then stopped. "There will be a next time, right, Sira? Soon?"

"Hayden..." Say it. Ignore the sudden nausea and just say it. "That's not really my name."

His smile grew. "I know."

"You do?"

"Of course." He came back to the doorway. "But it fits, don't you think?"

"Well, yeah. I mean, I like it. But—"

He stopped me with a kiss, his lips warm, his mouth tasting like coffee and mint and man. I put my hand on his chest, ready to push him away so I could speak. I should push him away.

I should.

I would.

I didn't.

He was the one to finally break contact. "I really need to go. Gotta take another cold shower before I go to the office."

I peeled my eyes open to see him walking away. I couldn't speak, my lips too busy rubbing themselves together, trying to hold on to the sensation his had left behind.

"Soon, Sira. Really soon."

"Soon," I promised. I'd tell him sooner or later. I waved goodbye as he pulled out of my driveway and drove off.

I'm a horrible person. I should've stayed where I belonged and never met him face-to-face. Then it wouldn't matter who I was or was just pretending to be. If I'd just kept everything professional, none of this would be happening.

Things were so much simpler online. You could be whoever you wanted to be. A person's name and past and baggage weren't important. If Hayden and I had never met, I could just be me, be Sira, his brilliant and amusing assistant, and that would've been enough. Now it wasn't. Now it was a lie. A lie I couldn't rationalize away.

Dealing with life through a glass screen made everything safer, easier to control. If I didn't like what I was seeing, all I had to do was press a button and it disappeared. That screen was my way of keeping a manageable distance from life and everyone in it. Maybe that's what was holding me back more than anything else—if I told Hayden my real name, that wall of protection would be shattered, and I'd have nowhere to hide.

I tried to focus on work, but my mind was all over the place. Eventually, my subconscious took over, and I found myself searching for information about the crime Detective Williams had told me about. The one I could possibly be blamed for. Yeah, that one. I didn't find anything more specific than what I already knew—not even the name of the security guard or what kind of information had been stolen. All I learned was that the unnamed guard had been struck and killed by an unknown driver of an unidentified vehicle outside of a big office building in the Financial District. Not helpful.

I could've looked deeper into it, but illegally hacking in to find out more about a hacking crime seemed a bit too much for my karma to handle.

I waited until the third ring before answering Emilia's call, not wanting to talk to her. I had too much crap to obsess over to go running or spinning or whatever other hell she had planned for us.

"We need to talk," she said immediately.

"We *are* talking. Right now, actually."

"Not on the phone. We need to talk in person, face-to-face."

"I'm really busy." Never going out in public again. The only things talking face-to-face got me were trouble or boob-sweat rings. Wow, did that sound wrong.

"Tough. I'm picking you up at seven and taking you to dinner. My treat."

"I can't—"

"Refuse. Yeah, I know. Wear something nice. Maybe something low-cut, so you'll remember not to tuck your napkin into your neckline."

"You mean they don't provide bibs?" I joked. "What kind of dive are you talking about?"

"The kind of place friends go when they have great news to celebrate."

She hung up before I realized she'd manipulated me into agreeing to go. I considered calling her back, but Emilia was a pro. I mean, in the last few months, she'd conned me into more hours of exercise than I expected to do in my entire lifetime. Besides, she'd said something about great news. And man, could I use some of that right now.

27

HAYDEN

IT HAD ONLY BEEN a few weeks since Clare and I had finally brought everything out in the open, but I was coming home to a different woman. I'd never seen her so relaxed, so happy. So...in the hallway.

"We're going out," she said, leaning up against the door of our apartment.

"Where?" I couldn't recall any parties I had to force myself to go to, and Clare knew better than to surprise me with social events. I needed at least twenty-four hours to gear up and pretend to be happy. Or at least not bored out of my mind.

"You're taking me out to dinner. Think of it as a celebration of our newfound honesty, and not like I'm trying to keep you out of the apartment until it airs out."

I groaned. "What happened?"

"I cooked." She grimaced and then shook her head. "No, that's not quite right. I charred."

"Should I call the fire department?"

"Nope," she said, unsurprised by the suggestion. "I already put it out. We may need a new pan, though. And potholders. Maybe counters."

With my eyes shut, I felt her take my arm and turn me toward the elevator. "Wait. Let me put my briefcase down." I tossed it through a narrow opening of the door, smelling 'dinner.' "We may need a new apartment, too."

"Yeah, maybe."

We went to one of the places Clare and her friends frequented and were seated near the window despite not having reservations.

"Throw enough money at something..." she said after I'd dismissed the maître d'.

I nodded at her favorite expression and pulled out her chair.

"Hayden, do you realize that the most normal night out we've ever had just happens to be after we've unofficially split up?"

"Maybe we should unofficially split up more often."

She adjusted her utensils unconsciously, keeping her head lowered until she spoke. "Thank you, Hayden. For understanding and sticking by me. I had no right to do what I did, and you had every right to walk out the second you knew I was lying."

"I made my fair share of bad calls and things I should've done differently."

"Like not marrying a lesbian?"

I smiled. "Actually, I don't see that as one of my bad calls. You've given me a lot, Clare. Whether you know it or not."

"You're a sick, sick man, Hayden Bennett."

I laughed. And agreed.

Until, over Clare's shoulder, I saw Sira, wide-eyed and staring at me from a table across the room. I moved to stand, but she shook her head and then glanced at the woman who was sitting next to her. I was at a loss, wanting to speak to her, but if the other woman was her boss, I'd only complicate things by going over.

"What are you looking at?" Clare asked.

I grabbed her wrist to stop her from turning around and then yanked my hand back. What was worse than Sira seeing me while being with her boss at a restaurant? Seeing me holding my wife's hand while being with her boss at a restaurant. Especially right after assuring her the divorce was pending.

"Hayden?"

I took the champagne out of the pail and refilled Clare's glass. "It's nothing."

"Well 'nothing' just put an endearing look on your face that quickly turned into panic, so—"

"Someone I work with is here. But she may not want to be seen with the person she's with."

"Oh," Clare said, tilting her head as if it was an everyday occurrence. And it was—ignoring the obvious for sake of propriety. I'd seen it in every woman I'd ever known.

I tried to keep my eyes away from Sira to prevent stressing her out more than she already was, but my gaze was drawn back to her every time I stopped concentrating on avoiding her. Now that I'd finally met her, all I wanted to do was study her.

She stood abruptly and turned away, bumping into the server.

"Okay, I guess I'll order for you," the other woman said to her.

Sira whipped around. "No, don't. Please, Emilia." As she met my gaze again, she shook her head, and then rushed toward the front of the restaurant.

I pushed my chair back and stood. "I'll be right back." When I got to the hostess desk, I looked around. She wouldn't have walked out of the restaurant without telling her companion, so I turned into the thin hallway leading to the restrooms. I passed the men's room and, glancing around quickly, opened the door to the ladies' room and whispered her name.

When no one answered and I didn't hear anything, staying near the door just in case someone screamed and I had to run for it.

"Are you in here?" What an idiot. I hadn't snuck into the girl's bathroom since I was seventeen years old and at boarding school.

"Go away," she said from inside one of the stalls.

"I just want to talk to you for a second."

"Go away."

"Sira, please." I flicked the deadbolt on the door. There were three stalls, each door going all the way to the bottom. I knocked on the first door and then jiggled the handle. Then the second. Both empty. "Can you please come out and talk to me?"

"You know what women do in here, right? Well, I'm doing that. So go away."

"I can wait." I wiped the edge of the vanity slowly and then leaned against it.

"Hayden, you need to leave."

"I will...just as soon as we talk."

Eventually, the lock clicked and she came out, looking furious. Her shoulders slumped when she glanced at the door. If she tried to run for it, she'd have to pass right by me.

"You didn't flush."

She glared at me. "I didn't pee. I was hiding, and you know it. Are you stalking me?" Her arms were wrapped tightly around herself, hip out, toe tapping—the complete package. And all I could think about was how amazing angry sex with her would be. All that anger lashing out toward me while she was naked.

"Right," she grumbled. "I forgot how well you listen. Should I repeat the question?"

"Can we just speak calmly?" It was all I could do not to blind her with my shit-eating grin, but I knew it would only piss her off more.

"How 'bout you start by calmly explaining why you're following me?"

"I'm not. You were seated after I was already here."

"With your wife."

I sighed. "Yes. Clare is here."

"Great. Well, I think that's enough calm and enough speaking." As soon as she moved, I stepped in between her and the door. She threw out her arms to stop her momentum, her palms landing on my chest briefly before she pulled them back as if I'd burned her. "What do you want from me?"

More than I could tell her. "To be in the same room with you. To not have you instantly run away. To have a conversation. Something. Anything."

"Look, the—" She turned her head, shying away when she saw our reflections in the mirror. "What happened between us—"

"The kiss or the whole evening?"

Her lips tightened. "What *happened* was that we both experienced a momentary lapse in judgment that lasted an hour more than momentary lapses should. It's no one's fault, but it was a mistake we won't be making again."

What? "You're telling me that kiss was a mistake? One you never want to feel again? Wow. *I* can't stop thinking about it. About you. I want to feel it again and again until—"

"This isn't going anywhere, Hayden. In case you've forgotten, you're my boss, my married boss. That's what we need to focus on. All the other stuff just confuses things." She held out her hands as if weighing something. "A little disappointment now, or a shitload of hurt later—guess which one I choose."

"I don't accept that."

"You don't accept it?" She laughed. "Well, tough shit."

"No. I don't accept those two things as our only choices." Not when there's even the slightest chance of having more. She knew there was, just as much as I did. "Do you know that you've never actually said no? Or that you don't want this?"

"I've told you this can't happen more times than I can count."

"That's different. That's situational. Letting other people determine our fate. But you've never said, 'No, Hayden. I don't want you.' Why is that?"

She stared at me long and hard. "Your wife's probably wondering where you are."

"I didn't lie to you about her." I moved a step toward her. Then another. "Please, if you want this even a fraction as much as I do, don't walk away."

She shuddered when I touched her cheek, when I cupped her chin in my hand, when I lifted it so she would look at me.

"I can prove I wasn't lying. Just give this a chance."

When my lips were millimeters away from hers, she spoke. "No."

I closed my eyes, dropping my hand from her face. But I didn't pull away. I couldn't. I wanted her to take it back, give me some kind of proof I wasn't in this alone. "Is that what you really want?"

"No," she whispered.

"I'm not sure what to do now."

She sighed and stepped backwards. "Go back to your wife, Mr. Bennett."

Then I realized something I should've already figured out—she really didn't see this like I did, not even close. She could keep me out, and I would never be able to do that, not with the way I felt about her.

So I stepped out of her way, her shoulder brushing my arm as she passed. Then I heard the deadbolt click and the door slam closed when she left me.

28

ANDI

"ARE YOU OKAY?" Emilia asked when I came back to the table.

"Perfect." I sat down with my lips curled up, but with no teeth showing because that's the kiss of death when you're trying to fake a smile. As soon as you show a little teeth, it ends up looking like disgust or a snarl. Two expressions happy people don't make.

Emilia stared at me, no teeth showing, but only because her mouth was open in confusion.

"Really, I'm okay," I said. "Not crazy about the bathrooms here, though."

"You've got to be the worst liar ever. What happened?"

I pressed my lips together to try and hold in my shame. Turns out, shame can escape in other ways. Like in watery eyes that can't seem to look anywhere but the tablecloth in front of you. Or the knife you should probably stab yourself with before you ruin somebody else's life.

"Can we leave?" I asked. "Go somewhere else?"

Emilia was out of her chair before I'd finished speaking. She grabbed our stuff and ushered me out of the place as if she were Secret Service and I was someone important.

She didn't say anything until we were in the car and pulling away from the valet station. "Wanna tell me what happened?"

I shook my head. I wanted to disappear and forget everything about my life. "Not right now. Still a lot to process." Like that Hayden had lied about getting a divorce and had turned me into a home-wrecker. In less than twenty-four hours. The sensible thing was to salvage the last remaining shreds of my dignity, start all over again, and find another way to make money. "That okay?"

"Of course." She put her hand on mine and squeezed.

Karma had just taken a huge bite out of my ass. No, that's not right. This was me making the same mistake I'd made four years ago. I'd trusted the wrong person again. I'd chosen a man over common sense. Back then, because of the transparency of my cluelessness, my punishment had been light—no jail time, and of course, no more internet access. It wasn't enough.

Don't get me wrong—I was very grateful not to have to wear orange, take group showers, or learn how to make a shiv, but I'd been responsible for ruining lives, and I should've paid more for that mistake. Guilt, shame, disappointment in myself, and a bunch of other great emotions, as well as all the cash I could return to the people I'd hurt would never be enough. Because no amount of money could repair those people's heartbreak, the violation they'd felt.

I was so sure I'd never be that big of an idiot again, but like the saying goes: 'Never say never.' Or 'always.' Or 'One more episode on Netflix, and then I'll go to sleep.' Because, as that other saying goes: 'The worst lies are the ones we tell ourselves.'

I deserved this.

"Do you know why I wanted to take you out tonight?" Emilia asked. "I heard something about Hayden Bennett from a reliable source."

My stomach clenched so hard, words and tears started

spilling out of me. I couldn't stop them. "OhmygodIshould-n'thaveandI'msosorry.Ittotallywasn'thisfault.Itwascomplete-lymine,and—"

"Andi, he's getting a divorce."

29

HAYDEN

I'm NOT sure how long I was in the women's bathroom, staring at the tiny dots of the granite countertop, trying to see a pattern where none existed. I didn't understand how I could've gotten so far off-course, imaging things that weren't there. Shocked and confused how I'd made it through this much of life being so incredibly clueless.

"Hayden?" Clare called from the other side of the door.

Time to go back to reality. I pushed off the wall and went to rejoin the land of the living.

"Where've you been?" She did a double-take when she saw the picture on the door I'd just walked through. "You getting in touch with your feminine side, Hay?"

I slowly followed her back into the dining room. One quick glance told me what I already knew—the table Sira had been sitting at was empty, the staff clearing off unused utensils and untouched water glasses. I took one last pity-me breath and refocused on the woman who wanted to be with me. Kind of.

"Remind me to never use the bathroom here," Clare said as I pulled her chair out for her. "Seems like a depressing place. You going to tell me what happened?"

"I'd rather not. Nothing personal. It's just—"

"Nothing personal. Got it." She emptied the bottle of champagne into my glass, filling it all the way to the top. Evidently I'd been gone long enough for our food to have arrived, so I used that as a method of conversation escape.

She watched me eat for a little while. "Hayden, I'm going to tell my family we're getting divorced at dinner tomorrow night."

Unless I was traveling, every Sunday evening I put on a suit and took her to her father's house. Oh, the fun.

"Not a bad idea, as long as you time it right after everyone's second glass of wine and your stepmom's sixth," I teased. "But are you really sure you want to? There's no rush."

"I've wasted enough of your life. We need to tell them, but I'm kind of chicken, so it'd be great if you were there, too."

"You mean so they'll have someone to aim at?" I wasn't sure if it was a good idea, but it was Clare's life, too. And she cared what her family thought of her. Luckily, I didn't have that burden with my own family. Not anymore.

I'd stopped caring what anyone thought of me the second time my father had tried to kill me. Or maybe it was a few minutes later when I'd let him die. I'd been pretty closed off before then, but that's when I stopped caring about everything, stopped feeling anything, and became nothing more than the person everyone expected me to be.

As soon as we got home, I tried calling Sira, but she didn't answer. Then I tried explaining myself over a few text messages. That failed to get a response, too. So I left a few more via the computer. I gave up after the second email, knowing anything more than that would only prove how pathetic I was.

Sunday morning, when I turned my laptop on, I saw a

message. It was short, much too short to warrant the amount of relief I felt. But anything was better than being ignored.

'A friend told me she'd heard a rumor that you're getting divorced.'

Wow, I'd underestimated the speed at which Clare's so-called friends' mouths worked. And had never been more thankful for it.

'But, even so, I still work for you. I hope you understand why I can't do anything to risk my livelihood.'

That was it? That was all?

I typed, *'Then you're fired. Problem solved,'* but then deleted it. That was hardly a good solution. By wanting to spend more time with her, I'd screw myself. I'd taken up so much of her workday, she'd become dependent on that income and had probably let other opportunities go. Since I relied on the quality and speed of her work too, dropping it all wouldn't help either of us.

Until now, I'd put off hiring an in-house assistant. That would change on Monday morning. I'd hire someone competent and keep Sira on until my new assistant could handle the workload and Sira had found other clients.

After that happened, she'd be out of excuses.

That night, on the long, anxiety-riddled drive over to Bart's house, Clare and I discussed scenarios, phrasing, etc. "Nothing should be this stressful, Clare. Why don't you just let me tell them?"

"No, I should. They're my dysfunctional family, not yours." Her pants were going to be stretched out in the shape of her fists if I didn't drive faster.

"It's not an execution. I'd be happy—well, not *happy*, but I'll tell them. As long as you're absolutely sure you want to do it *now*."

"As soon as I kick you to the curb, and some hooker takes

pity on your pathetic-ness and brings you back to her place to live, someone will notice." Her smile was tight, like her brow.

"When we get home, I'm throwing away your e-reader and ordering you another, filled with nothing but the classics."

"Just make sure *Moll Flanders* is on it. Talk about a tragic life. That kind of stuff happens all the time, Hayden. They even made it into a movie."

"And I'm canceling cable."

"I appreciate the bad jokes, but I'm serious. I may have accidentally mentioned our pending divorce to a couple of friends, and you know how my friends are, especially when they promise not to tell anyone."

Yes, I knew.

"I'd rather my dad hear about it from me rather than a tabloid," she said.

"We could claim it's a trial separation."

"What will that get us?"

"A chance to test out your father's reaction."

She laughed. "Are you that afraid of him?"

"I like to think of it as wary, not afraid." Sure, Bart held no real power in the company, but the board of directors didn't know that. Six years of mind-bending, soul-stealing work. I'd proven myself valuable, but Bart was fickle, unpredictable, and moody. If he went to the board, my career could be in jeopardy, and I would really prefer not to go job-hunting anytime soon.

But that wasn't why I was concerned. Clare's father already seemed to think that whatever his daughter did was exactly the wrong thing. He would take the news of a divorce better if *I* told him. It's a sad thing when a father trusts an employee more than his own child. Especially since his child had never actually done anything wrong. Other than not being who she really was for his sake.

Sunday dinner with the Chalmers was the same as every other time I couldn't get out of it. The only difference was Clare's hand on my thigh throughout. There was nothing seductive about her grip, though. Her fingers dug into my leg from fear and nervousness. If only it was another woman's hand for another reason, in any another place but this one.

When Clare's stepsister, her stepmother, and Bart's plates were taken away, Clare squeezed so hard I'd have bruises tomorrow. It was ridiculous for her to feel like this, and the sooner I got it over with, the better for her psyche, and the less blood I'd lose through the puncture wounds she'd make any second now.

"There's something I need to tell you—all of you." Once I had everyone's attention, I cleared my throat. "Clare and I—"

"I'm gay," she said.

All eyes beelined to her, including mine.

"I'm gay. I've always been gay"—her gaze darted from gape-mouthed family member to gape-mouthed family member —"and I always will be gay"—then finally moved to her father —"and I'm sorry I lied to you for so long."

No one said anything. But, to be fair, many of them seemed preoccupied with the napkins in their laps or the amazingly quick way their wine glasses had emptied. Clare looked at me and blew out a breath. Telling her she'd just made a colossal mistake would hardly be helpful, so with my eyes and a squeeze of the hand still denting my thigh, I tried to convey how proud of her I was. Because it was true. And I knew part of the reason she'd done it was because of me.

With a nervous smile, she said, "I know you must be shocked. But honestly, that was a lot easier to say than I thought it would be."

"I don't ever want to see you in this house again." Her father's tone was flat, dead.

Clare's smile melted. "And *that* was exactly as hurtful as I thought it would be."

"Cla—"

She cut me off with a look, placed her napkin on her plate and stood, staring at her father. "I've been your daughter for twenty-seven years. Gina has been your daughter for five, and in that time, you've paid for, and supported her through eight stints in rehab."

"Don't bring me into it," her stepsister snapped.

"I have nothing against you, Gina. I'm just asking for the same consideration."

"Maybe you'd get it if you weren't a dyke."

"Very mature."

And the laundry list cometh. My groan went unheard as a flurry of raised voices of varying pitches commenced. Every atrocity committed by a family member in the past thirty years was thrown out without a single one of them being heard. The only good it did was make me a little more grateful for my own family. Which, in itself, was disturbing.

"Stop it. Please, everyone, stop." I stood and put my arm on Clare's shoulder. "Calm down. No one is trying to hurt anyone else. If we all calm down and talk..."

Everyone suddenly shut up. The direction they were looking brought me to the reason.

When Bart threw his napkin into the ring, or onto the table in this case, people paid attention. His eyes were stone-cold, aiming straight at me. Me. Not any of the people shouting insults and slander. Me. "Did you know?"

"Yes," I said at the same moment Clare said, "No."

"Yes, Bart. I knew."

"You can clean out your office tomorrow."

As I nodded, Clare grabbed my hand, leaning around me. "I had no intention of telling anyone who isn't at this table right now. But if you fire Hayden, I'll take a full-page ad out in the Chronicle. The headline will say, 'I'm here, and I'm queer.' Explain *that* to your hate-filled friends, Dad."

"It's okay," I whispered, taking her hand. "Really." Then I looked at my ex-in-laws and said, "You're all intelligent people, so I'm a little confused how you've completely failed to grasp what a wonderful woman Clare is. All I hope for now is that you realize it before it's too late to have her in your life. Thank you for dinner." Then I pulled my wife away from the table.

Just before we walked outside, Clare turned back and yelled, "Oh, and by the way, we're getting divorced." When she looked at me, there were tears pooling in her eyes. "I sure told them, huh?"

"Yes, you did. Brilliantly." I put my arm around her shoulders and led her away from her nightmare.

When we got into the car, she said, "I'm so sorry."

I was reminded why I liked her so much—in the middle of possibly the worst night of her life, the one she'd been dreading for a decade, she was more worried about me than herself.

"You needed to tell them. The way they reacted is on them." I glanced at her and smirked. "Your timing probably could have been better, though. Next time, wait until they're drunk."

"You always give such good advice," she said smiling. "Someday, I might just start following it. So, what are you going to do now?"

"Me? Uh...I'm not sure." If Bart went to the board and lied his ass off, I might have to look for another job. He'd never tell them the real reason he wanted me gone. "But don't put that ad in the newspaper. It will hurt you a lot more than it will hurt him."

She nodded, wiping her cheeks. "I've always known how he'd react if I ever told him. But I'm glad I did it, and I'm glad you were with me." She was silent for the rest of the ride home, and I didn't press her to talk.

I pulled into the parking garage underneath our building and handed my keys to the valet. Clare held my arm tightly as we walked to the elevator.

"You should keep the apartment," she said, pressing the up arrow. "I'll find another."

"Why don't you wait until you've had some time to think things through before making any real estate decisions."

"No, it's better I move out." She looked at me, her expression serious yet peaceful. "I can't afford the mortgage payment."

"Do you even know how much it is?"

"No, but I'm guessing it isn't free and, seeing as how I'm penniless now, that means I can't afford it." Because of Bart's fact-proof delusion that his brilliant daughter couldn't possibly understand math or properly consult with an accountant, Clare's trust fund would remain under his control until his death. A day that, until listening to his outburst thirty minutes ago and seeing the effect it had on his daughter, I hadn't actually been looking forward to. Who knew what he'd do with the funds now that he'd disowned Clare, all under the pretense of her best interests.

"Whether we're married or not," I said, "you'll never have to worry about money. Understand?"

She dropped my arm and looked at me, her eyes filling with more tears. "Hayden, stop it! Stop being so goddamn nice. I ruined the last few years of your life because I was too weak to be honest. I don't deserve your kindness, or your help, or your generosity. I don't deserve any of it."

"You'd rather I was more like your father, then?" My voice was stronger than I wanted it to be.

"You'll never, ever come close to being the man my father is.

Thank God. You're too good, too accepting, too noble. But you need to stop using me as another wall."

"What does that mean?"

"Me. Our marriage. We were both hiding behind it, but at least I had Shannon. Excuse me for being blunt, but holy fuck, Hayden, what do you have? What do you *want*? Do you even know?" The volume of her voice increased with every word. I almost called her on it, told her that I wasn't the one she should be yelling at because I'd done nothing wrong. But I had. And everything she was saying was absolutely right. Absolutely irrefutable. Our marriage was just one more wall I'd built around myself. So I didn't have to actually *feel* anything, and I'd never have anything real to lose.

"I know you were staying with me for a lot of good reasons," she said. "And I love that about you. I really do. But now I understand what you meant by the wrong reasons. For all the risks you take at work, all the effort you put into it, you've never put anything even remotely like that into your private life. Why not?"

"I..." Didn't know.

"I get that you're afraid of getting hurt. And sometimes it *does* hurt. But it also feels amazing. It's worth any amount of pain to have those moments that take your breath away. That make you lose yourself and all your baggage and just be...happy."

"I am..." Even I couldn't stomach that lie. I wasn't happy. I'd never been happy.

The elevator door opened, and an elderly woman got on. She pressed the button for the lobby.

"We're going up, ma'am," I said. "You might want to wait for the next elevator."

"I hate waiting." She smiled at me. "This way, I'm moving, even if it's in the wrong direction."

When we reached our floor, I held the door and then

followed Clare into the apartment. I looked around the place, unsure what to do with it. It was too much for me, but if Clare didn't want it... "We could sell it."

"Where would you live?" she asked.

"Somewhere else. Where would you live?"

She smiled bitterly and tossed her bag onto a chair. "Somewhere else. I don't know how to not have money, but I hear some people do it. God, I never realized how ungrateful I am."

"I'll give you alimony." I had plenty of money, even without a job. When my father died, I'd inherited more than I could ever spend. Like my brother, I'd given most of it away, but I'd also invested some of it. Added to the holdings I'd accumulated over the years from other sources, and it would be a very long time before my grandchildren ran out. If I ever had grandchildren.

Of course, I didn't know what I'd do with myself if I didn't work. What could possibly eat up ninety-plus hours of my week? Then I thought of the one thing that could fill up that time and more, and keep me happy throughout. If only she felt the same.

30

HAYDEN

"What time is it?" Sira's voice was groggy.

I looked at my watch. "It's 1:00 am. I'm sorry. Go back to sleep." I should've called earlier, before Clare had broken out the drinks for our 'coming out, getting divorced, being disowned, and getting fired' celebration. But then, earlier, I hadn't had a half a bottle of champagne and a few glasses of bourbon in me, and would probably have thought it was a bad idea to call Sira at all.

"Is everything okay?"

Yes. No. Kind of. "It will be, eventually." *That was a good bet. Pat yourself on the back for that one.*

"Hang on."

I heard ruffling, probably of her bedding. I didn't want to think about it too much—her in bed, what she was wearing, how she looked when she first woke up. "Go back to sleep. I'm sorry I woke you."

"Shut up. I'm awake and won't be able to go to sleep until I know why the hell you called me this late. And it better not be that portfolio thing because I haven't finished it yet, and I will let you know when I do."

"I was fired."

"Seriously?" All remnants of sleep left her voice. "Oh, no! What happened?"

"I can't tell you everything because it's not my place to share certain information with you. I would if I could because I don't want to keep things from you, but I can't." Great, I had just enough alcohol in me to not make sense. "What I can tell you is that Clare's father is a complete and total asshole. He found out that I'd kept something from him, so he fired me over dessert at their house. Not literally over dessert, mind you."

She didn't answer right away, making me wonder if I'd over-explained myself into total confusion or an insult. But Clare wasn't ready to come out. When, or if, she ever was, I'd never keep another secret again.

"Wow," she said. "I can't believe you just called your boss an asshole."

"I think it all the time. I've just never said it before."

"So what does that mean for you?"

"That I'm beginning to trust someone with things I've never shared before."

"Actually, I meant about your career," she said shyly. "But thanks, though. That means a lot."

"And is something I probably shouldn't have said." I felt the heat the booze brought to my face get hotter from embarrassment.

"I'm okay with it."

Good. That meant I could try saying what I needed to. "The reason I called you is because, unfortunately and fortunately, I don't need an assistant anymore. Obviously, I intend to find other employment, but until then...you no longer work for me."

"Huh. Which means...?"

"Which means that due to forces beyond either of our

control, anything that happens between the two of us from this point on will have no bearing on your job."

"Huh."

"You already said that." I waited impatiently, not knowing what I expected her response to be, but hoping it would be more than 'huh.'

"So your boss fired you, and you're letting me go."

Never. I'd never let her go, not until I'd done everything in my power to convince her to at least try.

"But Clare still has her position, right?" she asked.

"Her position?"

"As your wife?"

Oh shit. "Damn, I meant to start with that. The reason Clare and I were at her father's house was to officially announce our separation. We're talking to a lawyer tomorrow. The paperwork might take a little while, but it will be simple and amicable. Although, we may have a rough Ro-Sham-Bo competition for the China."

"Huh."

I swallowed. Yeah, I'd really expected more than a 'huh' for that part. "In light of all this, I'd like to know if any of your guidelines are still standing, and if so, how I can rip them down."

"Have you been drinking?"

"Yes. But that's not—"

"How drunk are you?"

I sighed and closed my eyes. This wasn't going like I'd imagined it would. "Not enough to say things I don't mean."

"How much did you drink?"

"Four glasses of champagne and two small glasses of bourbon. But I'm a big man. Four champagne flutes filled mostly with bubbles and two short glasses filled mostly with ice consumed over a few hours isn't enough to make me say anything I don't mean."

"Maybe, but after being fired, making an announcement about the end of your marriage, and a few glasses of booze, you're probably not in a good state of mind to judge that."

I shook my head. It wasn't the alcohol that made me feel this way or know it was true. "Do you actually think these feelings are new? A result of some bad news and liquor?" I was tired of being in control of everything I said or did. Tired of holding it together for reasons I didn't understand. Clare had admitted a truth after a lifetime of holding it inside, knowing there was a big chance she'd lose. If there were a chance I'd win—a life I'd never expected with a woman I'd never expected—I had to go for it.

"I've never been happier," I said. "Because all I can see is a better future. Provided you're in it."

"I'd like to wait and see if you feel the same when you've sobered up."

"Nothing will be different."

"You've been drinking, Hayden. So hang up right now and call a cab. You can sober up on the way here."

"I—" Stopped. Did she just say—? "What did you just say?"

"I agree with you—you're a big man. Can you sober up in the twenty-minute cab ride to my house?"

I took a breath, a completely sober one. "Definitely."

"If you can't, then you can sleep it off on the couch. 'Cause I don't want a drunk in my bed."

"I'm going to hang up on you right now." I jumped out of my chair. "I have to call a cab...and find my shoes."

"You won't need your shoes, Hayden." She laughed. "I'll see you soon."

I ended the call before she could change her mind, then grabbed my wallet and headed for the door.

Clare stopped me, looking concerned. "Where are you going?"

My shoulders slumped when I saw my wife—ex-wife, for all intents and purposes. I couldn't leave her tonight, not after everything she'd gone through.

"Nowhere." I reached into my pocket for my phone.

"Really? Because it seemed like you were in a hurry to get somewhere."

"It's not important." Lie. Nothing had ever been more important to me, which was why I knew Sira would understand why I couldn't be there right now. "I was supposed to meet someone."

"Did you get a new job already?" she asked, smiling. When I didn't answer right away, she took a long look at me, ending at my feet. "No one forgets to put on shoes when they're going to an interview, Hayden. At least not you. Who were you going to meet?"

"She's someone I work—*worked*—with. But I'll reschedule."

"Oh, no. You're worried about me, aren't you?" She rolled her eyes. "Well, stop it. You've rescheduled your love life for three years, Hay. I'll be fine. You should go."

"Are you sure?" I pressed my lips together so they wouldn't give away how desperately I wanted to go.

"Of course. Besides, I told Shannon what happened, and she's coming over. Just to talk, but with you gone, who knows. Maybe we'll both get lucky tonight."

"Damn, I hope you're right."

"Go make your woman happy. *Really* happy."

I kissed her on the cheek. "You're amazing."

Before I closed the door behind me, I heard her say, "It's been a couple years, Hayden. So make sure you think about baseball because I don't want to see you until tomorrow." And then she laughed.

Baseball. Right. I really hoped that worked.

31

ANDI

I STOOD in the middle of my living room, glancing around to check for anything with my name on it, kind of hoping there was. Maybe if Hayden just happened to find something incriminating, then I could come clean. As many times as I'd wanted to tell him, I hadn't. Because I was terrified of what came after. The name itself wasn't a big deal—why I used it was.

And now, in the smartest/dumbest move I'd ever made, I'd basically promised him sex if he hurried over. A horny man wasn't something to be trifled with. His ability to converse would be at half-capacity. Max. And, with the idea of us sleeping together bouncing around *my* head, there went the other half.

I blew out a breath. Obviously, I had to tell him. It didn't matter that it hadn't already happened—that was in the past. If we had any chance of a future, I needed to be honest.

I jumped when I heard the knock on the door. Did he pay the cabbie extra to drive at light-speed? Crap, I wasn't ready. I hadn't decided what to say yet, and I was still in my pajamas— boxer shorts and a tank top. Maybe my incredibly un-seductive clothing would temper the mood enough so we could talk before anything else happened. Right.

I needed another few breaths, another few days, and another few brain cells before opening that door. Hopefully, he'd brought some of that booze with him.

Hayden stood there—no smile, no booze, but so incredible I wondered if I'd actually fallen back asleep and was just dreaming again. I opened my mouth to say hello, but the next thing I knew his lips were on mine, blocking any speech or thought. His grip was firm on the nape of my neck, his tongue like silk on mine. He bent slightly and slipped his arm under my knees, scooping me up and kicking the door shut behind him. Mumbling what I thought was the word "control," he carried me to the couch and sat down, setting me beside him and pulling his mouth from mine.

"Were you going to say something?" he asked, running his thumb across my lower lip.

Do it. Say it. I adjusted myself to face him straight on, sitting on my heels. "Hayden, I need to tell you something."

"Okay, but before you do..." He held up a finger. "I really want to hear whatever you're going to say, but, a big part of my focus is on your mouth, and it's...um..." He leaned toward me then shied back, clenching his teeth together. "Your mouth is... damn, your mouth is...very distracting." He blinked. "I'm having a really hard time focusing on words right now—yours *and* mine. This is something I've been fantasizing about since what seems like forever ago, and now that it's even remotely possible, I'm...um..." He shut his eyes completely. "I want to know what you were going to say, so I think it would be better if you slid over to the other end of the couch."

I smiled, feeling incredibly powerful. I'd brought Hayden Bennett to the edge of logical behavior. "Should I cover myself up with a blanket, too?"

"That'd be great. Thanks."

Instead of moving away like he'd asked, I threw my leg over

his and straddled his lap, enjoying his rapid inhalation. "How's this?"

His hands moved to my waist, feeling their way, bunching up my tank top as he caressed up my side and then halfway up my back. When they came back down, they made it all the way to my ass. He lifted me slightly and slid down on the couch a bit so his cock rubbed against me. We both groaned.

"I thought you wanted to talk," he said, his eyes clenching even tighter.

Did I? "What about?" There was something I was going to say.

"I'm not sure," he said, opening his eyes only to go right back to staring at my lips. "But you'd better remember quick because your mouth is about to be busy."

"With what?" I teased, licking my bottom lip and looking down at his cock.

"Stop making it so much harder—"

"I don't think it can get any harder."

"—for me to be a gentleman."

"I don't want you to be a gentleman, Hayden." I laughed and ground against him, daring him, wanting him.

"Good. Because I'm tired of pretending to care what you have to say." His smile only lasted a moment before his lips crashed into mine. He took hold of my jaw and forced my mouth open for his, tilting my head at the same time so his tongue could reach deeper into me.

I'm not sure how long we kissed and pulled at each other's clothing before I realized I needed this man naked.

Now.

I unbuttoned his shirt, pulled it open, and slipped it over his shoulders. His body was a *very* pleasant surprise, not that I'd thought it wouldn't be great, but I mean, come on. "When the hell do you have time to work out?"

"Exercise is a great form of stress relief. I have a stressful job and need an outlet. But you've made me think I may take up other activities from now on." He looked up, and a flash of color hit his cheeks. "It's been a long time since I've..."

"Since you've what?"

"Been with someone."

Huh? "But you're—" I didn't want to say the word, as if not saying it would help us forget.

"Married to a wonderful woman who's been in love with someone else the entire time."

"Oh." Well, that put a few things into place.

His hands slid off me. "I ruined the mood, didn't I?"

"Yes." I took his hands and put them on my ass. "So you're going to have to work extra hard to get it back."

"Extra hard. Got it." Smiling, he pulled me closer, rubbing his cock against my core. "But if I..."

"It's like riding a bike, Hayden. Plus, if you do anything really wrong, I'll let you know. Consider yourself in training."

His smile grew until it hit his eyes. "Like riding a bike, huh?" When he moved his hand up my ribcage to my breast, he sighed contentedly.

"Is that all it takes to make you happy?" I asked, my smile just as big.

"I'm an easy man to please. But I'd like to stick around to see what else is going to happen."

"You're lucky then, because I'd like to show you." I rocked my hips against his.

Closing his eyes, he groaned. "I hope you don't have any plans tomorrow."

"Hmm...tomorrow is Monday, right?" I tapped my chin. "Actually, since I'm no longer working for an impatient jerk, my schedule's pretty open."

"I'm still impatient," he said with a grin.

"Bring it, Hayden."

He slipped his hand around me again and yanked me into him, our mouths landing together, hard. I pulled away long enough to stand and drag him with me toward the bedroom, our feet tripping over each other's, teeth bumping and hands clawing at clothing.

As soon as we got to my bedroom, I shoved him backwards and spun around to my nightstand. I knew I had some condoms in there at one point, I just hoped they wouldn't be expired.

"What are you—?"

"Condom." I glanced at him. "I know I had a couple."

Relief filled his face. "I can't believe I forgot about that. Thank you."

"Anytime. Really." I started tossing things onto the floor—a magazine, iPod, vibrator. Doh! I kicked it under the bed so he wouldn't see it. Where the hell were the condoms? I flung a book over my shoulder, hearing him grunt.

"Sorry!" I said without turning. Yesterday I was desperate. This was way beyond that.

"Keep looking." He caught me from behind and slid his hands into the waistband of my boxer shorts, pushing them down my legs. My underwear went along with them. I froze, bent over, completely exposed, my arms barely holding me up.

"I said keep looking," he growled.

Easier said than done.

When he kissed the back of my thigh, I gasped. When he ran his lips across my skin, I moaned. Then, as the heat of his mouth inched closer and closer to my core, I made a sound only dogs could hear. I let my head fall, smacking my forehead on the nightstand. But it didn't hurt—all my nerve endings were too preoccupied with what Hayden was doing to me. I'd always known he was talented, but never imagined he'd be *this* talented.

"Hallelujah." I finally felt the edges of a small cardboard box at the very back of the drawer and pulled it out, holding it up for him to see. He grunted his approval, his mouth too busy for speech.

Without being able to see what he was doing, every touch of his tongue and his fingers came as a surprise. A *damn* good surprise. If I died right now, they'd have to shove me in a closed casket, because they'd never be able to get this look off my face.

Before I'd realized my legs had given out, he caught me and lifted me into his arms.

He smiled and licked his lips. "I wasn't done yet."

"Neither was I," I teased. "But I was pretty close."

"Patience is definitely something we both need to work on." He smirked. "Starting tomorrow."

I could taste myself when he kissed me, while we explored each other's mouths. I wrapped my arms around his neck, forcing him to follow me as he set me on the bed.

I squeezed my hands in between our bodies and fought with his belt buckle for a few seconds until I gave up and pushed him away a little. Thankfully, he took over pants duty so I could focus on the rest of him. His chest and abs and neck and—

Damn, was there nothing imperfect about this man? Oh, wait.

"You have an outie," I said happily, poking his bellybutton.

"Disappointed?" he asked, yanking his pants down and wiggling out of them with my help.

"Complet—" The word died halfway out of my mouth because at that very moment, I saw his cock. No disappointment there. None whatsoever. "Nope."

Swallowing, I tried to stop staring, stop drooling. He helped by kissing me again, using my mouth for something other than gaping. He pressed his body against me, grinding into me, his erection caught between us. I pushed myself up higher on the bed until I felt his length between my thighs. Both of us moaned.

When he released me, I took a deep breath, making up for the last few I'd missed. I ripped open the box, quickly checking the expiration date—thank the heavens these things had a long shelf life—and slipped the condom on him.

I shouldn't be doing this. I should stop him until we'd had "the talk." And if I were smart, that's what I would've done. But lust and logic rarely happen concurrently. Speech and thought were impossible, as if my brain had taken a siesta in everything but its response to pleasure.

"I've been waiting so long for this," he said quietly, brushing my hair off my face. "I'm having a hard time believing it's real." He looked at me with such softness, such care, I didn't know how to react. This was more than just two people wanting a physical connection. This was two people who'd already connected mentally, emotionally, and who were about to express it physically.

Honestly, it was a little terrifying.

"This *is* real, isn't it?" I asked, running my hand down the side of his face to his shoulder. "What we have?"

"It's the most real thing I've ever experienced."

I let out a breath, grabbed his ass, and then smiled. "Good. Then I think we should do more experiencing, don't you?"

"I love it when you get bossy." He sighed. "But we have all night, so if I... Like riding a bike, right?"

"Right."

He eased himself into me so slowly, it was frustrating as hell and still completely perfect. My eyes closed as he filled me, pressing all the way in. Neither of us moved, allowing our breaths a chance to synchronize. Each exhalation drew him in, each inhalation forced him back. Tiny movements that felt endless.

"You are as perfect as I knew you'd be," he whispered. "So warm. So beautiful."

When he started moving his hips, I focused on holding back, not to give in to the pleasure because I never wanted it to end. As soon as he reached under one of my legs and pulled it up so he could get closer, deeper, with every thrust, I knew I would fail epically.

I shouldn't have been surprised at Hayden's ability to multitask. He was still fully capable of speech—in the dirtiest sense of the word. Damn, this man was impressive. For the life of me, I couldn't figure out why he'd been worried—if he actually had forgotten how to do it, and this was his version of a refresher course, no way would I have been able to take him when he was at his peak.

"Holy hell, do you know how to ride a bike, Hayden!"

The vibration of his laugh bounced around my entire body until all the sensations merged into one bolt of energy so strong I think I blacked out for a second. When I came to, I was still moaning, the orgasm still pulsing through me.

Through the haze, I realized he was speaking. At first, I could only pick out a few words. Then I caught a full sentence.

"If you squeeze me again like that, I'm...aah...going to..." *Almost* a full sentence. Because the second I contracted my muscles, he lost the ability to do anything other than lose it. I guess those boot camping and spin classes were useful after all.

Power could make a woman do awfully good things.

32

HAYDEN

THERE WAS nothing left of the old me in the morning. I woke up revived, reborn, with her naked body tucked against me, my arm curled around her, her leg on top of mine. I'd been to four out of the seven wonders of the world, piloted a helicopter over the Grand Canyon, but I'd never seen anything more beautiful than she was. Last night had been unbelievable, the perfect way to begin a new life—nothing to weigh me down and everything to look forward to.

She'd come into my life so unexpectedly, so innocently. And thankfully, despite my countless mistakes, it had worked out even more perfectly than I had a right to. Thanks to lots of thinking about baseball, every muscle in my body ached from hours of lovemaking, almost as much as the muscles in my cheeks from smiling. Incredible, inexplicable fortune.

Without opening her eyes, Sira ran her hand across my chest then patted me in various locations as if she were trying to feel for something.

"What are you looking for?" I asked.

"I'm just making sure you're really here before I open my

eyes. Because if I opened my eyes and you were gone, I'd know it was just a dream."

I smiled and kissed the top of her head. "Do you have a lot of those kinds of dreams?"

"Far more than you could imagine." She smiled, her eyes still closed. "And before you ask—yes, they are all about you."

"I wasn't going to ask that." But it was nice to know. I rolled on top of her, supporting myself with my forearms next to her shoulders.

"I know you weren't, but you were thinking it."

"Open your eyes." I wanted to see them—my way of knowing we were both living the same thing.

"No, I'm trying to sleep."

"With me on top of you?"

She threw one hand over her face and pushed my chest with her other. "Do you think I can't?"

"I think you can do whatever you set your mind to. But then, so can I." I rolled my hips against hers, pressing my erection farther into the thin space between her thighs. Moaning, she opened up for me, spreading her legs and wrapping them around me. "I win."

She laughed. "You cheated."

"Open your eyes, Sira." When her face tensed for a moment, I thought I may have hurt her. I pushed up onto my hands, and swung off her. "Whatever I did wrong, I'm sorry."

She opened her eyes slowly, looking at me with a sadness I didn't understand. "You didn't do anything wrong." Her smile stayed tight as it grew until she finally shook her head slightly as if releasing whatever she was thinking of. "In fact, you did many, many things right. With a little training, you might be worth keeping around."

I laughed at my own words being thrown back at me. "I get

an hour for lunch and every fourth Sunday off. But otherwise, I'm available at your convenience."

"Well then, you'd better get to work. We only have four hours until lunchtime."

I reached over to her nightstand, making a mental note to pick up more condoms the first chance I got. Because I intended to spend every waking moment with a part of me inside a part of her—my fingers, my tongue, or my cock.

I couldn't get enough of her taste, her warmth, the jerk of her body whenever I reached a particularly sensitive spot. The right side of her ribcage was more ticklish than the left, and every time I ran my lips below her bellybutton, her toes curled and she whimpered. When I settled myself between her thighs, she tensed, then went limp and groaned as soon as my tongue touched her core. A moment later, she tightened again, running her fingers through my hair and pulling it.

It had been a long time since I'd touched a woman's body, but I don't remember them being so much fun.

She swatted at me, laughing. "Stop, Hayden. You have to stop."

"Can't hear you," I mumbled against her, pointing to her thighs that were squeezing my head and covering my ears. When she released me, I didn't stop. After all, I had two years of no sex and a lifetime of mediocre sex to make up for.

After we'd flipped over and repositioned ourselves, I watched her as she slowly slid down my body, her lips dragging across my abs and hip. Feeling the heat of her mouth around my cock was something else entirely. I lost the ability to express my gratitude with anything but a moan. This was perfection. *She* was perfection.

Baseball was no match for this woman. "Oh, fuck!" The orgasm hit me before I could stop it, shattering every nerve receptor in the same moment, leaving me unable to breathe or think.

"I win," she teased, looking up at me and wiping the corner of her mouth.

"Yeah, you definitely won that round." I pulled her up next to me and held her to my chest. "But I'm not giving up yet."

Her laugh vibrated against me. "Seriously?"

"Well, I'm giving up for the next half hour." I brushed her hair back and kissed her forehead. "So enjoy your victory while it lasts."

I was too exhausted to move. And, at the same time, felt more awake than I ever had. Awake and free. Immortal almost because nothing could take this away from me—not the lies my father had told me, the lies on a piece of paper, or the lies I'd been telling myself for the last decade. I deserved this, to be happy, to be with someone who cared about me and who could love me the way I needed her to. And who I could trust enough to love back.

33

ANDI

I COULDN'T REMEMBER the last time I'd felt no inclination to turn on my computer, check my messages, and work for a couple of hours. Maybe it was due to all the times Hayden and I had 'connected' last night and this morning. So I stayed in bed, dozing, until I heard him curse. Not from next to me, like he should've been, but from the kitchen. Where he *shouldn't* have been. I jumped out of bed, threw on my robe and went to go find him before he found out anything about me I should've already told him.

I suck. How could I have slept with him before doing the whole confession—I'm-not-who-you-think-I-am thing? What kind of person did that? A selfish one. A scared-as-hell one. One who wished there were a way to not have a past at all, and just live in the moment. Wasn't that the advice shrinks gave—don't live in the past and all that shit. And, here I was, doing it again—except this time, I was dragging someone amazing down with me.

"Hey!" I got to the kitchen just as he poured two cups of coffee into the sink.

"I'm not coming back here again—"

I inhaled.

"—without a decent coffee maker. I can't even bring myself to call this coffee." He grimaced. "Let's go out to breakfast."

"You're not my only client, you know. It's Monday. I have to get some stuff done." Like sitting down and figuring out a way to explain all my lies in a way that wouldn't make him hate me. That kind of shit took focus—something that was hard to come by while he was within groping distance. Speaking of...I removed my finger that had somehow found its way to his abs, tracing the little squares that intensified every time he exhaled.

He nodded silently. "I'm moving too quickly, aren't I?"

"You? No. Well..." No, but last night had. "This is all a little unexpected. And there's a lot we need to talk about."

"I'm not sure what *you* do when you go to a restaurant with someone, but I tend to fit in some talking as well as eating." He ran his fingers through his normally slick and perfect hair, messing it up even more perfectly. "And I'm fairly sure I can keep my hands off you through most of it."

Ugh. "I can't go out with someone who looks like they just got out of bed."

"Since I wouldn't want to embarrass you..." He slipped his arms around me and picked me up. "Let's jump in the shower. Then you can take out someone who looks like he can't wait to go *back* to bed."

Shockingly, he got both of us into the bathroom without smacking my feet or my head into any walls. He set me down and turned on the shower. Thirty seconds later, he stepped into it and shivered. Maybe rich people's water actually did get hot while they watched it.

"You must really be in a hurry to get that coffee," I said, laughing.

"Actually, I'm really in a hurry to see you naked and wet. So..."

"You saw me naked and wet all night long." As he groaned, I wiggled my eyebrows, shrugging my robe off one shoulder and rolling it. Then I heard the doorbell. "Oh, shit." I tied my robe back up tightly and shut the shower curtain on his disappointed expression. "I'll be right back. Don't go anywhere."

Smiling, I opened the front door, expecting to see my mailman or UPS or someone with a big package of something I'd probably ordered and paid for myself. But packages, in any shape or size, were always fun. Could this day get any better?

Why yes. Yes, it definitely could. When I saw Detective Williams standing there, all my positivity disappeared.

"Andi." He nodded. "I'm going to have to ask you to come down to the station tomorrow afternoon."

"What for?" I asked, gnawing at my lip and wrapping the belt of my robe around my hands. I let it go when I realized how close it felt to being cuffed.

"You know what for. We have a few people we're looking at, and...." I was one of the 'few' people. "Did you find yourself a lawyer?"

"I'm working on it." But I wasn't. Not really. Maybe because things had been going so well. I'd just sent out a large number of checks to the people I'd hurt years ago, I had amazing friends, and Hayden was soaping himself up in my shower as we spoke. I should've known it was all about to crumble.

"Time's up."

I'm not sure how long I stood there blankly staring. The detective's face blurred as I tried to get my head around this horror. It was bad enough being brought up on charges for something I did without meaning to. Turned out that being a suspect in something I *didn't* do was way worse. But I didn't fight it—I hadn't done this wrong, but I'd done so much other shit. Knowingly. What was that cliché about just desserts? And why did I suddenly have a donut craving?

"I didn't have anything to do with it, Detective. They can't possibly be that far down the list of suspects yet." Since I'd seen how the detective had put all the pieces together in the last case, I figured the same thing would happen with this one—and in about the same amount of time. Cybercrimes took a lot longer to investigate than others because of the subtle differences in each hacker's signature. It couldn't have been done in just a week.

"I don't know what to tell you, other than I think it would be a good idea for you to...make a statement so they can move on to other people." His hesitation before the word was tiny, nonexistent to anyone who'd never been in trouble before. I heard it with perfect clarity. He'd been about to say 'be interrogated,' and that was an entirely different thing. But I trusted him, and heaven knows my paranoia could get the better of me, so I'd take him at his word for now.

He wanted me to make a statement. Which only meant that someone would ask me a couple of questions, and I'd answer them. At least, I had my story straight, so my friends wouldn't get in trouble. I'd be as helpful as I could be, which wasn't at all helpful because I really didn't know anything about the crime. But once they'd ruled me out, they could go find the person who really did it.

"I'll let you go before you run out of hot water."

I blinked him back into focus. "Huh?"

"Hot water. Your shower's on, isn't it?"

Oh fuck. Hayden. "Yeah, I should go take care of that," I mumbled. "Thanks."

He nodded stiffly, obviously not expecting me to thank him for stopping by.

"Oh, shit." When the detective's eyes bulged at something he saw over my shoulder, I knew exactly what he'd seen. Hayden's cursed apology only verified it. "You two are—"

"Okay, bye." I slammed the door in the detective's face and

spun around.

"I'm sorry. I didn't know he was...I got impatient." Hayden blew out a breath. "Is everything okay?"

"Yeah, everything is fine." I kept my gaze on the purple towel wrapped around his hips. I didn't have the guts to look him in the eye. He was just something else I didn't deserve, and the sooner he realized that, the better. For him. "That was...um..."

"Officer Williams."

"Detective," I corrected. "Do you know him?" Great. Great. Great.

"Not too well. He tried to help my family when I was a teenager. Nice guy."

"Yeah, he's great." Great. Great. Great. "Seemed great anyway in the two seconds I spoke with him. Right then."

He waited, not asking the very obvious question: Why did a cop just knock on your door?

So I didn't ask the other very obvious question: Why did your family need a cop's help?

There's no such thing as a lie. Singular. Because as soon as someone lied once, inevitably, they would be forced to lie again. And again. And again. Until their life was filled with more lies than truths. And every day felt heavy and miserable because it took so much damn energy to maintain all of them.

"Shit. I just remembered that I'm supposed to be somewhere in, like, twenty minutes." I picked up my sloth-ish pace so the comment made sense, even though my body fought me on it, wanting to curl up in bed, close my eyes, and pretend this life had never happened. But first, I had to get rid of the most incredible man I'd ever met.

When he took me by the waist and pulled my back to his chest, the warmth and dampness of his body seeped through my robe, and I almost lost it. I almost let everything go, spilled all my sins, my lies, my mistakes. Almost. But I knew that as soon as

I did—if I could even get the words to leave my mouth—he would disappear. And even though it was for the best and it would happen eventually anyway, I just needed it for a little while longer. It was greedy and selfish and so unfair, like everything else I'd done, but I needed it. Like an addict.

"I'm not a good person, Hayden."

When he didn't react, didn't speak or let go or hold me tighter, I realized I hadn't said it out loud. I was too much of a coward to admit what a coward I was.

"Hayden?" My voice was barely audible but I forced it out because he didn't deserve this mess I'd dragged him into. I remembered how it felt to find out what you thought was perfect was actually one gigantic lie told by someone you trusted. I remembered how that felt, so I knew how he'd feel when I told him the truth. *Tell him. Now. It will never be any easier.* "I need......"

"Time and space. I know. See, sometimes I actually *do* listen." After another second of stillness, he stepped away. "Can we do a late dinner or something?"

"Sure." That was a good idea. By tonight, I should at least be able to look at him without bursting into tears and actually speak versus grunt and do that weird high-pitched whiny talking thing. Or the three words—then sob—three more words —another sob thing that no one could understand.

Actually, I might need a little longer. "Tonight's not good. Tomorrow?"

"If that's your best offer..." he said as he got dressed. "Was it my singing that freaked you out so much? I really should know better."

"Yeah, you really should."

I hurried around, getting ready for my nonexistent appointment, and trying my hardest to act like everything was okay. All I probably accomplished was to make him think I had some kind of obsessive-compulsive disorder.

When I told him how tricky bus schedules were, and that if I missed it, I'd have to wait twenty minutes for another, he offered to take me to my appointment. I couldn't exactly refuse, so I gave him the closest logical place I could think of.

We ended up in front of Emilia's country club. If this wasn't an example of crappy karma, I didn't know what was.

"Thanks for the ride."

"Thanks for the ride?" He looked at me confused, under-standably so. "Which one are you thanking me for?"

We'd just shared the most incredible night of my life, and I end it with 'thanks for the ride.' Very cool.

"All of them," I said quietly. "Look, I've never had anything like this before, and I'm not sure the best way to handle it."

"I feel the same way, but I think we're supposed to figure it out together. You need to talk to me."

How could I when, every time I looked into his eyes, all I could do was picture him naked?

"You're right. We should talk. But not right now." I took a deep breath and waved to my old spinning instructor, who was next to the club's entrance, digging something out of his duffel bag. "He hates it when people are late for class." As soon as I opened the car door, Hayden grabbed my arm, twisting me around to face him.

"We're still on for dinner tomorrow?" Then he kissed me. One of those kisses that shuts out the rest of the world so completely you wonder if it will still be there when you open your eyes. He cupped my breast with one hand, held my chin with the other. I groaned when I felt his erection. Um...actually. I busted up laughing as soon as I realized my mistake.

"I thought..."

He got it as soon as he saw my hand groping the car's gearshift. "I've never been jealous of a car before."

"Well, next time I see you, let's do something to make the car jealous of *you*." I'd meant it to sound seductive, but what the hell? We had a simultaneous moment of trying to imagine how that could possibly work before both of us were laughing.

"I'm sure we'll think of something," he said. "Get to class."

Right. Class. When I climbed out of the car, the instructor was staring at me, holding the club's door open. Oh crap, I think he was actually waiting for me. Or maybe he was just checking out Hayden. Either way, I had to walk through that door.

I'd planned on waiting in the lobby until Hayden drove away. But my luck being what it was, the spin torturer whisked me by the front desk before they could ask me for a membership card I didn't have and ushered me right into class. I even got a front row spot. Yeah, really not my day.

Although, maybe for once, exercise would be good for me. I could focus on the pain instead of the pleasure of last night. Feel the burn in a productive way.

For an hour, I forgot about everything other than how much I hated my instructor. Unfortunately, as soon as I slumped off my spinning bike and hobbled to the bus stop, it all came back.

This screw-up trumped the one four years ago, that was for sure. Because now I couldn't even claim to be young and stupid. Now I was just stupid. This time I was hurting people who knew and cared about me. For years, it had felt like no matter what I did, I'd never be free of my sins, and so eventually, I stopped even trying. Pretending I'd never gotten into trouble made it okay to work for Emilia even with the risk she was taking. I'd told myself it was okay to use a computer or to accept the one that Hayden had given me, it was okay to keep information about who I was from a man I was falling in love with and who obviously had feelings for me.

That was the biggest lie of all. None of this was okay, and it was no one's fault but mine that everything was about to fall apart.

I wanted to call Hayden, hear his voice, ask him to come back so I could hide in his arms for the next decade or two. I was sure he could somehow make everything bad disappear. But I couldn't call him. Because I was a liar and, as soon as he found out all the wrong I'd done, *he* would disappear. And he'd feel the same betrayal and humiliation I'd felt after I found out what my ex-boyfriend had conned me in to doing for him. How could I have done that to Hayden? *Knowing* what it did to me?

As soon as I got home, I called Emilia, still feeling like the worst person in the world, although now it was for putting yet another burden on my friend. But I didn't know what else to do.

"Em, don't freak out, but I have so much to tell you. First, Hayden stayed over last night."

"Finally," she teased. "Let me guess: he was amazing. The earth moved, and the seas parted. No, wait, it was your legs that parted, wasn't it?" She laughed. "Okay, tell me everything."

"I'm in trouble, Em," I whimpered. "But I don't want you to try to fix it. Okay? And you have to *promise* not to tell Rob."

"What happened?" she asked, instantly on high alert.

I filled her in on the situation—the first visit from the detective that I'd been too embarrassed to mention to this morning's unhappy visit. Emilia sighed and said, 'Oh, Andi,' or 'I'm so sorry' a lot.

"I have to go to the station to answer some questions. Williams didn't give me any details, and I think that means I might be in more trouble than I thought."

"You don't know what that means. He could've just not been in a chatty mood. You said he's nice, right? That he seemed unhappy about telling you that he had to investigate you as one of many options?"

"Yeah."

"Well, that's probably all it is. Don't freak out before you know for sure. Meet me at the park in a half an hour. We can talk and run—two times the stress relief."

"I don't really feel like running." Unless it's away. "I need donuts."

"No, donuts are just fluffy, delicious balls of evil."

"Exactly why I love them. Besides, I actually already worked out today."

Her shocked silence didn't last long. "How 'bout we do brunch at Morning Grill tomorrow—my treat."

"My last meal?"

"No, stupid. We use an exorbitant amount of food to gather your courage, and then I'll take you to the station."

"Thanks, but I don't want you to go with me. It's humiliating enough without you actually being there."

She scoffed. "Do you honestly believe that you're the only one who has things from their past that they wish hadn't happened? I'm your friend, Andi. All I'm doing is paying you back a tiny bit for what you've done for Rob and me."

"You don't need to pay me back for anything."

"Oh, but I do. Do you already have a lawyer?"

"No." I'd just sent out a big batch of checks, and the cupboards were bare. "I'm going to tell them the truth." And if they didn't believe me, the state would appoint a lawyer.

"Andi." Emilia's voice was sharp, a warning. "I'm calling Rob."

"No!" I didn't want either of them more involved in this. They'd already done way too much for me. "I meant yes before —I have a lawyer. He's great, actually." How many times did I need to prove I was a terrible person before they'd stop believing in me?

"What's his name and his firm? Rob knows a lot of the criminal firms in town."

"Matt Something-Italian-Sounding. Small firm. Young, so he's not too expensive."

"Young and not-expensive aren't good qualities in a lawyer, Andi. Let me find you someone. Or maybe Hayden knows a good one. You can tell him it's partial payback for all the crap you've had to put up with from him."

"He doesn't know."

She signed. "About the interview?"

"About anything. He doesn't know what I did. He doesn't know about this case or the old one." My chuckle was more sob than laugh—like a sad clown, crying on the inside. "He doesn't even know my real name."

"Oh, shit." Then a lengthy silence. "When were you planning to tell him?"

"A billion different times, in a billion different ways. But every time I could, I couldn't. You know?" Yeah, awesome excuse.

"So you slept with him but couldn't tell him your name. Wow. So not cool, Andi."

"I know," I whined. "And I feel awful. I kept waiting for the right moment, but it never happened." Duh, the right time to tell someone you're a total screw-up and have been lying to them since you met... Is that before or after 'never?' "I was going to tell him last night, and then this morning... It was on the tip of my tongue, closer than it's ever been. But he just lost his job and his marriage, and I made him happy. He was so happy, Em, and I knew it would all change as soon as I said the words."

"Are you ever going to tell him? Or are your kids going to think their mom's name is Sara?"

Sira, actually. Not that it would be an issue—Hayden wouldn't want me for that long. But I deserved Emilia's disappointment and condemnation, just like I would deserve Hayden's anger when he found out the truth.

"I'm going to end it. I will." Then I won't have to tell him why. I'll just say the obvious—it was never going to work out anyway. Biggest chickening-out ever, but better than actually hauling out all my baggage, unpacking it, showing it to him, making him feel extra awful, and then having to pack it up all over again before I left. Right? Left. "Oh man, I'm a mess."

"What you need to do is stop being an idiot."

"Thanks?"

"You made a mistake, yes. But how long are you going to punish yourself for it? Forever? Stop being so afraid of who you are. Stop hiding. And when something good comes along, accept that you deserve it."

"Okay." What else could I say? "I'll see you tomorrow. Thanks, Em."

After I'd hung up, I stared at the phone, wondering what to say to Hayden, if there was a way to make it all right and what he'd say to me once I confessed. I had to figure out how to do it in the least hurtful way. Of course, the least hurtful way was actually a few months behind me now.

When my eyes got dry and tired, I started to pace. Then I took a shower. And then went to the donut shop. I kept myself busy for the rest of the day. The only thing I didn't do was pick up my phone.

34

HAYDEN

I'D NEVER COME into the office later than nine before, and those occasions were only because of a morning meeting or something similar. So going up in a full elevator and entering a busy building was a first. And maybe a last. Ironic that by the time I had something worth taking time off for, I didn't have a job to return to. But walking through the maze at my former workplace didn't bring great sadness or regret. I had acquaintances here, peers, people to run ideas by or say hello to, but no real friends. Here or anywhere else. So leaving wasn't hard.

Endings aren't painful. They're only nerve-wracking because of what follows them—beginnings. Beginnings are packed with doubt, the knowledge that you'll have to relearn everything you thought you'd mastered. Hope is the most terrifying thing in life. Because hope makes you ripe for disappointment.

But not today. Today hope had filled me with nothing but excitement. I knew there would be challenges as Sira and I moved forward, but she'd hog-tied me, just like Carson had predicted. And I'd never been more happily trapped.

I took the elevator up to the fifth floor, walked through reception doing the same thing I always did—nodding hello to the same people at the same desks through the same glass walls. Funny that I'd never noticed how many walls there were in this place. Glass walls that kept us separated, everyone in their proper place. Something to hide behind that provided no protection at all.

Bart's secretary stared at me from her desk. I tried not to be bothered by it. Tried and failed.

"Is there something I can help you with, Ms. Beasley?" I asked, flipping to face her.

She rocked back in her chair at the tone of my voice. "He wants to see you."

"I don't give a shit if he wants to see me." I dropped my head forward. "I'm sorry for being crass." I looked up at her large eyes, her knowing and condescending look. "No. No, I'm not sorry. Please relay the following message to him, if you don't mind." I cleared my throat, knowing I was about to commit professional suicide but unable to find a reason to care. "Please tell him that I don't give a flying fuck what he wants. However, if he expects me to be contrite and kiss his ass, then I will change my mind and happily give said flying fuck to him—as long as he uses it to go hang-gliding with." I smiled stiffly at her and walked away.

On the way to my office, I grabbed a cardboard box from the copy room.

I saw Bart through my office door. My ex-employer was leaning on my ex-desk in my ex-office of my ex-job.

"Wasn't sure you'd be coming in today, Bennett," he said. I wondered how long he'd been waiting for me to show up. Hopefully a while.

"Really? The last time we spoke, you were pretty clear about where you thought I should go. But don't worry—I'll be quick. I actually just left a message for you with your secretary." I started taking books off the shelves, reading their spines to decide which ones I wanted to keep and putting those into the box. I didn't want many of them. They were reminders of this place and all the mistakes I'd made to get here. The less I remembered, the happier I'd be.

Bart cleared his throat. "The board overruled me. They want you to stay."

I didn't respond.

"Did you hear me?"

"I did."

"They tell me you're doing better than I knew."

I laughed, not amused. "Are you here to congratulate me before you call security?"

"I'm here to tell you that things have changed, and you can have your damn job back."

I turned around to look at him, my boss of six years, my father-in-law of three. "Clare is still gay. I still knew. And you're still a bigot. So I'm not sure what has actually changed."

"Damn it, Bennett. Don't be an idiot. I'm offering you your job back. Your dad's company back."

I saw the fear in his eyes—he'd finally figured out what he'd lose when I left. All my clients and contacts, including those involved in Inspex, along with my father's name and all the status it had provided.

He ground his teeth together. "If you think I'm going to get down on my knees and beg, you've got another thing coming."

"Frankly, Bart, the idea of you on your knees for any reason is pretty damn unpleasant. So I think we've finally found something we both can be happy about." I grabbed the box and went behind my desk, picking up the stapler just because. I'd never actually been fired before, so this was all new. Wasn't I supposed to steal something trivial? Out of a sense of spite I didn't feel? Now, if I were required to take something out of a sense of relief, that would be different.

"You and Clare will get a divorce, go your separate ways. Fine. But it doesn't mean you should screw up your life."

My life? I had no intention of screwing up my life. In fact, I was here trying to salvage it before it was over. I stopped packing and looked at him. "Don't spend too much time worrying about me, Bart. I think you'll have other things that will need your focus as soon as I step out that door."

"You've spent six years here, Bennett." Yep. Six years stuck in this glass box. "Don't throw it all away."

I chose to assume he was talking about the pens and notepad in my hand, so I pointedly tossed them into the garbage can. "I need to ask you something, Bart."

He nodded, spreading his legs as if we were about to go three rounds and he needed more balance.

"Do you think I should get angry? Belligerent? Throw things around?" I asked. "You're right—after being here for six long years, I'm at a bit of a loss as to how to react. Primarily because I don't seem to care all that much."

Bart narrowed his eyes and breathed out long and loud. "I'm giving you another chance, you idiot. You have two days to decide. Then the offer is off the table."

"The board was right—I'm good at what I do. To prove it, in a way you'll understand, I'm going to counter your offer. I'll come back on the following conditions: You take an ad out in the newspaper, admitting exactly who you are and expressing your commitment to becoming a decent human being. And then you beg your daughter to give you another chance. If she agrees, then I will too."

"You can kiss my ass."

"You're not my type, but should I take that as a sign you're trying to be more open-minded?"

He stomped out, probably angry the door was impossible to

slam. I watched it close slowly and quietly before gathering the rest of my things and leaving. The stapler stayed behind.

I dumped the box just inside the apartment door, content with the idea that I wouldn't be working tonight. Or tomorrow. Sira had said she needed to do a few things—

I couldn't call her Sira anymore. That was a nickname born out of our working relationship when I'd never imagined I would ever meet her. She was no longer a bunch of words that popped up in a chat box or a voice on the other end of a line. She was real, and beautiful, and not the slightest bit submissive or obedient.

"Sara." I tried it out a few times as I walked through the foyer. "Sara."

I wonder if she'd notice the next time we saw each other. I knew *Sara* was trying to take things slow, something I respected as much as I hated. I was past going slow, considering every possible consequence, showing caution. If it were up to me, I'd stay with her until things were settled with Clare, and then I'd ask Sara to move in here. But telling her that might be a little too forward, so I'd be patient. Until she gave me the slightest hint I could stop.

The second we said goodbye, all I could think about was taking her out for a quick dinner and then taking her back to bed. Therefore, my big plan for this evening was to go to sleep, so I'd be rested when I saw her tomorrow.

"Clare," I called out as I walked into the living room. "Your father offered me my job back."

She poked her head out of the kitchen. "Did you take it?"

That's when I realized that the apartment smelled amazing. "You're not cooking, are you?" I rushed into the kitchen because Lord knew what would happen if I just walked. I stretched my arm out to navigate the corner and slid on the hardwood floor. Clare stood beaming next to a woman with short brown hair. "Shannon! I— Hello." I hadn't spent too much time with Shannon—standing in a room with the two of them had always made me feel like I was forcing Clare deeper into the lie.

"How are you, Hayden?" she asked, turning only for a moment before going back to the stove.

"Fine. Especially now that I know Clare isn't in the kitchen unsupervised."

"That's not nice!" she said, tossing a towel at me. "Did you get your job back or not?"

"It was offered. And, if I'd waited just a few more minutes before insulting him, I think he would've actually gotten down on his knees and begged."

Both of them laughed. "Damn you and your impatience, Hayden!"

I blinked because my world had just gone out of focus. I was unemployed, my soon-to-be-ex-wife and her girlfriend were cooking dinner, and I couldn't remember a happier time. Except when I was with Sara. Which I would try to be as soon as possible.

Clare handed me a glass of wine and then took a sip of her own. "Shannon and I aren't back together, nor are we into threesomes, so you can quit smiling like that."

"No, I was thinking of something else." I came around the island and peeked over Shannon's shoulder.

She elbowed me. "Great, now I have *two* people hovering. It will be ready when it's ready. Now go away. Both of you."

I spent the rest of a very pleasant evening with my ex-wife and her ex-lover, ignoring the small voice in my head warning me that things were about to fall apart. That life didn't offer happy endings for any of us, and that there was a very good reason I'd built the walls up around me.

When we finished eating, Clare set her glass down and cleared her throat. "Hayden, I have a proposal for you."

"Okay."

She glanced at Shannon, who gave Clare a 'just get on with it' expression. "Since I've been disowned and am going to be on my own for basically the first time ever, I need to support myself. I've never had a paying job, and my college diploma looks great on a wall but is totally useless, so I started weighing options."

"I think that's great, Clare. Let me know if I can help."

She smiled. "I was hoping you would say that."

"I thought you might be." I'd never seen her more nervous or more talkative, but I wasn't sure where the conversation was going. So I waited for her to get through a speech she'd obviously prepared with Shannon's help, ready to help her the second I knew how. Our marriage had been a burden for both of us, a continual lie to live and slowly die from, but I still had nothing to blame her for.

"I want to start my own business, Hayden. After going through all of my many talents with Shannon"—she winked —"I came to the conclusion that I'm at my best when I'm living other people's lives." They both looked at me expectantly, as if I were supposed to understand what she was talking about. "I want to help people organize their lives—like a freelance advice giver-slash-stuff doer. I can plan their parties, tell them what to wear, how to get things done. Those kinds of things."

I couldn't count how many of the Bennett Foundation events Clare had set up, so turning it into a business would barely be a stretch for her.

After I had agreed it would be perfect for her, Shannon cut in. "Clare needs money. I've already spoken to Frank, and we're going to invest enough for some start-up costs. But I can't offer as much as she needs for ongoing cash flow. So my end will be more of the gathering clients and pimping her out as loudly as I can."

"It's perfect for you, Clare." I nodded slowly. "But I'm not going to loan you money. I think it's important that you earn it on your own."

"Hayden!" Shannon snapped, glancing to Clare whose jaw had dropped.

"I'm going to hire you. For Carson. He and Laney need to get married. Those two are so in love, they can't even think straight. So you should do it for him."

"You're such a good man, Hayden." Clare's smile hit me hard, but it was what she said next that was so overwhelming, I had to look away. "You deserve that kind of love too, you know?"

Did I? I'd spent my life doing the right thing, or what I thought was the right thing at the time. Living up to other people's expectations. Professionally, I was everything my bastard of a father would've wanted. Privately, too. Probably. He didn't know how to love someone, and neither did I. His marriage wasn't happy, and neither was mine. He was dead... and, until recently, so was I.

But I wasn't six feet under. I hadn't hurt the people I care about. I hadn't abused them. And I was still breathing. I still had a chance to live and be happy. And be loved.

"You still have our checkbook, right?" Then I quickly gave her a number her budget should stay below. I had enough money to be jobless for a long time, but having lived her entire life without ever wondering where the money was coming from, Clare would probably need help with her books. I might even hire someone to advise her while I took a month-long trip to Bora Bora with a certain little brunette I was going to meet tomorrow.

Screw patience—I'd used it all up over an hour ago.

After we'd gone over some details, I excused myself and took my phone into my home office. My *only* office currently. I wanted to talk to Sara, to hear her voice, now that I could call her freely without worrying about all the things I'd been afraid of disrupting before.

She picked up right away. "Hey, what's up?" There was an edge to her tone that I didn't expect. Or understand.

"Is everything alright?"

She paused. No, she *hesitated*. And I felt that hesitation in my gut. "Listen, Hayden, I made a mistake last night. I didn't mean to be confusing or make promises I couldn't keep, but I can't see you again."

"What? Why?"

"What happened between us isn't right. It's just not...right."

"Is this about Clare? I told you I'm not very married anymore. Not even mostly married." My attempt at a joke fell flat before I'd even finished the sentence.

"Even so, maybe you should take some time before you start a new relationship."

Time? No. I'd already wasted too much of that. "I thought you understood. My marriage was over before it began. It should've never happened. I've had years of waiting to start a new relationship, a real one, an honest one." It was hard to speak because it was hard to breathe. My chest, my gut, too tight for air to pass through.

She wasn't supposed to do this. She was supposed to be my chance, my life. My body held on to my breath as my mind realized everything else was slipping away. "I've waited so long for this already. I thought I was beginning again."

"You are. You'll find a new job and can have any life you want. And I'm really happy for you."

"How about being happy *with* me?"

"I...I can't. It's not right."

"Stop saying that!" I shouted. "Clare and I aren't together.

We've never been together in anything other than name." On a piece of paper, a commitment held together by loyalty, not love.

"I can't."

"If it's a matter of you not believing me, I could send you proof. A note, maybe."

"From your mom? 'I give my son permission to get into your pants?'"

I cursed. "This isn't about getting in your pants. Why would you say that?" How *could* she say that? "I don't know how else to prove to you that my marriage is over. I want—"

"To give me a note from your wife." She laughed.

"Stop! It's not funny. It's just making the situation even more confusing."

"That's because this is so insane. So stupid. You don't even know me, Hayden."

"Not everything, obviously. But I know enough to know I want to get to know you."

"Wow, there were a lot of 'no's' in that sentence."

I sighed. "All I want is a chance to see if it would work. It's a few dinners out, not a proposal."

"Of course, it's not. Because you're already married!"

I bit down hard, not understanding why she said she believed me but still used it as an excuse. Why she *needed* an excuse. "I get that you're having trouble taking my word for it. I do. It probably happens all the time to you—men you work for wanting more and lying to get it. But this doesn't happen to me. Ever. I don't know how else to convince you. What can I say to prove I'm telling you the truth?"

"Why are you shouting at me?"

"Because you infuriate me, and I'm not used to people doubting my word"—my voice trailed off—"and I want this so badly."

"I shouldn't have slept with you, Hayden. It shouldn't have happened. It was unfair to you, and I'm sorry."

"Then you're sorry for giving me the best night of my life." I waited, listening to her shallow breaths but not knowing what else to say. After a few seconds, it stopped. No, it hadn't stopped, it had just continued somewhere I couldn't hear.

She'd hung up on me! Damn it, she actually hung up on me. I stopped myself from hurling my phone across the room just in time.

Yes, I was being unreasonable and demanding and acting like a total child. But I was so far out of my element, I didn't remember where my element was.

I was being a complete idiot. An obsessed idiot. But if she wasn't so—

Another breath, deeper this time. She'd slept with me, not committed the rest of her life to me. Even if it had meant more to me than to her, I knew she didn't think it was a mistake. We fit too well to be a mistake. There was nothing holding us back now.

I needed to think, be rational, figure out why she was still fighting it. Step back and treat this with the same kind of logic I would any business negotiation. Because it was a negotiation at its core. And if I ever acted this way in a boardroom, my ass would be out on the street before my coffee got cold. *Don't be an idiot.* I'd never been this desperate for anything in my life, and desperation is hardly an attractive attribute.

In a deal... Who was I kidding? If this were a deal, I'd have already given up, have been out the door and working on something else. But there *was* nothing else. This was the biggest deal of my life, and I couldn't lose it.

Think, you idiot. Do what you're good at. Objectivity. When the other party holds most—if not all—the cards, you don't allow them to stay angry. Anger breeds resentment. Resentment is an impossible hurdle, an unscalable wall. I picked up my phone and quickly dialed her number. Which I knew by heart because I was a complete idiot.

When the ringtone stopped, I knew she'd answered, but she didn't say anything.

"I'm sorry," I said calmly. "I didn't mean to yell at you. I need this to work, so tell me what I have to do to make it happen."

"It won't. Because I screw everything up." Her voice was small, weak-sounding. "Even if it's as good as I think it would be...if we were together, I'd screw it up."

"Prove it."

"What?"

"If you're so sure you'll screw it up, then I want proof. A week. No, a month. Be with me for a month and let me see first-hand how you screw it up."

"I know what you're trying to do, but I think it would be worse."

"Worse than this?" I shouted, frustrated beyond my breaking point. "You think *anything* could be worse than this?" All I heard was a muffled hiccupping breath. Oh shit. I'd made her cry. "Sara? I'm sorry." Still no answer. "Sara?"

"That's not my name," she said softly.

"What?"

"My name is not Sara."

"I...I don't understand." I looked at my phone, even more confused than I was a moment ago, which shouldn't have been possible.

"My name isn't Sara. It's a fake name for a fake person. You want a fake person, Hayden. Not me."

"We need to talk about this."

"I'm not a good person. You deserve better." And then the line went dead.

I sat back in my chair and scrubbed my forehead with my

hands. I didn't understand. Not a single thing. I was so sick of people telling me what I deserved. I deserved a great career, a great life, a great love. Really? If I was so fucking deserving, then why the hell was I sitting alone in a room with nothing?

Clare knocked on the door and then stuck her head in. "Shannon and I are going out for more champagne. Do you want anything?" Then she rushed forward, her face full of concern. "Hayden, what's wrong?" I shook my head, unable to speak. She knelt down in front of me, her hands on my thighs. "Hayden? What happened? Are you okay?"

Confusion had numbed my mind, but I could still feel the pain everywhere else.

"Oh, baby. What happened?" She pulled her sleeve over her hand and wiped my cheeks and just under my eyes. "It'll be okay."

"I'm...fine, Clare." I pushed her away. "Everything is fine."

What a lie. Fine meant nothing. And nothing would ever be better than fine.

35

HAYDEN

CLARE LEFT me alone for the rest of the night, bringing me food I didn't touch and drinks I downed as soon as they were in my hand. I was no better in the morning, only getting out of bed because I had to answer the damn door buzzer that wouldn't shut up. I dragged myself to the door, wondering where Clare had gone this early. Maybe she'd forgotten her key?

I woke up as soon as I opened the door and saw Officer Williams standing there, his hands in his pockets.

"Glad to see you again, Hayden."

"And with pants on this time." Pajama pants I had every intention of living in until my life came back into focus again. If it never happened, at least I'd be buried in something comfortable.

"Yeah, that's a definite upgrade." Williams laughed. "Sorry about that interruption. And this one."

"No problem." I shook his hand, knowing it was too much of a coincidence that I was seeing him twice in the same number of days. "Been a long time. Should I call you *Detective* Williams now?"

"'Williams' works, just like it used to."

"Alright." I nodded. "Anything I can help you with?"

"The woman from the other day..." He hesitated, maybe wondering how well I knew her. Although, maybe I just assumed that because I was wondering the same thing.

"I think I'm in love with her." Oh, shit. Since when did my mouth stop running ideas past my brain before sharing with veritable strangers?

"She's in a lot of trouble, Hayden, and I don't know if she'll be able to handle it by herself. How much has she told you?"

I hesitated, my mind overwhelmed as it sorted through all our conversations, looking for any hint that she was in trouble with the police. Shit, all it came up with was...nothing.

"She didn't tell me anything. What's going on?"

His raised an eyebrow. "I should probably let you talk to Andi first then."

"Who?"

"Oh, jeez, I'm sorry." He shook his head, turning to leave. "I thought—"

"Wait, please. Whatever is going on, I want to know." It would be a nice change. "I'd like to hear it from you—less chance of getting the facts wrong."

He nodded warily and then followed me through the apartment into the living room. I offered him coffee while pouring some for myself. He refused the splash of bourbon I added to mine, so I helped myself to his share and took the chair opposite his.

"When I saw you with Andi..." He continued the sentence, but it took me a moment to follow. He saw me with *Andi*? Did he mean Sira?

It hit me.

Oh shit. When she'd told me Sira wasn't her real name, and I'd assumed she was referring to the nickname, I'd assumed wrong and hadn't let her finish. So her name was Andi. And that wasn't the only thing she hadn't told me. I rubbed my neck when I felt it heat, but anger wasn't relieved so easily. We'd slept together, had talked all night, and she'd never thought to give me her real name.

Wow. "Sorry," I said, raising my hand. "Can you start over? I lost focus for a second there."

He took a sip of his drink and set it down on the table between us. "Are you really in love with her?"

"I thought I was." No, that wasn't right. Despite the new feeling of distrust, that emotion hadn't gone away. "But I'm just now finding out that there's a whole lot she hasn't told me about herself."

"Have you told her everything about you?" His question was vague, but we both knew exactly what he was referring to.

"No."

On the last night of my spring break from boarding school, my father had been particularly unhappy with me for a reason I can't even remember. At some point during my punishment, Carson had called the police. Until that point, my parents had been able to control everyone who suspected what was going on inside our home.

Williams and his partner came to our house and interviewed us. The happy Bennett family. All four of us telling the same lie, my father standing behind me, digging his fingers into my shoulders and my mother's arms wrapped around Carson as she whispered God knows what into his ear.

'I'd never lay a hand on them,' my father had said. *'Boys just get a little rowdy from time to time.'* As if the visible marks on my skin had been caused by my terrified little brother and not by a man who knew exactly when to hide his rage and when to unleash it.

Williams had stopped by again the next day on his own time and in plain clothes while my father was at work and I was packing to go back to school. He'd told me he could protect me if I told him the truth. But I couldn't. Not with Carson still at home. A week later, my father came to my dorm, wanting to know if I'd been the one who called the police. I'd almost died protecting Carson because he'd been trying to protect me.

In the universe's twisted sense of irony, the effort my father had put into beating the truth out of me had been too much strain on his heart. He might've lived if he'd been given CPR.

But I would never lay a hand on him.

"I've been doing this a long time," Williams said, bringing me back to the present. "I'd like to think that makes me a pretty good judge of character. Andi's a tough girl, but she's out of her league with this one, and she needs help."

I nodded. Whatever happened between us, I wanted her to be safe. "Tell me how I can help."

"Well, for starters, this entire conversation is off the record. If I wasn't so sure she had nothing to do with this, I wouldn't be here."

I finished my drink in silence, listening to Williams and piecing together tiny bits of information about the woman I'd planned my future around. His confidence in her innocence only reaffirmed my own—she may have done some stupid things in her life, but murder wasn't one of them.

"Thankfully, there's no connection between her and the security guard who was killed, and she doesn't own a car."

"What was stolen?"

"Nothing from what we know, which makes things a lot harder. Seems that whoever broke in knew the security code and the guard's route. It was only bad luck that he found them in Brecken's office."

I stopped him. "Brecken Shipping? How did I not hear about this before now?" Granted, I'd been preoccupied with every-thing *but* work lately.

"Lots of moving pieces to sort through, and even law

enforcement moves slower on weekends. They're still collecting statements from Brecken employees, trying to figure out what the perpetrators were looking for on the computer, and who inside the company had a motive."

"Sadly, espionage seems like all the rage nowadays." Before long, they'd start looking at the company's competitors, the biggest of whom was Conure. Then I remembered another connection. Eventually, he'd find out about Tim, but I could save him some time.

"About a week ago," I said, "a Conure employee was fired for sharing confidential information with Brecken. Would the threat of prosecution be enough to make someone try to bury evidence that could be found on Brecken's computer?"

He perked up at the suggestion. "People have done much worse for less cause."

"I know." I trusted the man enough to tell him the truth about all of it. When I hesitated, he added what he knew, filling in blanks about Andi—damn, that name was going to take some getting used to. But now wasn't the time for name calling. She needed my help, and I owed her. If nothing else, she'd forced me to wake up and live.

A half hour later, the detective shook my hand and thanked me for my help. "I'll be in touch, but you may have just made things a hell of a lot easier on everyone."

"Except Tim Carpenter, of course."

"Yeah, except him." He stopped at the door. "Look, I don't know what's going on between you and Andi, but you've both had a rough time of it. It'd be a nice change to see two good people actually get what they deserve."

"Yeah," I said slowly. "Yeah, it would."

36

ANDI

AT THE LAST MINUTE, Emilia texted me something about Morning Grill being closed, and asked if we could meet at her favorite lunch spot instead.

Unfortunately, she'd neglected to mention the dress code of this particular lunch spot. Since I was heading to the police station right after brunch, I had on my best slacks and a silk top, but the only jacket I owned was old and, unlike every other woman in the place, I didn't have a single diamond anywhere on my person. At least, I'd stopped crying and, as long as Hayden didn't come up as a topic of conversation, I could control myself. Most of the day yesterday—and all last night—had left me too dehydrated for more tears. No more liquids for me today—I shouldn't refuel. And, hey, if all this ended up with me going to prison, at least the system would save money on water.

Every time I thought about how Hayden's voice had sounded when I'd told him it wouldn't work out, my chest felt like it was wrapped up in a python's coils, and I lost the ability to breathe. He'd be fine, though. He'd look back on me and our night together as a small stepping stone to a more plausible relationship. And eventually, I'd be able to breathe again.

It was a cruel irony that on the day I might be arrested for murder, other things weighed more heavily on my mind. I actually *wished* I could start worrying about the police. But Hayden had taken control of my thoughts just like he'd controlled my body. If anyone could help me refocus, Emilia could. She'd probably lay out a few scenarios that all had happy endings.

I told the hostess who I was looking for and was led through the crowded restaurant. Food I wouldn't be eating looked incredible, but I applauded myself for being such a mess that I'd killed my appetite. At least I'd be a skinny mess.

Emilia lifted her hand as soon as we saw each other. A woman I'd never met but who looked really familiar sat next to her. The woman was gorgeous—long blond hair, flawless face, perfect teeth. I smiled back as I thanked the hostess and sat down.

"I'm so glad you could come," Emilia said. "Order whatever you want, it's on me."

I cringed inside. "I'm good. Thanks." I wasn't embarrassed about being poor, but I didn't want strangers to hear about it. If nothing else, it made them look at me differently, like I was a stray dog Emilia had picked up somewhere and was now feeding regularly. But the woman didn't look surprised or pitying. What she looked was nervous, intense. Strange that Emilia hadn't introduced her yet. She was usually the epitome of social skillfulness.

To fill the awkward silence, I faked a grin and stuck out my hand. "I'm Andi."

The woman glanced at Emilia, looking confused. Emilia nodded and put her napkin on the table. "She goes by both names."

Oh, shit. Why hadn't Emilia mentioned that this was a work meeting? If I'd known, I wouldn't have used my real name. "Andi is a nickname I use with friends." Crap. With all the lying I'd done, you'd think I'd be better at it.

"Then that's what I'll call you," the woman said as she shook my hand lightly. "I'm Clare. Clare Bennett."

My heart stopped for a moment, and my stomach dropped a lot. I knew my face must have gone white, and all I could do was concentrate on not throwing up. Granted, the last time I'd seen her was only the back of her head, and the time before that, I'd been too busy gawking at Hayden to really notice her in the picture, but crap!

Hayden must have lied about his marriage being over. Why else would his wife want to talk to me? Served me right.

"I'm glad I could finally meet you," Clare said, taking a sip of water as if this were something she did every day—the talking to the woman who'd slept with her husband, not the water.

I didn't know what to say. *'Glad to meet you, too,'* or *'Your husband talks about you a lot,'* or...

Oh, man. How bad would it be if I just got up and left now?

Before I could decide, Emilia stood. "I'm going to let you guys talk. See you later." She nodded at me and smiled. What the hell? She'd just set me up for a roasting, and now she was leaving? With me on a spit with an apple in my mouth. I watched her walk away without saying a word. But I stayed. Because I deserved whatever tongue-lashing Clare would give me. If she threw a glass of water, or even a fist, in my face, I would accept it. I hoped Hayden had gotten worse, but I knew what I'd done. And now I had to pay.

"You know who I am?" Clare said.

I kept my gaze down. "Yeah, I know who you are."

"I've wanted to meet you ever since I found out about the two of you."

"I'm..." I looked her in the eyes because it was the right thing to do. And the least she deserved. "I'm sorry. What happened was..." I glanced at the fork in front of me. Would it be more or less painful to end this conversion by shoving it in my eyeball? "I'm not sure what Hayden told you, but I know he loves you very much and doesn't want to hurt you. But regardless, he did. *I* did. And I'm sorry. It's over now, though. I mean, it barely began really, but it's totally over now."

"Oh." Her brow furrowed. "That's too bad."

"Excuse me?"

"What did he do?"

"Um..."

"It couldn't have been *too* bad because I don't think Hayden *can* do anything too bad, but then, he *is* a man and men are stupid. Even the good ones. So what did he do to you?"

I shook my head. "He didn't do anything to me."

"So *you* screwed it up?"

I wanted to say no, wanted to *scream* no. But it would be a lie. "Yeah, I screwed it up."

"Okay," Clare said, leaning forward. "From what I know about Hayden and from the look on your face right now, my guess is that you don't know very much about our marriage. I bet he did that annoyingly noble thing he does and didn't lay it all out for you. I swear, sometimes he can be the biggest idiot on the face of the earth."

"No, I am."

"You guys can fight for the title if you want to, but that's not why I asked Emilia to set this up." She sighed. "Right now, Hayden is a total mess. I've never seen him even close to this, and he's been through a lot. I want him to be happy. He's been nothing but great to me for years, and I've been nothing but a burden to him. I need to make it up to him somehow, and the only way I know how is through you. So...if that means I need to help you get your shit together, then that's what I'll do."

Hearing the word 'shit' come out of such a sophisticated

woman's mouth threw me a bit. But not nearly as much as the rest of what she'd said. "I'm sure there's another way to help him that doesn't involve me."

"You are the first thing he's shown any passion about in... probably ever. He liked his job, and it won't be long until he finds another, but he can do that kind of thing in his sleep. In fact, until recently, I think he *did* do it in his sleep. He did *everything* in his sleep. But he's awake now, and you're the reason he is. So, now that you understand I'm not in the picture anymore, what's the problem? Are you mentally unstable? An ax murderer? Frigid?" Her jaw tightened. "Gay?"

"No." I took a breath. This was all so surreal—Hayden's wife, or ex-wife, trying to figure out a way to get us together. "I lied to him."

She shrugged. "So did I. For a lot longer than you could have. But he forgave me. Just tell him the truth."

What could she have possibly lied about? Whatever it was couldn't have been as bad as what I had. Our entire relationship, if you could call it that, had started with a lie. "Did you lie about your past, your problems, your life? Who you even are?"

"Yes, yes, yes, and yes. And Hayden forgave me because that's who he is. Because he can look through all the bullshit and find something in you that you didn't know existed. Because, even though he'll never admit it, his heart is as big as the ocean. The problem with Hayden is that he doesn't let people see it. His walls go on for miles in all directions. But for some reason, he let the two women sitting at this table in. So don't screw that up because it may never happen again. We can't do that to him. He deserves to be happy. Really happy. And something in you makes him happy." She sat back and studied me for a moment. "Well, it did until yesterday. I didn't understand how much I was holding him back, but now I do. Now he's finally free to think of himself and what he wants. And, in case you missed it, he wants you."

"I didn't mean to hurt him. I want him to be happy, too."

"Then what's the problem?"

I wrung the tablecloth in my hands. "I don't know if I can tell him the truth."

"Here's what you do: You suck it up and do it. Either he forgives you and all is well, or he doesn't." She sat back in her chair. "Am I supposed to call you Andi or Sara?"

"I'm Andi." For better or for worse.

"Andi," she repeated, nodding. "One honest conversation with that man changed my life. It could for you, too."

The server came over to take our order, but Clare shooed him away. I just sat there. Even if she was right, I couldn't do it. All I wanted was to run away and not deal with it—my lies, his disappointment, our feelings.

"If you tell him and he ends up hating you," she said, "then you go your separate ways, never see each other again, and be miserable for a long time. That's what you're planning to do right now anyway, isn't it?" Gee, that was an awesome way to look at it.

"I guess."

"But if you tell him and he forgives you, then no one has to be miserable."

I hated that she made sense. But these were emotions, and since when did emotions ever make sense? "It would never work out between us. We're too different."

"I think that's why he fell for you. *Because* you're so different." She took out her wallet, tossed enough money onto the table to cover the bills of our table and the one next to us, and stood. "Come on."

I got up slowly. I wanted to leave, but not with Clare. "I need to think about it."

"Time for thinking is long over, my dear. All thinking does is confuse things. Now we act. Well, *you* act, and I block the door so you can't escape."

"I really need to think about it first. Plus, I need to be somewhere in a little while. But I promise to call him." Eventually.

"One thing you need to know about both Hayden and me is that we don't give up. So if you're planning to sneak away and never be heard from again, you should come up with a better plan. It's like I always say: if you throw enough money at something, you'll eventually find what you're looking for."

"I'm not something you can buy," I snapped.

Clare smiled. "I know. If you were, he wouldn't want you so much." She slid her hand into mine as if we were old friends and led me out of the restaurant.

I was too confused to react, to pull away, to question what Clare was planning. By the time I found my voice again, the valet was pulling Clare's Mercedes up. "I can't go with you. Not now." Or hopefully ever. "I have to be somewhere."

"I'll take you there."

"No." The last thing I needed was Clare hovering over my shoulder during an interrogation. Although after *Clare's* interrogation, I think I'd feel more comfortable with the cops.

"Where is it? I'll drop you off. Around the corner if you want me to. Unless you're going shopping—then I'm going with."

I stopped. "Why are you doing this?"

"I owe him for the last three years of his life. I'm counting on you to make the next three better."

I slipped into the passenger side. My heart was racing for all the wrong reasons. Primarily because it was encouraged, hopeful even, and that wasn't good. Because it meant that I had to come clean to someone who currently believed I was a decent person. And as much as I would love to be with him, I hated the idea that his belief, even from a distance, would no longer exist.

"Where to, Andi?"

Clare's expression—calm, determined, relentless—gave me strength. I didn't ask what she'd lied to him about for so long because then I'd have to confess my own sins. And if I could build up the courage to tell the truth, it was going to be a one-shot deal. And it would be to *him.*

I took a deep breath and gave her the street address, then I added, "It's the police station."

Clare's only reaction was a single nod. "So who is Sira?"

37

ANDI

"LIKE I SAID, if you throw enough money at something, you can get whatever you want." Clare's longer legs meant she only had to take one stride for every two of my shorter ones, but she still struggled to keep up with me. My steps were louder, too—the added bonus of stomping in boots. "Can you slow down a little, Andi?"

Nope. I was too furious. And the faster I got out of the police station, the faster I could freak out without getting shot.

"What is wrong with you?" she asked. "Burton is a great lawyer."

"Yeah, but he's not *my* lawyer. I didn't hire him, and I can't pay for him."

"Andi, you need to calm down. So what if someone else hired him? He's going to handle everything for you." Then her voice dropped to a mumble. "If you actually talk to him, that is."

"He wouldn't even tell me who was paying him. How am I supposed to trust someone who won't be honest with me?" Forever trapped in that fucking irony, wasn't I?

I'd gone in prepared to speak to the police. Instead, some guy in an expensive suit who I'd never seen or spoken to before came in claiming he was my attorney and that I had nothing to say. But I *did,* and it was so simple, even an idiot like me could've done it without assistance. I hadn't done what I was being accused of. I didn't know anything about the hacking or the murder. That's it.

Instead, my new lawyer who wasn't my lawyer—and whose name wasn't something Italian sounding, although his suit probably was—shuffled me outside, refusing to let me speak and telling me I should meet him at his office in two hours to talk about the case. My first thought was that Clare had hired him, but she didn't know anything about me or why I was here. When I saw her in the lobby, unfortunately waiting for me, she looked as lost as I did...almost. The lawyer had files and information on the case, which meant he'd known for at least a few hours.

It had to be Emilia. Again, Emilia had stuck her well-meaning but completely inappropriate nose into my business. I already owed her way too much. Honestly, if I went to jail for breaking the conditions of the agreement I'd signed, that was no less than I deserved. All she was doing was getting herself more involved and making it harder for me to prove that she didn't know what I'd done.

I glanced at my watch. She'd be heading to the park for her run now. If I waited until she was back home to call, I'd have to steam for another hour. And taking the bus to get there would probably take most of that hour.

I turned to Clare. "If I talk to Hayden in the mood I'm in right now, there's no way I'll be able to stay civil. I need to calm down, talk to Emilia, and then calm down some more. Maybe with a drink or two. So can you drive me somewhere else first?"

Clare grimaced. "One stop?"

I nodded.

"Had I known I would be driving so much I would've worn

different shoes." She rolled her eyes. "Okay, one stop, but then no more stalling."

After we'd driven around the park for about ten minutes, we saw Emilia. She was sweating and oblivious to the wrath that was about to outrun her. Clare pulled over to the side of the road, and I jumped out. I stood in the middle of the path, waiting for Emilia to see me. As soon as she did, she slid to a stop, took her earbuds out, and walked forward hesitantly.

"Since you look like you're about to kill me," she said breathlessly, "I'm taking that it didn't go well with Clare."

I didn't say anything because what I had to say wasn't the kind of thing that should be shouted in the middle of a public place.

She stopped just a few feet away. "I knew you wouldn't be happy I set it up, but I didn't think you'd be *this* unhappy."

"Clare's really great."

"Then why are you looking at me like that?"

"I met my lawyer."

"Good. What'd he say?"

"Not enough." Out of the corner of my eye, I saw Clare get out of her car and stretch her legs. "I know I have a lot to be thankful for, Emilia, and most of it is because of you. You have done more than I could ever repay."

"Nothing more than you deserve," she said as we both stepped off the path. "So why do I think there's a 'but' coming?"

"Because there's a big but coming, and don't you dare laugh at the pun." She didn't. "I hate that you feel like you have to take care of me all the time. I screwed up. Me. And you trying to fix everything, while appreciated, makes me feel less like your friend and more like a charity case." Embarrassment heated my skin, made the blood pound in my ears. Emilia shouldn't have to constantly take care of me as if I were a child. The fact that she felt like she *did,* made my humiliation unmanageable. "When my best friend doesn't have enough confidence in me to let me figure things out on my own, it says more bad things about me than good things about her."

She scratched her head. "I'm not sure what we're talking about, Andi. Everything went well with Clare, but you're mad at me?"

"Not about Clare. About the lawyer. Why did you hire him?"

"Now I'm more confused. I didn't hire you a lawyer. You said you already had one."

Who else could it have been? I only knew a few people who could pay four-hundred dollars an hour for an attorney, and two of them had just denied having done it. After glancing over to Clare, I closed my eyes. "Hayden." He already knew. He knew, and he'd tried to fix it with his money. He'd tried to fix *me* with his money. "How did he find out who I was?"

Her brows came together for a moment, and then her mouth opened a bit. "Oh." Her cheeks, already reddened by exercise got even redder. "Oh, yeah. Now it makes sense."

"Not to me it doesn't."

"I overheard Sara talking on the phone at the office. It sounded like a personal call and, since you know Sara, you know how hard I try to not hear her personal calls. So I only heard a little, and it didn't make any sense unless Hayden was on the other end of the line. She says her name at the beginning of every call, so maybe he thought she was you for a second?"

"What did she say?"

"I don't remember." Emilia shrugged. "It made no sense, so I shut my door and went back to work. I don't know what she told him."

"It doesn't matter." I couldn't be mad at Sara—she probably thought she was helping. She couldn't possibly have known what she was damaging.

Hayden knew. I'd told him Sara wasn't my real name, and

he'd figured it out. Somehow. Maybe by my address, or my cell number, or any other way I'd let him into my life. He'd taken that and found out everything else because he never gave up. Throw enough money at something...

But he hadn't called me—he'd hired me a lawyer. Tried to solve my problems while keeping his distance, being professional. Somehow, that made everything worse—no one in my life thought I could solve my own problems.

No, what made it worse was that they were right. I'd been hiding behind a glass screen for so long, pretending *that* was reality, that I was safe and in control. But the only reason I was safe was because the people in my life kept sweeping up my problems for me. All so that I didn't have to deal with them. So I could stay hidden and not face them.

"I love you, Emilia," I said. "And I think you're amazing. But I can't keep hiding behind you. I need you to be my friend, not my keeper or my shield." If I was ever going to live, I had to stop hiding behind other people. I had to stop depending on them and start depending on myself.

"Do you know what's going on?" Emilia asked Clare as she walked toward us.

"I'm taking her to see Hayden."

I shook my head. "That's not going to happen. He already knows what I lied to him about." I'd lied to him about my name, but never about who I really was. Not that it mattered to anyone but me. "He's better off not hearing from me again."

I wished...I wished I could start over, not be ashamed to tell him who I was, not hide online because I could be whoever I wanted to be, not who I really was.

It was so easy to pretend your past didn't exist when you weren't standing in front of someone, when all they knew was who you were at that exact moment in time.

From behind a screen, I'd been able to spend the last four

years of my life actually being me. I could ignore the person I used to be, the stupid, insecure one who wanted to be loved so badly that I'd gone against everything I knew was right.

Clare and Emilia argued and came up with all sorts of scenarios, none of them plausible. I'd told Hayden to go away, but he hadn't. He'd found out who I really was. What would meeting him accomplish? I didn't have to stand in front of him to apologize. Plus, I was pretty sure he wouldn't want me to, now that he knew. He hadn't called, and I didn't blame him. Would he really want someone with my past, who'd broken the law again just to be able to work? Reasons were irrelevant, intention useless. I'd deceived him, put Emilia's ass on the line, and really fucked things up all in the name of doing the right thing. Which was just hilarious, really. Hilarious in an I-want-to-cry-but-not-from-laughter kind of way.

The feeling that overwhelmed me wasn't disappointment or anger, though. It was shame. Shame for what I'd done four years ago, shame for all the lies I'd told since, shame for allowing Emilia to risk everything she'd built, shame for leading Hayden into thinking that someone he shouldn't want was someone he *did* want.

"Emilia, how long will it take you to divvy up my clients among the other assistants?"

"Why would I do that?"

"Because I think I've finally learned my lesson." I heard them call my name as I walked away. But I didn't turn, and thankfully, they didn't try to catch up. Because then I'd have to run away, and I didn't want to do that anymore.

38

HAYDEN

WHEN SIRA'S name popped up on my cell phone, reminding me to change the name in her contact info, I was in the middle of lunch with the president of a small manufacturing business that might be able to help me salvage the Inspex deal. I waited as long as two vibrations before excusing myself, knowing I was probably screwing everything up just so she'd have another chance to tell me to go to hell. But since it seemed unlikely that she would call to tell me to leave her alone, I would answer the phone.

By the time I was far enough away from the table, I'd missed it. So I called her back, hoping I hadn't blown my last shot. She picked up on the first ring. That was a good sign, wasn't it?

"I met Clare today."

I inhaled. "Did you? Why's that?"

"She wanted to let me know that she supported whatever happened between us."

"Hopefully, she was more specific than that because I'd hate to think she would support you telling me to fuck off."

"Yeah, she was more specific."

I waited. There was so much uncertainty in her voice, so much tension, that I couldn't tell which way this was going to go. I braced myself for either.

"I'm..." she started. "I can take care of myself."

"I know you can." I wanted to say more, but held back, knowing that if I didn't let her lead, she'd just disappear again.

"Then why did you decide to stick your nose into something you know nothing about?"

"I'm afraid *you're* going to have to be a bit more specific now because you seem to know exactly what you're referring to while I'm not as sure." She could've been talking about her, love, or life in general.

"I don't need your lawyer, Hayden."

Oh, that. After Detective Williams had left, I'd called the virtual assistant agency and spoken with the real Sara, just to have a few separate points of reference, to know I wasn't going crazy and imagining all of this. Unfortunately, as soon as I'd mentioned the name 'Andi,' it became pretty clear that I was finally hearing the truth. So I'd called an attorney friend, hoping he knew how I could learn more about the woman I wanted and how I could help her. Even if she didn't want to be in my life, I wanted her to have a good one.

"I was trying to help," I said. "I'm sorry if it didn't."

"I didn't do it—what they're accusing me of. I wasn't involved at all."

"I know."

She laughed. "That's it? 'I know?' How could you possibly know?"

"Because I've spent I don't know how many weeks giving you every reason I could think of for us to be together. And I've spent the same amount of time listening to you tell me that, despite what you want, what I was trying so hard to give you, you won't take it. Because it would be wrong. So knowing what I know about you—as little as that may be—I know you'd never be involved in someone's death."

"Why would you believe anything I've ever said? I lied to you about everything—who I am, my past, my mistakes. Even my fucking name."

"I didn't fall in love with your name. I don't lay in bed all night thinking about your past or the mistakes you've made. I think about *you*. Your laugh, your body under mine, your cruel comebacks and how they make me feel more alive than I ever have. Those things aren't fake. They are *you*." I swallowed. "I love your mind, and your spirit, and the way you make me feel. I don't just believe them. I *know*."

"I've made so many mistakes, Hayden." Her breath hiccupped. "So many."

"Yes, you have. You've also paid for them. They've made you who you are, and I love who you are."

"You don't love me. You can't. You're just mixing your feelings up. So now that you know I'm full of shit, you should go. You should run away as fast as you can."

"I want to be there for you."

"I don't need you," she whimpered. "I'm not going to thank you for the lawyer. I'll pay you back, but I won't thank you. I don't need you to rescue me."

Ah-ha. "That wasn't my intention. It's obvious you can take care of yourself." As soon as I said the words, I wished I could take them back. Because they sounded flippant, bitter, sarcastic. I was none of those things. I was only confused and afraid of hurting her.

"I never asked you to take care of me," she yelled. "I know I screwed up. I think about it every single day. I can't *stop* thinking about it. But I never asked you for help so you can keep your sarcastic comments to yourself."

"I wasn't being sarcastic. You're misunderstanding me, Sar
—" My head flopped back on the wall. I should really start
listening—not to what she said, because I already did that, every
syllable she spoke. But to what she *hadn't* said. For months, I
didn't even know her real name.

I didn't care about the lie itself. But, sadly, it was a sign. A
sign that she didn't trust me enough to come clean, that she
didn't see a future for us. If she had, she would've told me. "I
want the best for you, and unfortunately, I don't know what that
is. I don't want to fix you—I think you're perfect just the way you
are. But I would like to help if I can. In any way I can."

"I don't need your help."

"Okay," I said on an exhale. "Then what do you want me
to do?"

"I want you to erase my number and my email address from
everywhere they are. I want you to forget my phone number.
And if you see me in public, I want you to walk in the other
direction. That's what I want you to do."

"Don't ask me to do that."

"I'm not asking. Goodbye, Hayden."

"Andi, come on!" I yelled into the phone, her real name so
foreign on my tongue. But it was too late. She'd already hung up.

After staring at my phone for a while, I started walking. I
wasn't sure how long, and I wasn't sure where I was going. When
the sun started to go down, I raised my gaze from the sidewalk
and looked around. No idea where I was. I had my phone and
my wallet but had left my briefcase in the restaurant.

All that walking and still no closer to a way out of the hole
I'd dug my way into. Like a grave. I'd fallen a lot in my life, busi-
ness dealings that failed, personal relationships that fell apart.
But I'd always prided myself on being able to pick myself up.

I finally understood why it had been so easy. Because I'd
never been that far off the ground. I'd never felt free. Not being

fully alive had kept my feet firmly planted. She'd changed that—
Andi. Andi had made my chest fill with laughter, my soul fill
with hope. So that when I fell, it was from a much higher place.
And it hurt a hell of a lot more when I landed.

39

ANDI

EVERY PART OF ME ACHED, and I was only about halfway through packing up my stuff. Ironically, I used to think of myself as a minimalist. Although, most of it wasn't mine. Grandma had left lots of souvenirs from a life well-lived, a full and happy one. Those memories needed to be carefully wrapped and labeled for storage until I could afford a place larger than a postage stamp. Selling the house wouldn't give me all the money I still owed, but after I paid off the mortgage, the rest would help a lot of people regain what they'd lost.

It hurt to sell something that meant so much to my grand-mother, but what else could I do? I needed to start over, and hopefully, there was enough fun stuff to do in heaven that Grandma would never notice.

I'd stopped checking my phone, letting all the calls from Emilia, Sara, and Clare go to voicemail. Once a day, I texted a quick, *'I'm alive, but can't talk now. Need more time,'* message back to them so no one would decide to come over to see if I was still breathing.

I wasn't sure I still was.

Not surprisingly, Hayden hadn't called. It was fitting that the one time he listened was the time I'd told him to erase me from his life. I told myself the pain in my chest was guilt, not disappointment. Not sadness that I'd let someone down again. Not anxiety over imagining him cursing my name—my *real* name—and thinking what a fool he was for believing me, trusting me, wanting me. Because if I thought too long on any of those things, I'd start crying. And crying only made the packing go slower and the nights seem longer.

The only thing I had to celebrate was that I wouldn't have to pay Hayden back too much for the attorney. By the time I'd called the guy to tell him I wouldn't be needing his services, I was no longer a suspect, and the police had a lead on someone else. I didn't ask for details—it was hard to care about anything anymore.

Unfortunately, fifty years of clutter covered up a lot of dust, and moving Grandma's things stirred it all up. When I could no longer stand the taste in my mouth, I walked down to the donut shop. The place seemed different this time, not as safe anymore. Maybe because I knew this neighborhood wouldn't be my home much longer.

As I passed a liquor store with my half-dozen beauties, I decided I was thirsty. Hell, why not? I grabbed a six-pack of the cheapest beer they had. Maybe I'd just have one, or maybe I'd have all six beers and all six donuts and then spend the rest of the night crying. Ain't life grand?

When I got back to the house, I saw him. Hayden was sitting in the swing on my front porch as if it was just another night and this was just another visit. As if he'd been here countless times before and had done exactly the same thing. But he'd only been here a couple times...that felt like they'd been seared into my memory with a branding iron. Painful reminders of who I'd almost belonged to but never would.

What is it like to have memories that don't hurt?

Hayden wore jeans and a sweater, by far the most casual thing I'd ever seen him wear, but nothing could make him look bad. He looked gorgeous, confident, powerful, completely out of my league, so much more than I'd ever deserve.

Under the weight of his stare, I dragged my feet up the sidewalk, words darting around in my mind but not sticking long enough for me to figure out something to say. I slipped my key into the lock and opened the door. I didn't need to explain myself to him—he knew what he needed to know, anything else would only make him hate me more. And that wouldn't do either of us any good.

"Can I have one?" His voice made me flinch, cringe, shiver, feel lots of unpleasant stuff.

"Um...sure," I said. I wanted to just run inside and lock the door behind me, but instead, I tossed my wallet, keys, and donuts inside, pulled a beer from the plastic ring, and handed it to him. Then I grabbed one for myself, set the rest down at my feet, and leaned up against the wood railing.

When he examined the label, I instantly knew he'd probably never had beer in a can before. He cracked it open and took a cautious sip, then another.

"Is Andi short for anything?" he asked calmly.

"Andrea." I took a long swig—partly so I didn't have to look at him and partly hoping the alcohol would hit me really fast.

"You got in trouble with the police, what, four years ago?"

I gagged, the beer in my nose instead of where I needed it to go. After my coughing fit was done, I looked at him and nodded. He deserved to know. "My boyfriend at the time asked me to do something for him. I was stupid and was sure he loved me and would ever ask me to do anything that was wrong, so I did it. Turned out only one part of that was true: I was stupid."

"But you're paying back what he and his friends took?"

How did he know that? "Clare was right. Throw enough

money at something and you can find out whatever you want."

He shrugged. "You'd be surprised how easy it is. And how inexpensive." He took another sip of beer. "I spoke to a few of them."

"A few of whom?"

"The university employees who are receiving funds from an unknown source. They're very thankful. Why didn't you ever tell them what you were doing for them?"

I'd never contacted any of them. Never had the guts to. "How do you tell someone that you're the person responsible for their life savings being stolen? They all saw me at the trial, and they have every right to hate me. So what's the point of taking credit for the small amount of money I've given back to them?"

"Just over eighty-five thousand dollars isn't a small amount of money."

"I've never added it up." I kept records of every payment and every family they went to, but tallying it up didn't seem like anything but a reminder of how much *more* I owed them. "Doesn't seem like a lot over four years, though. I wish it could be more." I wasn't sure how much longer I could stand to talk about this, but his pause made me even more uncomfortable— wondering how badly he was judging me.

"Why were you so afraid something had happened to Sara the night we first met?" I might've been thankful for his switch of topic, but all he'd done was move from one awful discussion to another.

I felt my eyes water. "She trusted the wrong person and got hurt. I don't know who it was, or what exactly happened, but I understood how she felt because...because I'd done the same thing. Trusted the wrong person and got hurt. But I hadn't just hurt myself—I'd hurt other people. Even though I can't stop those people from being hurt again by someone else, I can make sure Sara doesn't. At least not..."

When he nodded, I took a breath of relief that I didn't have to keep talking about the past. Until he started speaking again—no subject was safe anymore.

"Only four people know what I'm about to tell you," he said. "But I want you to know that I don't expect reciprocity. I'm telling you because I trust you, and I hope that someday you'll trust me."

I took a sip and waited for whatever would come next.

"When I was eight, my father almost killed me. I spent four days in the ICU. Eventually, I came home with casts on both of my arms and one leg. But it was fine because my family was rich. We could hire people to push my wheelchair around. We could pay for the best surgeons to make sure there would be no lasting damage. We could donate enough money to the hospital so that people forgot to file a report. So everything was fine."

He took another drink. "When I was about eleven, I missed a month of school. I couldn't go because I couldn't sit down or bend at the waist or knees or take full breaths. But everything was fine, because we had servants who could bring me what I needed and my parents didn't have to deal with me. Eventually, they sent me away to a boarding school in Connecticut...so they didn't have to deal with me. I was mostly healed and, by then, I'd learned how to not let the pain show on my face. So everything was fine."

He stood up, shaking his can slightly. "Can I have another?"

"Sure." I bent down to get him one, and when I straightened, he was next to me. Not facing me, though. His hands were on the railing, and he was looking out at the street.

"When I was sixteen, Detective Williams was called to my home for a domestic disturbance. That's how we met, and why he told me about you. Because he's a good man who tries to help people when they don't know how to ask for help. A week later, my father came to visit me at school because he thought

I'd told Williams about the beatings. That visit led to two weeks at a private hospital because I needed time to heal, and my family was in mourning." His knuckles were white on the rail.

"Mourning?"

"My father had a heart attack in my dorm room. I was a certified lifeguard and knew CPR, but I watched him die on the floor next to me." He rubbed his lips together. "I could've...I was bleeding and had a few broken ribs, but I could've helped him. I chose not to. I chose to let him die."

I was frozen, listening to his every word, still holding the beer he'd asked for. He seemed to have forgotten about it, too.

"I told my mother it was because I was injured—my father had gotten upset and had beat me pretty badly, and I was still sore from the last time. But that's not why I didn't help him. I didn't help him because I wanted him to die. I wanted him to leave me alone, and Carson, and my mom. I knew that if I gave him CPR, there was a chance I would save him. Save him, after everything he'd done to us. I couldn't. So I did what he'd taught me to do, what my family had always done—look away, pretend things were fine and that my father wasn't using his last breath to curse my name. Pretend I couldn't feel his grip on my pants weaken and go limp when that breath was over."

"I'm sorry, Hayden."

"Me, too. At least, part of me is. But the other part understands why I made the choice I did. That I did it to protect the people I loved." Blinking, he looked down, his brow tightening when he saw me still holding the beer.

"Am I boring you yet?" he asked, taking the can out of my hand and cracking it open.

"Not at all." As much as I knew this man, there was so much more to learn. So much that explained why he was the way he was. The more he spoke, the more I respected his strength, and the more courage that gave me. "You can keep talking...if you want to."

A smile flitted across his mouth. "When I graduated from high school, I went to college at my father's Alma Mater. I'm not sure if I was a good enough student to be accepted, but I was. And, even though I wasn't under my father's fist anymore, I followed his rules, his expectations—my fraternity, area of study, sports, and girlfriends were all exactly as he would have wanted them. He had been successful, and if I wanted to be successful, it was wise to follow his example. And I was fine with that because I *did* want to succeed. I think. After grad school, I got an interesting job that I was good at and married an amazing woman, whom you met. Everything was...fine.

"Then I met this amazingly smart and funny woman who challenged everything I knew. And in between making fun of my typing speed and driving me a little crazy, she helped me realize that everything *wasn't* fine. It had never been fine and, if I continued living my life the way I was, it never would be fine. Because now...now I want more than fine." He finally turned to face me. "I want you. I want us. I want a chance at a life I've never even dreamed of."

Until that moment, with him looking at me so intently, so humbly, so honestly, I'd thought I wouldn't cry. But I felt tears slide down both cheeks. I didn't know what to say. How to tell him how sorry I was for all that he'd gone through. How hard it was to believe he could still care about me after everything I'd done wrong.

He took a deep breath. "If that's not something you're interested in pursuing, that's..." His jaw clenched. "No, that's not fine. It's not." His hand darted around my neck and pulled me into him. Our lips met already open, filled with regret for time wasted and desire for what was to come. I threw my arms around his neck and held on as he lifted me into his arms and went to the door. I reached behind me, banging my hand against the wood until I found the doorknob and turned it.

He tore his mouth away from mine, and we stumbled inside, slamming the door behind us. "I want more. I want this. Not just partway. You and me. Completely. I need to see if it can be what I think it could. Do you understand?"

I nodded, relief and disbelief making it impossible for me to say anything.

"You have the next four seconds to stop this, Andi. After that, I'm not listening to you anymore."

We stared at each other, our breath shallow. He held me—eyes, body, and heart.

"Your time's almost up," he said, his eyes studying my face for signs.

"Actually, I promised Clare I'd give you three years." I swallowed. "Anything longer than that will have to be negotiated."

That might not have been the answer he expected because it took a second for the smile to show up. "I'm really good at negotiating, you know."

"So I've heard."

Then my back was against the wall, my legs around his waist, his hands in my hair. Our clothes came off piece by piece somehow, but I didn't know whose hands did what. My fingers traced the muscles on his chest and abs, while my eyes stayed closed and my lips stayed on his. I unbuttoned his jeans and yanked down while he pulled my dress over my head. He shuddered and pulled back slightly, holding me by the waist and looking at my body with dark, needy eyes.

"Damn, you're beautiful."

"You're such an easy man to please," I said, smiling.

"Only by you, Andi. Only by you."

Somehow, we made it to the couch, and then a little later, we got to the bedroom...with a few stops along the way. Maybe even a couple breaths. He was more than I'd ever wanted. More than I'd ever dreamed of.

Every kiss, every thrust, every second brought us closer together, until I couldn't remember a time without him. He'd given me nothing but pleasure, respect, and trust. And, thank the heavens, I'd finally figured out I deserved it. I'd messed up so many things in my life, but he'd refused to let me mess this up. And Hayden Bennett always got what he wanted.

After what seemed like hours—and *was*—we separated. "I should start calling you Lance Armstrong, you bike so well."

"I think we should stop using nicknames altogether, actually."

I grimaced. "Good point."

"Besides, Andi suits you. I never did think you looked like a Sara." When he reached out for the glass of water on my nightstand, his arm bumped into the computer monitor that had been resting on top of it, waiting to be packed up. He tried to grab it but missed.

I cursed when I heard it shatter on the hardwood floor.

"Oops," he said shyly.

"Oops? You destroyed $300 worth of equipment my favorite client gave me, and all you can say is 'oops?'" I climbed partway on top of him to look down at the damage. "You're just lucky the monitor isn't where the important stuff is."

"I know." His lips ran across my collarbone, over my heart. "*This* is where the important stuff is." Then he took my face in his hands, forcing me to look into his eyes. "The monitor was what you used to hide behind. But not anymore, got it?"

"Got it." I had to speak, tell him everything. So while we were both still catching our breaths, I told him. Everything I kept hidden, everything I'd screwed up, everything I was. And he didn't hate me. He didn't pity me.

Nope, he loved me.

40

HAYDEN

I GRABBED Andi by the waist and pulled her away from the trays. "You're going to make Clare regret having the party catered if you eat all the food."

"I can't help it." Slipping something into her mouth, she spun around and looked up at me with those dark brown eyes I'd never get bored of. "I'm nervous," she mumbled after swallowing. "And I eat when I'm nervous. Normally, I have to make do with chips, but this is way better, which is perfect because I'm *really* nervous."

"I can tell—it also makes you talk a lot."

She smacked my chest. "Be nice, Birthday Boy, or you won't get your present after everyone leaves. And believe me—"

I meant to shut her up with a quick kiss, but found myself, once again, losing track of everything else as soon as our lips touched. The last few months had been spectacular, so much more than I could've ever imagined. The Inspex project was in final negotiations, my new company was well on its way to becoming a force, and every day I got to come home to a beautiful, intelligent, spirited woman who drove me a little crazy in the best possible way.

"Break it up, you two," I heard Clare say behind me. "Your guests are getting restless."

"I'm the worst hostess in the history of hostesses, aren't I?"

Clare glanced at me for help. "Should I lie to her?"

Andi groaned and swiped another *hors d'oeuvre* off the tray.

"Ignore her," I said, taking Andi's hand. "Besides, this party isn't about you. It's about me."

We followed my ex-wife into the living room. With a lot of updating and construction, Andi's house had become ours, at least until we outgrew it. Obviously, we could've afforded a larger place closer to my office, but I knew how much this place meant to her. I just hoped that by the time we needed a few more bedrooms and a playroom, she'd be okay with the move. But that wasn't a concern...yet.

With an arm around Laney, my brother stared out the window, looking a bit lost. It wasn't like him to be uncomfortable at a party or anywhere else, for that matter. But as soon as he'd stepped through the door, I'd known something was off—he held Laney a little tighter, didn't make any lame jokes, and his smile seemed pasted on. When there weren't this many people around, I'd have to ask him what was wrong. Maybe it was time for some more brilliant advice only a brother could offer.

"Does everyone have a glass to raise?" Clare waited for everyone to nod and pick up their champagne flutes. "Great. I'd like to make a toast to a very special man, who—"

"Is this going to make me cry?" Carson grunted as Laney's elbow met his side.

"Hit him again, Laney. Only harder," Clare called. "Like I was saying, Hayden is a very special man, who—"

"Could I say something when you're done?" My stepsister Anna had an incredible ability to appear completely innocent with enough sass to convey her obvious guilt. It was her own special kind of skill.

"I want to, too."

"Can I go next?"

I lost track of who was speaking—Emilia, Laney, Real-Sara, Carson, Shannon. One by one all the incredible people in my and Andi's life spoke up and over my poor ex-wife, until even Clare was laughing.

"Seriously, people? Back off." Clare downed her remaining champagne, refilled her glass, and held it back up. "Hayden-I-love-you-Happy-Birthday-You're-the-best-ex-husband-I'll-ever-have," she said, all in a single breath. "Now which of you jerks is next?"

"I'm next," Andi said firmly and then grimaced. "Not that I'm a jerk, but..." She cleared her throat and started over, turning to face me. "Hayden—"

"Will you marry me?" It came out as a surprise to everyone, including me. This wasn't at all what I'd planned. The program I'd contracted someone to build and install on her laptop was almost done. Flowers would be delivered to the house. But not tonight.

All I had was the champagne, the woman I loved, and the ring.

"What?" was said in multiple voices, but only one mattered.

"What did you say?" Andi asked again.

"I was going to wait for the perfect moment to ask, but then I realized that *every* moment with you is perfect. Because *we're* perfect together, and I want it to last forever." I brushed a misbehaving lock of hair out of her eyes so I could see them. They were shining. "I want to marry you, Andi. I want you to be mine, forever."

Andi pressed her lips together and looked around the room at our friends, who were quiet for the first time in their lives. When she took my hands, I realized what was missing.

"Wait here," I said quickly, ignoring the communal groan as I ran to our bedroom and grabbed the small blue box I'd hidden in my drawer. I opened it up, took a picture, and then texted, *'Marry me.'* Then, to make sure she saw the message, I yelled, "You'd better answer that!"

I stared at my phone, waiting. Held my breath when I saw the gray bubbles appear. Closed my eyes and let out a shuddering breath when I read her reply:

'Yes.'

And then another popped up, *'Now, get your ass in here and seal the deal, Bennett.'*

When I came back into the room, everyone was staring at me. None of them knew what had happened and, as much as I loved all of them, I didn't explain. I focused solely on the woman I was going to spend the rest of my life with.

As soon as I took the ring out of the box and slipped it on her finger, everyone cheered. Someone patted me on the back, while Real-Sara and Emilia pulled Andi away from me to hug her and admire the ring.

Clare held both my hands, squeezing them with excitement. "Please tell me I can plan your wedding. I know you said I should work on Carson's, but I swear, he's impossible. So who knows when that'll happen."

"Wait, he said what?" Carson's eyes were enormous as he looked at Clare, then me, then Laney, who thankfully hadn't heard the comment. "Dude, seriously?"

"Relax, little brother," I said quietly. "I didn't set a date or anything."

"Yeah, well... Still not cool."

"If you wait too long, you know that Laney could come to her senses, right?" I laughed.

"Thanks, Hay. Don't think I won't remember that." He turned his back on us, grumbling, "Like I need more pressure," under his breath.

After a lot of toasts and glasses of champagne, I finally got my hands back on Andi.

"That was by far the best text ever written," she said.

"And the longest wait for a reply."

She shrugged. "You should really work on your patience, Hayden."

"My patience? And here I was assuming you were considering other offers."

"No way," she said, smiling. "In business, when you see something you want, you need to move in fast before anyone else swoops it up. But you can't let anyone know how badly you want it, or you get screwed in negotiations."

"Oh, you'll get screwed all right, my love." I kissed her. I kissed my fiancée. "In fact, I think it's time everyone went home, don't you?"

"Patience, Mr. Bennett."

When Real-Sara asked where we were going to get married, all other conversation stopped.

Andi looked up at me. "I've heard good things about the Maldives." She wiggled her finger, asking me to bend down a little so she could whisper in my ear. "No extradition."

"Please tell me you're joking."

"I don't mean like that," she said, her lips warming my ear. "But I kind of love the idea that I can keep you there for as *looong* as I want, and no one can do anything about it."

That sounded perfect.

"Pack your bags, everyone. We're going to the Maldives."

Once Upon a Time...

THERE WAS a woman who lived in a glass box, believing she would remain there for the rest of her days to pay for mistakes of long ago. And there she stayed until she met a man who had been living in another cage built by his and the hands of others. Wall after wall after wall. Until it was impossible for anyone to get through. But when he heard the woman's true voice, he knew her to be good and kind and caring. And because his desire to reach her was so great, he broke down wall after wall after wall of his prison.

And though she feared him getting too close, she knew he would never be able to see through her glass, and thus he would never see what a horrible thing she was. But the man wasn't content to stand outside her cage, knowing she was suffocating within it. So he began to chip away at the mirror. Day by day, hour by hour, he toiled.

And when he finally got through, he didn't think her ugly, he thought her the most beautiful thing his eyes had ever seen. To help her understand her beauty, he brought her to the other side of the glass and stood beside her. Piece by beautiful piece he showed her that she was no longer the woman she had been, and no longer deserved to be punished.

And when she looked at the glass from the outside, she saw the man holding the hand of a woman she didn't recognize. Only understanding after she looked down and saw that the hand the man held was hers...and he would never let it go.

The End

Thank you so much for reading *Virtually Impossible*. If you enjoyed the book, *please* consider leaving a review.

Seriously, for authors, reviews are like gold or little blue boxes from Tiffany's (although we'll take those too).

∿

Want more?

Visit my website to sign up for my newsletter and get exclusive extras from the *Once and Forever* series (including an interview with Carson and Laney) and be notified when future books are available.

Deeper Water, Once and Forever #3
~ *Carson & Laney's* After *Happily-Ever-After* ~

Two people can only tread water for so long.

Carson and Laney are back! Take a peek into their *after* happily-ever-after and be there for Hayden and Andi's island wedding!

My name is Carson Bennett.

The first time I slept with Laney Temple was two years ago.

At the time, I thought I deserved a medal for all the effort I put into making it happen. What I ended up with was a million times more valuable.

Now, with everyone and my brother getting hitched, I think I'm finally ready for the next big step. To make what Lane and I have better and stronger. Deeper. I'm just not sure if *she's* ready.

Unfortunately, life isn't all bacon and glitter just because we say three little words to each other.

When we're horizontal, our communication couldn't be better. And the other forty-nine percent of the day—when my pants are zipped, her bra is hooked, and nobody's hands are anywhere fun —it's still easy and full of laughs.

It's just that last one percent we haven't quite figured out yet.

Time's ticking. And if we don't repair the cracks soon, water is going to rush in and break this whole damn thing apart.

~ No, a novella continuing Carson and Laney's story wasn't in the original plan. What can I say? I'm weak and gave into peer (reader) pressure. The fact that I absolutely loved writing this couple and didn't want to say goodbye to them yet might have also had something to do with it...possibly. But I prefer to blame other people since I'm not 100% sure about that last part.

~

Immaterial Defense
(Once and Forever #4)

Two strangers meet in a karaoke bar.
She's all alone in the darkness.
He's lighting up the stage.
It's going to take a whole lot longer than one night to get all they need from each other.

Book #4 is a party-girl/rockstar twist on The Emperor's New Clothes. And this is how Sara's fairytale begins...

Once upon a time there was a woman whose life had been blessed from the moment of her birth. She wore beautiful gowns and went to fancy balls and danced with handsome princes and hated every second of it. For though none but the woman knew it, these things were not real but imagined. And the reason she understood this was because she wasn't real either, having been unmade in a single moment in time...by an enemy she hadn't foreseen...in a way that left her body wounded and her soul scarred.

The Heights

Unseen, Vol 1

Job security isn't something Addison is all that concerned with. Death, however? Yeah, death is a major concern.

While a prophesied war brews in the Heights, Addison and Rhyse must decide which carries more risk—trusting someone who could destroy you or trusting someone who could *love* you?

Unearthed, Vol 2

What would you give up for freedom? Even if it wasn't yours?

Two people from opposite sides of a war will discover the price of freedom and what they're willing to pay for it. But in the Heights, nothing is ever fair. For something they both want, one of them will pay with their eternity.

Unwanted, Vol 3

The werewolf pack doesn't want Noah almost as much as he doesn't want to be one of them. Until he discovers what he really wants and where he truly belongs - next to the daughter of his enemy.

This series is a mixture of urban fantasy and paranormal romance with multiple interlocking stories and characters and plot lines as well as different races of supernatural beings, each with their own cultures, hierarchy, and attributes. It's not a series about only two people, or three, or even four. This is a world in which everyone will have to pick a side.

The Hyde Trilogy

Hyde ~ Jekyll ~ Strange Case

The Complete Hyde Series Box Set

"...my favorite series of the year...a perfect blend of what makes a book go down in history."

— Ohhh My Shelves

Dark and light, good and evil—mankind's universal struggle.

But what if you're not a man? Or can never allow yourself to be kind? What about on those nights when you're not quite human?

Two people bonded by a curse of heredity and the manipulation of an unknown entity. When the truth leaves them nothing to hold onto, they will be forced into a partnership neither expected...or wanted.

Because in life, who you trust is as important as who you *are*. And when you can't even trust yourself, sometimes the only person you can rely on is the last person on earth you should be falling for.

~ All three full-length novels are intended for adults because of very naughty language, biting sarcasm, and descriptive love scenes. They are not a retelling of the classic story. Not even close.

Second Bite

A second chance...

A second lifetime...

Can Daniel overcome two lifetimes of guilt and be the man Olivia needs? Or will both of them lose everything?

There will be more.

Much more. More in The Heights, Once and Forever, Summer Rains, a spin-off of the Hyde series, an as-of-now untitled YA paranormal series, and a billion more projects all impatiently waiting their turn. So stay in touch to find out what's next.

ACKNOWLEDGEMENTS

To my Stewartists, readers, bloggers, and friends, including the magnificent Nadine Colling and Aestas Cross:

Last year was a very difficult one. I'm not sure I would've made it if I hadn't had you at my back - encouraging, supporting, and nagging me. Thank you for making this series so much more than I ever thought it would be, for sharing *Darker Water* with others, and for allowing me to be a part of your lives.

To my incredible therapists/critique partners, Christina McKnight and Olivia Rivers: Your talent is only surpassed by your kindness. This book wouldn't exist if not for you.

To Katy Regnery: When you first contacted me, I thought you were a little nuts. Now I know you're a lot nuts, in all the best possible ways. Thank you for your advice, support, and friendship.

To my incredibly talented and patient graphic designer Amanda Simpson who puts up with *way* too much of my crazy: Sorry. :)

That apology goes out to my editors, Jen Blood, Chelle Olson, and Anja Pfister, too. I should probably warn you that my next project will be coming soon.

Oh, and Amanda? Make sure my room is ready.

A NOTE FROM THE AUTHOR

Anyone who's ever been to YouTube knows that good things rarely happen on a dare. This series is the exception.

You see, when I fall in love with my characters, I have a hard time saying goodbye until I've tortured them through at least a few books. But, one day, a close friend wondered aloud if I could ever just get to the damn happily-ever-after in only one book. Since I wasn't sure myself, I decided to take that challenge, and Darker Water was born. It was so much fun that I decided to keep going, wrote seven more fairytale beginnings and plotted out stories to go with each.

So *Once and Forever* will be a series of at least seven stand-alone novels. Each story uses a theme or symbol from a fairy-tale, but only as a starting point.

Because while fairytales aren't real, love *is*.

ABOUT THE AUTHOR

Lauren Stewart lives in Northern California with one teenager, an almost-teenager, a mellow cat, and a very high maintenance, very large puppy. On the nights Lauren doesn't collapse from exhaustion, she reads almost every genre so, naturally, her writing reflects that. With every book and every story, you'll find elements of other genres—fantasy, mystery, romance, paranormal, suspense, YA, women's literature, all with a touch of humor.

Because what doesn't kill us should make us laugh.

**How to help your favorite authors
& make them eternally grateful**

*Leave reviews
Tell your friends
Share their posts on social media
Recommend their books to readers' groups*

CONTACT ME

Need to get hold of me? Email me, like me on Facebook, follow me on twitter, visit my website, or meet me at Starbucks.

I've set up a Facebook "support" group called the Stewartists. We do a lot of chatting, laughing, and random giveaways. Go to my Facebook Author Page if you'd like to join us!

email: LaurenStewartAuthor@gmail.com
facebook: www.facebook.com/LaurenStewartAuthor
Stewartists: www.facebook.com/groups/LaurenStewartAuthor
twitter: @ReadLaurenS
website: www.LaurenStewartAuthor.com
Starbucks: pretty much everywhere